COMMANDER

In Commander the story picks up with Dance, investigating into his Dad's holdings in the Philippines.

DORSE DUBOIS
WITH ROYAL CONNELL

FOCSLE

Published by Focsle, LLP, Annapolis, Maryland
Copyright © 2024 by Dorse Dubois

The Catalog-in-Publishing Data is on file at the Library of Congress.

ISBN
Hardback: 979-8-9860857-9-1
Paperback: 979-8-9906543-0-3
eBook: 979-8-9906543-1-0

About the cover: For Hod in Chief, the Elly Mae was central to his development and growth as a Navy Chief Petty Officer. There was no single ship that was similarly central to the life of Dance.

Instead it was his twelve seasons of rowing Crew at the Naval Academy as well as the four years spent by the Bay as a Midshipman.

The author was the second boat stroke oar. I did little time in the first boat, but the team lost once to only one school in four years, and that school was Harvard. Because 2nd boats race first, my boat was the first to beat Harvard Lights in eleven years.

It was that expectation of always winning and training to make that possible that formed me for life. The picture is of our Crew in that boat

Cover credit:
Chesapeake Bay nautical map provided by NOAA Office of Coast Survey, nauticalcharts.noaa.gov

Commander is dedicated to my Partner, Royal Connell, the most determined, courageous man it is my honor to know.

ACKNOWLEDGMENTS

Commander came to life as the result of a partnership with Royal Connell, who edited the book, pulled it together with fantastic chapter names and offered encouragement and dogged determination to complete the book, even as he recovers from life threatening surgery.

Nancy Blankenship Jones, who by her many encouraging responses through the years to my FaceBook postings caused me to raise my level. Thanks for your encouragement and for your efforts as a proofreader of Commander.

And there is a startling contribution that comes from cyberspace; for it was in FaceBook over a period of several years and perhaps 500,000 "likes" that I honed my craft. There I learned to connect at the heart and benefitted from instant feedback, thousands of times. There was the closed group of Parents of Naval Academy Midshipmen in particular that read my stories and encouraged me to write more.

"You oughta' write a book," they said.

Just sayin'
Dorse DuBois

For this and all my writing projects, I dedicate my effort to my father.

Royal Connell

PROLOGUE

The funeral for Hod Dantes, retired WWII Chief Gunner's Mate and GS-14 Civil Servant, was held at Fort Sam in San Antonio. He had been active in competitive running well into old age and was very popular, locally. Seated with the Family under the tent were Vice Admiral John Lodge USN (Ret.) and his wife Lydia and their son Hod Lodge. A Navy Commander in Service Dress Blues knelt on one knee before Dance Dantes and offered the thanks of a grateful Nation as he reverently handed over the precisely folded colors to the Chief's oldest child. Admiral Lodge stood to speak and was reminded of another time at his Dad's funeral when he spoke in Boston. "I was privileged to serve with the Chief at several points in our careers. In fact he saved my wife Lydia's life in a daring rescue in the Philippines and also served at Normandy in the destruction of German tanks and gun emplacements. Those were tough times that called for the very best we could put forward. Hod Dantes was certainly that, a genuine unassuming hero to whom I will always be grateful."

Finally Dance Dantes stood to speak. "Thank you all for coming," he said. My Dad was a genuine hero who would've scoffed at the word. He grew up on his Grandma's farm in Lockhart, Texas and then upon graduation from High School in Beaumont he enlisted in the Navy. He felt lucky to have a job during the great depression and over a period of years, ship after ship, he grew to be a skilled Gunner's Mate, proud of his service and the chance to fight against our enemies. Hod Dantes rose through the ranks to become a Chief, one of the honored cadre that turns orders into action in the Navy. As a Navy kid I didn't get to see much of him, especially during the war years. I knew this. All I ever wanted to be was a Chief in the Navy, like my Dad. He served and it has been my honor to follow in his footsteps and along the way to hear stories of his exceptional service from his shipmates, such as Vice Admiral Lodge, here today." Dance turned to the Admiral and, even though in civilian clothes, gave a salute. Admiral Lodge and his wife stood and returned Dance's salute. Smiling now, "My Dad used to host a feed of pinto beans and tamales after Saturday runs," and here several in the crowd chuckled. "So we'll do it for him one more time. You're all invited down to the house for some Mexican chow, Texas barbeque and Sea Stories."

In going through his Dad's things that week after the funeral Dance discovered some letters from a law firm in Manila. A Ricardo Verdad, Esquire had reported every ten years or so about his Dad's Estancia in the Baguio District of Luzon. "*That's funny, Dad never mentioned business interests in the Philippines.*" Detailed in the correspondence was the running of an Estancia and an accounting of several financial interests. The profits had generally been plowed back into the ranch and its various businesses including real estate. It seemed that property in the Baguio area was very valuable and his Dad had owned some four thousand acres of it.

Dance contacted a local lawyer to discuss with him the legalities of making a claim for his Dad's assets. A letter was subsequently sent to the Verdad Law Office with notice of his Dad's death, including the Death Certificate and suggesting a meeting in their offices in Manila. Dance decided to take a week or two and flew to the P.I. and set up in the Manila Hilton. He had pulled into port in both Subic and Manila when he was on active duty and was amazed at the growth and amount of commerce.

At the Verdad Law Offices the managing partner, greeted him with a firm handshake, "Welcome, Commander, how was your trip? Coffee, Sir or something stronger? I'm Consuela Verdad, my Father founded the firm and he actually knew and very much admired your Father." "Yes, well my Dad never talked much about his wartime service. If you have it a rum and coke would be nice." "I do have a small lunch coming when we're ready for it and I've blocked out the afternoon for our discussions." "That sounds fine to me," Dance replied.

They proceeded into the firm's conference room and took seats in a luxuriously furnished space. Ms. Verdad went to the bar and mixed a drink for the Commander and drew a coffee for herself. "Am I to take it that you don't know very much about your Father's time in the Philippines?" He laughed, "Until a month ago I knew only the sketchiest details of his early service in the Navy; I was just a boy during the war years, and I had no idea he had these sizeable holdings in the

Archipelago." She smiled, "I think all of those heroes, the Greatest Generation, tended to do the impossible and then think nothing of it. My Father, though, never tired of telling us stories about your Father. When your Father was here he was but a young sailor. She smiled at a memory, "Commander would you like to hear some of the stories that are still being told in my family?" Dance grinned, loosened his tie and allowed as how she ought to just call him Dance, she insisted on being called Connie and joined him in a rum and coke.

Connie suggested a visit to a local place of business still being run by the original Mamasan, Rosario Gabangabang, and her husband Gunny Clancy. She had called ahead days earlier to let them know that a Commander Dantes, the son of Hod Dantes, was going to be visiting. In the event they took Connie's car and went downtown to the place and went in. The Gunny stood slowly, "Getting kinda creaky in my old age," he said as he held out his hand. "This is my wife, Rosario." "Commander it is an honor to meet you." "Thank you. You know until fairly recently I had no idea of my Dad's activities in the Philippines." "I would love to hear about him during those years. He didn't talk about it. I've read about the property and the accounting of its operations over the years. Tell me is it still in operation, people living there under ten year agreements like the original contract stated?"

Putting down her Kirin beer, Rosario smiled, "It has changed quite a bit since the days when I actively ran the businesses. There is extensive acreage under cultivation and yes there are dwellings there for the workers and their families." Gunny spoke up, "Did the reports you read say anything about what took place, mention anything about why Hod got all of that land?" "Just a hint, Gunny, enough to make me want to hear the whole story." Both Rosario and Gunny leaned forward in their chairs, talking over one another. They couldn't say enough about his bravery, coolness under fire and decisiveness in life and death situations.

Dance mentioned that he'd spent time with the lodges, The Admiral and Mrs. Lodge, and that they had only good things to say about his Dad. Gunny sat back in his chair and told them about the last time he'd seen Hod. "On the roof of the Manila Hotel he was only a kid, a Seaman who was a crack shot with a Colt .45. Much later, toward the end of the war he came back as a Chief aboard a tin can that carried Commodore Lodge as the Squadron Commander. He came in to shore to pick up Lydia Lodge, a Navy Nurse who served with us in the resistance. He was cool under fire and totally devoted to the Lodges." Dance took it all in, these people who had thought so much of his Dad. "Thank you so much for telling me about him. Connie and I are going up to Baguio to tour the place, would you like to join us?" They looked at each other and said thank you for the offer, we think we'll let Connie take you there."

At the Estancia they met the family of Rosa, the original overseer and the one who had been granted permission to live and support herself on the property. There was even a short hike up to the top of a tall foothill where they viewed the hideout used during the war. It was a whirlwind two day tour of mostly business sites and enterprises and at the end of his tours Dance decided to extend his visit for a more in depth inspection of the region in order to get better acquainted with property values and start evaluating what he'd like to keep and what he might liquidate. Besides, Rosa Vasconcellos' family had offered to show him more of the sights and they'd quickly set him up in one of the houses he owned, a very nice place out in the country with gorgeous views of the mountains.

Two of Rosa's grandchildren, took charge of him and showed him all of the places neither he nor his Dad had ever seen. Both Hod and Dance had spent time in Subic during their careers, of course, but neither had made the trip to Baguio. The grandson, Horatio Calderone pointed to a large park in the downtown area. "The Japanese leveled the city and there was wide spread ruin after the war. "My Grandmother and Auntie Rosario bought several properties in the ruined areas after the earthquakes leveled the area for a second time." His sister, Arsenia added, "We think you might like to go out to the mines. Gold is mined on some of the land you own." There was a dinner every night and usually a single lady or two was invited. Altogether it was a very relaxing and enjoyable time in Baguio.

After his tours and back in the Verdad law Offices, Dance asked "Connie, I think it is time to put these affairs into some sort of more permanent order." "I agree, what do you have in mind?" Dance replied that he thought that the people who had lived there for so long and worked the property would have certain legal protections and that in any case he wanted to do the right thing by them and not see it get down to a legal fight over squatter's rights. "I agree with you and we would be pleased to continue to represent you here, in these matters. Give me a couple of weeks and I will present you a plan for formalizing ownership in your name of all of the businesses as well as settling equities with the people who have lived there." Dance agreed and they shook on it. "Connie , I've been to the mining properties and understand there is interest in them. I know nothing about mining except that it is pretty risky. I'd like to sell them before they run out of pay dirt. I'd also like to consider developing the land in the city that currently looks like a park. Let's see what kind of interest there is." Connie cocked an appraising eye at Dance, "Can do, Boss." "And considering the cool climate and pine forest growth, there's a potential for tourism. Please check into how the zoning is now set up and let's look at tax structure and do some strategic planning to do some investing in the areas of agriculture, tourism and real estate."

Connie Verdad sat back with puffed cheeks and let out an excited laugh. "What are you, a mind reader?" "Why, you've thought about some of these moves?" he asked. "Of course, but I've had a few years to do it; you've only had a week!" "Whom do you think I might engage to honcho this operation," he asked. At that Connie paused and leveled her best twin barreled look at him and said, "I think you're looking at her." They spent another week in discussions in Manila and Baguio getting comfortable with each other. Evenings were spent in the law offices going over the research produced that day by Staff. "Connie, something has been on my mind. I want to know what Philippine law has to say about the passage of real estate, land grants, even, in cases like mine, where for purposes of these properties my Dad was intestate. His will did not mention any of these holdings, in fact I imagine he only knew about some of them. Part of it is Granted from centuries ago to the Calderones by the Spanish, the rest is all over the place and maybe not so critical." "You may be surprised to know that I have looked into this. Law in the P.I. directs passage of the block grant holdings to the eldest surviving male heir. Which of course, is you. You are the owner. Failure to have made your claim would have no doubt drawn interest from the politicians. As soon as I earned of your Father's death I filed your claim, as your legal representative.

"I think it is time to fire you as my lawyer." She held her emotions in check, noting that he'd not finished his thought. "And hire you as my Partner. You should know that I will first settle some fair amount on my Sister, who should share as our Dad's beneficiary, let's say twenty percent." With a serious look he asked, "Are you interested?" She came around the table and didn't know whether to kiss him or shake his hand. She held her hand out and he hugged her. "Fifty-fifty with what's left?" he asked. Then she kissed him and said, "Yes, but you're too generous." And he said "no, actually your Dad earned this for you. There were stories in the Vasconcellos family of your Dad's honesty and fearlessness in looking out for my Dad's interests. It was touch and go with the Japanese during the war years.

Before he left to return to the States, Connie documented the partnership, which merged the Law Offices with Baguio Enterprises and asked him how much money he might like to withdraw initially as a disbursement, Connie said, *before* they signed the papers. "That's not necessary," he said. But she insisted. That integrity streak ran deep in the Verdad Family. He finally agreed and when he boarded his flight home it was with the very pleasant knowledge of a one million five Swiss account with his name on it and a feeling of total confidence in his Partner.

CHAPTER 1
THE ASSASSIN

"Senator Jonathan Riggs was shot and killed today as he entered his car, returning home from a short stay at Bethesda Naval Hospital. The assault occurred in the restricted access area behind the hospital, often used by high-profile patients. A highly placed source at the FBI stated that two tires of his vehicle were shot out, then the Senator was struck. It is believed that a high-powered rifle was used in the attack. No one saw the gunman or men. The senior senator from Massachusetts, a Democrat, was scheduled to sit in consideration of another of President Jameson's judicial appointees next week. Speculation now is that those meetings will be delayed. More bulletins and updates on the investigation as we receive them. Meanwhile, in other news..."

Not old, not young, he sat for a while, staring at the screen neither seeing nor hearing. A tape played in his head—the corpulent Senator and his party turning at the sound of the first two shots, then his silvery mane jerking spasmodically to the shots delivered to his chest and his head. Crack! Crack! White shirtfront punched in crimson, flying fragments of his suddenly dissolving expression spraying onto the car. His mind's eye saw the shocked reaction of hospital staff as they took cover. Before they could respond he had broken down the rifle and secured it beneath his jacket, picked up his spent brass, turned and angled through the wooded area toward the sidewalk. Four blocks away he caught the next bus and rode it to the stop where his car was parked. He'd gotten home in time to catch one of the first reports on CNN.

He flipped the TV off, went to his computer and brought up the "theliberallist" web site, He slowly scanned it for new entries and messages, read them and closed out the site. He turned in and was soon sleeping soundly.

CHAPTER 2
THE LIBERAL LIST

Dance Dantes glanced at the caller ID and thumbed the line open on his cell phone. "Hey, bud. What's up?"

"What's up? Don't you watch TV anymore?" It was his long-time buddy and classmate from the Boat School, Wade Bates. "I guess all you look at is that web site of yours."

Dantes waited patiently, a tolerant smile on his face to go with strong, regular features and bright blue eyes.

"Just that last night, your favorite senator was shot and killed, that's all."

"My fav… you can't mean *the* senior senator from Massachusetts?"

"That's exactly who I mean, the Chief Obstructionist in the U.S. Senate."

Dantes flicked on CNN and dropped into the soft leather oversized sofa in his study. "Wow, hard to believe, but there must have been many who would've been willing to do it, Wade."

"Yeah, I know. Hey, what number was he on your list?"

"Well, let's see. He had been No. 1 for a couple of months there, but lately had slid to something like three or four... *wait* a minute, you're not implying anything, are you?"

"No I'm not; but that hasn't stopped your liberal buddies in the press from making some typically dumb statements."

It was coming across on the TV now. "Senator Riggs was rather highly placed on the ultra-conservative web site, "The Liberal List," right up there with radio personality Howard Storm, movie actress Fanny Goldman and ..."

"Hey Wade, you're right! Looks like I'm finally getting some media play. Not sure I like the implied connection between my web site and what's happened to Riggs, though."

"Well, rotsa' ruck, buddy. I've got a feeling this is only the beginning."

————

It had been a wild ride. Only six months ago he had put up the web site. He did it out of frustration, fed up and angry with his and most Americans' inability to get any unbiased information about important current events.

Horace Howard Dantes had lived a varied and lively career in the U.S. Navy, Lockheed and finally IBM. He had maintained a strong interest in national defense and had developed a growing interest in politics. It bothered him that the press labeled all conservatives like him extremists, and reported critically on their activities, while essentially giving liberals a free ride. Although retired now, he had decided to do something about it, even if only in his own small way.

He'd contacted friends at IBM Global Services and gotten some "on demand" services. They'd set him up with a domain name and web site, "The Liberal List," that included a lot of really neat features. He'd started out with the voting records of the members of the House and Senate, ranked from most liberal to most conservative, with the cut-off being at the 90 percent mark for liberal voting. There were biographical sketches of the top several liberal voters, one of whom was Senator Riggs. Then he'd added names from the world of entertainment. Movie actors and actresses and rap musicians, shock jocks and porn stars, even a Supreme Court justice or two. IBM had included, almost as an afterthought, a portal to make donations to the web site, as a means of helping to pay for it.

A poll was included along with the one-vote, one-dollar rule, so that anyone accessing the site could vote for his or her top ten liberals. It had been a good thing that he had opted for 'on demand' expansion, because what he'd gotten was an explosion in hits as well as donations. In three months he'd gone to 2,000 hits per day. Anyone could submit a statement, limited to 250 characters. He'd had to put in a disclaimer as well as a warning about content. The readers and writers and donations kept coming in large numbers. It was unfiltered, and it was passionate. They were all over the map. No telling what they would say, pouring out pent-up emotions and frustrations on his site, telling it all to those who would read "The Liberal List."

Incoming copy was left on the site for only a week and then flushed. Income outstripped costs significantly and he was banking some five thousand a week. Unlike the cable network that prided itself on being fair and balanced, "The Liberal List" trumpeted that it was "fair and biased." Dantes saw this bias as necessary in order to restore any sense of balance to the whole media system.

Dantes had gone into the Navy at the University of Texas NROTC unit in Austin, Texas where he had taken the Naval Academy entrance examination, coming out second in the state. He got two first alternate appointments but when Lyndon Johnson learned he had two, Johnson withdrew his. Unfortunately his roommate had gotten the primary appointment from then-Senator, soon to be Governor, Price Daniels, and that left Dance out in the cold. He went on his ROTC Summer cruise without an appointment, but had been swept up into the group of qualified candidates whose Parents were Service retirees. This group was eligible for a Presidential appointment and Dance got one of them. When his ship pulled into Rio de Janeiro, orders were cut for him to fly back to Annapolis for duty as a Midshipman. He transferred from his summer cruise aboard USS Iowa (BB-61) in the summer of 1957.

CHAPTER 3

THE ADVOCATE AND THE ADVERSARY

Jennings Carson sat in the Café Normandie, on Main Street, Annapolis, sipping some strong French roast, black. Across the room a TV was on with the volume low, as she totted up in her head the results of the day so far. Her struggling weekly publication, the *Anne Arundel Advocate*, was consuming all of her time, she thought, and wasn't making it. *"Don't know why I got into this—yeah, I do, but I had no idea it was going to be so tough."* Her interview subject, an Anne Arundel county exec, was already 20 minutes late. Her calls on advertisers had yielded only one new account to offset the loss of three the past month. It wasn't looking good.

Upon graduation from the Georgia Institute of Technology with a bachelor's in aerospace engineering, Jennings had landed a job in the aero design engineering section at Lockheed, in Marietta, Georgia. She had been bored out of her skull. Wing-foil shapes, wind-tunnel tests and lift and drag coefficients were not her cup of tea. What she really enjoyed was people. And they enjoyed her. After two years of engineering anonymity she chucked it in and took off for a year to Europe, using some of the money her grandmother had left her.

One year turned into three years and two French lovers. She banged around working to stretch her funds. She taught English at the Lycee. She waited tables at Le Meridien Etoile, just minutes from La Defense and the Champs Elysees in Paris, before moving to its Lionel Hampton Jazz Club as a cocktail waitress. Finally she wrote several investigative pieces for *Le Monde Diplomatique*, English version from the Congo, covering the AIDS epidemic and terrorist trade in diamonds, gold and uranium.

When she came back stateside she knew what it was that she wanted to do—journalism. Turned away at several newspapers (an engineering degree wasn't what they had in mind, and a French résumé wasn't too popular nowadays), she'd found a small weekly publication for sale on the web and ended up buying it. The *Advocate* had bumped along for thirty years, sometimes in the black, sometimes in arrears. She'd taken what was left of her bequest from Grandma Bam and made a down payment on the *Advocate*. The bank owned the rest and she was in business. It wasn't as alluring as a posting as an international correspondent, but it was close to D.C. and, who knows, things had a way of becoming interesting when you least expected it.

———

The drone of the TV rose above the level of her introspection. It was an interview with someone who had actually shown up for the TV guy—Dance Dantes, a local boy retired in Severna Park, and Jeff Prather, network talking head for ABS.

"How do the names get up there on your web site?" Prather stared accusingly.

"The first batch I selected, Jeff, the rest came from my viewers."

"Viewers?" as if the riff raff that went to Dantes' site could be called viewers.

"Hits, eyeballs, people who come to theliberallist.net for something different," said Dantes.

"Different, as in to read instructions for the next person chosen for a 'hit'?"

Dantes frowned slightly at Prather, "Would you like to rephrase that, Jeff?"

"There are many who think that what you put out there is tantamount to shouting fire in a crowded theater," said Prather, ignoring the question and looking down his nose.

"*How* many, Jeff? Do you have any direct quotes, or is this just more innuendo? As you probably know my viewership rivals yours. The thousands upon thousands who make their remarks on my site put their name to what they say. Have you been to theliberallist site, Jeff?"

"Well, actually…"

"I thought not. Let me give you a personal invitation…"

"Frankly, Dance, your reputation precedes you. It's not necessary to go there to know that it is filled with conservative hate speech." His tone was one of moral superiority.

"Hate speech? I think, in a way, you're right. A lot of conservatives hate the kind of irresponsible speech that liberals such as you ritually and routinely make."

It was obvious that this wasn't going the way that Prather had expected at all. Most interviewees on his program quickly ducked and ran when politically correct labels and issues were brandished. It was also obvious that Dantes was every bit as fixed in his views as he accused the liberals of being. As the program drew to a close, Dantes flashed a placard with "theliberallist.net" printed on it, with a big grin on his face. Prather frantically motioned to the producer to take it off…

Dantes had a few years on him, but Jen kinda' liked his grin. And his attitude. *In fact, he more than slightly reminds me of my last Frenchman.* Jen pushed her chair back and rushed out of the café. She had an idea. She didn't see the sweating and puffing gentleman in the rumpled suit who came into the café ten minutes later, looked around, checked his watch, and then left.

————

Jeff Prather strode the corridor between the studio and network offices deep in thought. He could barely avoid scowling. Forty-five years old, he was just at his peak in terms of influence and popularity as a broadcast news personality. He had the Hollywood good looks and resonant baritone and twenty-three years of media experience behind him. Ratings had been better, but they were still not bad. He'd been thinking of a new issue, one that would grab his audience and flood the network with e-mails—e-mails in praise of his vigilant service to the American public. The spot just concluded with Dantes wasn't one of his best. He'd let it get out of hand. *He* was supposed to be asking the questions. Dantes was better prepared than he thought he'd be. Jeff decided to have the staff dig up some stuff on this Dantes guy. Maybe he'd turn out to very useful in the weeks and months to come.

He popped into the conference room for the usual postproduction meeting.

"Hi, Jeff." A respectful chorus from the crew already assembled.

"Hi, guys." Uh-oh. Sitting at the table was the network vice president to whom he reported, Mike Madden.

"Hey, Mike, what's up?"

"Oh, just thought I'd sit in on this one."

"Okay, well let's get to it." And they went around the room, taking comments from each person there. "Little ragged in switching active cameras at the end," he said to the producer.

"Yeah, I wasn't ready for the give and take between you and that Dantes guy." People exchanged looks around the table. Jeff didn't really see any challenges from any of the people he had on the show, probably didn't even dignify what had happened as 'give and take.' Still, in the silence, an uncomfortable tension grew. Clearing his throat and with his voice a little more clipped, Jeff asked if anyone else had any input, with that famous 'look,' eyes squinted just a tad and jaw thrust forward a bit, a look that said that he didn't expect any.

"No? Well then, until next time. Thanks, folks."

As the last of the group filed out of the room, Jeff turned to Mike and smiled, "Little surprised to see you down here, boss." He waited while Mike, fingers steepled, a little frown developing just between his eyebrows, let the silence expand.

"Yeah, well, we need to talk some." It was dawning on Jeff that this was not going to be fun. "Jeff, it's about the numbers you're hanging up. They're just not what they have been, not what they have to be."

"Now wait a minute, Mike. They've been holding pretty steady and…"

"Yeah, steady at about seven points less than they were last quarter and you know that Cox is grabbing *all* of that market share. They've passed us in ad revenues and are on the upswing. And if that's not bad enough, rumor is that they're hiring that hot chick Riley Berry who does the magazine pieces for CNN. Ought to bring them another point or two after she settles in. I hear she's going to go against you, in your time slot."

"Heyyy, look, boss," said Jeff, feeling a pool of sweat beginning to form inside his collar on the back of his neck. "You know I've never failed the network, I'll be back up there. I'll be back soon. I have some ideas."

"Yeah, well you'd better get better-looking at the same time. That Riley is one fine looking girl. We tried to get her on board ourselves, couldn't match their offer. You still working out?" Quick stabbing glance at the paunch pushing at Jeff's belt—quicker yet, Jeff sucking it in. "I'm telling you, we don't have much time on this. Don't know how long I can keep J.D. from getting involved."

J.D.? Network news president? This was turning nasty. In his twenty-plus years with the network they'd never threatened him in this way. "Heyyy, not to worry, boss. Let's do lunch next week and I'll go over my plans with you then."

"Good idea, Jeff, only let's do it on Friday, so I'll have the weekend to prepare for the corporate review coming up."

Friday! He didn't yet have a clue how he was going to handle this! "No sweat, Mike, Friday it is!

———

Prather had planned to get his staff to dig up some useful material on Dance Dantes, but the more he thought about it, the more he didn't want his staff to know about this project. *Instead, I'll get staff to do some background checks on a private investigator. Need to be sure I've got the right guy; then I'll get the P.I. to do the spadework.* It would be better not to just rush into this; he could sleep on it overnight.

Buzzing his administrative assistant on the intercom the next morning, first thing, he said, "Nancy, please come in."

"Sure, Jeff."

"Nancy, could you please get our undercover expert in here? I need to talk with him about some background work."

"Right away." Only a few minutes later, the man was there.

"Yeah, Jeff, whatcha got?" 'Knucks' Halloran, a beefy former club fighter who was known for his persuasive and thorough approach to matters of some discretion, sprawled in the chair across from Prather's desk. He had a whiskey rasp to his voice, which rumbled from deep in his chest like rocks breaking up.

"Look, you know a few P.I.'s, don't you?"

"Yeah, who doesn't?"

"Well, but I mean you might know or could find out a lot about some of them, right?"

Where's he headed with this? "Well, Jeff, you know that I pride myself on being able to get answers, even from 'uncooperative subjects.' If there's something we want to know about someone, even a private eye, I'm sure I can get it."

"Yes, well, I want to select a private investigator to handle a potentially explosive situation. I need someone whose loyalty to me will be greater than I could buy with money alone." He looked at Halloran steadily.

He wants to be able to blackmail *a P.I.,* thought Halloran. "Look, I think I can get the skinny on a couple who might fill the bill nicely. Let me check around and I'll be back with a rundown and you can pick the one you'd like."

"That's super, Knucks. And if it's not asking too much, could I have your reports before close of business tomorrow? Sorry to put such a rush on this."

"Not a problem. Ought to be able to put it together in no time."

———

The quickly assembled dossiers sat on his desk the next morning, handwritten sheets clipped securely into folded manila with two-hole keepers. One described an older, broadly experienced investigator with a liquor problem. He periodically abused his wife as well as the bottle. Canned from the D.C. police force fifteen years ago, he nonetheless had friends there who still threw him the occasional job. His really dirty secret was that he had an extensive collection of kiddie-porn.

The other subject was distinctly different. He was single and thirty-five. His experience wasn't in police work at all. In fact, he'd had a hard time developing the investigatory skills required in his line of work and his annual income showed it. Based upon the extreme difficulty that Knucks had in getting any background information on him, it was likely he had been employed by one of the intelligence agencies. Knucks explained that any attempts to confirm this might in fact unnecessarily alarm the subject, probably a mistake one would not want to make. He added his opinion that having a struggling business coupled with a desire to keep his past quiet; this P.I. ought to be very cooperative. *A nice touch, that, on the part of Knucks, putting all of this down in handwriting... no sense in having it saved somewhere on somebody's machine.*

Jeff made his decision and swung around to his telephone, punched in the number. After the third ring he heard, "Starzinger Investigations, how may I direct your call?"

CHAPTER 4
THE PI

"Hey, Dixie, hold my calls until noon. I'm going to be tied up here."
The slightly past her bloom receptionist, secretary, bookkeeper and
mother of two tossed her head. *Hmmph! It'll be the first time he's been
busy in the last six weeks.*

"Gotcha covered, Dick." *And that's what he'd been acting like lately, a
prick, ever since he lost the Williams security job to the big firm across
town.* A giggle escaped her as she pictured what she'd just said and
thought for just a moment about actually "covering his dick." *Well,
now. And wasn't* that *a tingle-inducing thought to get you going in the
morning!*

Work for the firm had been hard to come by and it had Dixie
somewhat concerned for her own security. She glanced at her reflection
from the glass covering the framed portrait of her boys on her desk.
A sigh escaped her nicely endowed chest as she minutely examined
the accelerating signs of age in her face, framed in natural blonde hair.
Focus shifting from her own image to her boys actually in the photo,
she reminded herself that they really needed a dad. She thought of the
handsome lug behind the office door and sighed once again. Then she
straightened her skirt, got more comfortably disposed at her desk and
picked up the phone to make the rounds, yet again, of all the creditors
and debtors that held Richard Starzinger Investigations in thrall.

Dick Starzinger was poring over the articles in this morning's
Post on the Riggs murder. Personally, he wondered how an assailant
could've gotten so close and then gotten away so fast, without arousing
suspicion. Flipping through the associated stories, he noticed one on a
guy named Dantes who ran a web site of some sort. The article made
vague suggestions, implications really, that the web site actually targeted

national figures for this sort of treatment. *Interesting! I need to check this site out, and see for myself.* The name of the site wasn't given in the article, but he'd Google Dantes and web site and was sure he'd find it. Come to think of it, he *had* heard about it—Liberal List or something like that.

Dixie picked up the phone on the third ring. "Starzinger Investigations, how may I direct your call?" she said, as though there were more than one place to connect the call. She looked puzzled as she heard the voice, which seemed familiar, though she couldn't place it.

"Hello, I need some investigative work done and would like to talk with Mr. Starz-injer, er, uh, about it."

"Mr. Starzinger is in a meeting, may I take a message?"

"Actually time is short and I need to meet soon on this matter."

"Perhaps I could interrupt. Whom shall I say is calling?"

"Oh, sorry. Uh, Jeffrey Prather."

I knew he sounded familiar! "*Oh, Mr. Prather, I'm such a fan,*" *she thought;* "*I watch you every night!*" *she wanted to say.* She pictured him, the most famous of the talking heads, and in a twinkling of an eye was imagining another sort of head, *You've got to* stop *this!*

In her most professional voice, Dixie said, "Why of course, Mr. Prather, let me just check with Mr. Starzinger." Shaking her head and fanning herself, she placed the call on hold and went straight into Dick's office. Out of breath, she said, "Dick, you have a very interesting call you've got to take!"

"Dixieee, I told you *no* calls."

"I know, but this is *Jeff Prather!*"

"Jeff Prather?" He quickly suppressed a quizzed look and said, "Put him on."

"Dick Starzinger here, Mr. Prather. How may I be of service?"

"Well, Dick, if I may call you that?"

"Sure, Jeff."

"I have the need for some investigative services, something outside of our normal corporate channels. And, of course, I need to keep it entirely off the record."

"Of course. Why don't we meet and discuss what it is that you have in mind?"

"Exactly. I can be in your office this evening, say eight? If that works for you."

"That'll be fine, Jeff. See you then, at eight."

"Oh, and I expect that I can rely on the discretion of your assistant; I don't want my name repeated outside our conversations."

"No problem there, she's very discreet, but I'll speak to Ms. DeLight."
"Thanks, Dick." And the line went dead.

———

"Nancy, thanks for staying late; I'm packing it in."
"Certainly, Jeff… before you go, I didn't want to upset you with this earlier.
"What?"
"It's about Mr. Halloran."
"Knucks? Why, anything wrong?"
Sniffle, "Oh, Jeff, he's had an accident, a car accident."
Prather had been standing on one foot, ready to head out the door. Turning to Nancy, he dropped his briefcase and put both hands on her desk, a flash of fear causing him to shudder. "A car wreck? He's okay?"
"No, Jeff. It was a single-car accident and they think it happened some time ago. He was found in his car, run off an embankment and into some trees, up near where he lives—lived."
"My God, this is terrible… he was in here just, what was it, yesterday? Look, Nancy, set a meeting for tomorrow morning. We'll want to get everyone together and handle this appropriately. Knucks was married, wasn't he? Let's put together a draft letter of sympathy, and we'll… gosh I just can't think all of this through. We'll check into this more tomorrow. Thanks for letting me know, of course. You drive carefully going home, okay?"
His hand was shaking as he retrieved his brief case. *Christ, this is mighty close to home! This can't be just a coincidence! Maybe I shouldn't keep the appointment with this Starzinger guy. What was it that Knucks had said, "Might not be a good idea to get him riled…"*
"Still, there's nothing overt that ties me to Knucks. He was certainly more careful, more discreet than that," he muttered under his breath, unlocking his car and hurriedly swinging behind the wheel. Another shiver, this time convulsing his whole body as he gripped the wheel. *Knucks Halloran, dead!*

———

At 8:18, he pulled into the parking spaces by Starzinger's office in a strip center across from a weedy used car lot. He noted that there was only one car out front. *Good, the fewer who are aware of this business, the better.* Then another thought hit him. "I wonder how smart it was to set this meeting this late—and with him alone, at that," talking to himself again. *C'mon... You're running out of time to get some stuff together for Mike Madden. I have to have a plan, based on some real stuff, at least some stuff that raises questions.* He hesitated, stared up at the lighted office and, mind made up, started for the door.

Zinger glanced at his watch, grunted in exasperation, *twenty minutes late!* He'd noticed Dixie hanging around after she'd normally have left, probably wanting to catch a glimpse. Still, he wasn't surprised when Prather hadn't shown up at eight. Prather had more than his share of arrogance, must be used to having others wait for him. Restless, Zinger went over to the window that overlooked the parking lot from his second-story office. The streetlamps cast their light onto the asphalt like curved wave patterns at the beach. As he was wondering how much a light source that small would heat up a stretch of pavement, he heard the knock, just a double knock, abrupt and guarded.

"Thanks for waiting, I appreciate it." Prather sat across the desk from Starzinger, a serious man, he thought, who looked like he could take care of himself in a brawl. Confident with close-cropped hair and unsettling eyes that bore in on him.

"No problem at all, good to meet you. Any trouble finding the place?"

"No, not at all. Sorry to be late. Last-minute stuff at work, couldn't get away when I'd planned."

"I know how *that* goes," Zinger grunted. "But, tell me, just curious… how did you find *me*? As you can see, my offices are small and my business activities are relatively small in scope."

Careful here! "Actually I wanted one of the smaller outfits, thought my business would be handled best by a single individual and I preferred to work directly with the person I chose. How'd I find you? I picked you out of one of the single-line listings in the Yellow Pages."

Zinger paused, just slightly, as he considered Prather. From his non-verbal signs, it was very plain that this man was lying. Prather had looked down and to the left as he mentioned the phone book. Come to think of it, "Jeff" wasn't fitting the profile Zinger had expected. He was actually somewhat deferential, and appeared uncomfortable. The discomfort was routine in a setting like Zinger's office. The obvious care with which Prather was conducting himself as a 'good guy' didn't fit what Zinger knew about him. He'd done some checking around, largely on the web, and there really were a lot of folks out there who didn't care for "Jeff." Other facts that Zinger had gleaned about Jeff were that he was divorced and an avid hunter and sportsman; he had some nice boats, had even raced them for a while. So, it was a mixed bag; this guy was interesting.

Curiosity reinforced, Zinger leaned forward onto his desk, forearms resting on the edge, hands folded together and asked, "How may I be of help?"

Prather's thoughts skipped back to the reasons for his overture, the appearance on his show of Dance Dantes and his meeting with VP Madden. An eerily similar set of feelings had been engendered by all three encounters. Dantes, then Madden, and now Starzinger had all made him feel uncomfortable —uncomfortable and out of control. *Christ, I've got to get a grip!* He took a deep breath and took the plunge.

"Yes, well you see, I'm concerned about a conspiracy, a congealing of suggestion and violent action that I think is more than just coincidental. I'm referring, of course, to the recent murder of Senator Riggs and the fact that the victim had been targeted, in open forum, on the web. I think that Dance Dantes, who runs that vicious attack web site, is responsible, in some direct manner, for the Senator's death. There may even be something intended against me; as you know, I've had Riggs on my show, several times."

Actually, I don't *know, you little prick. You must think everybody watches you on the boob tube.* "This killing is shocking, to be sure," replied Starzinger. "But there's a police force and FBI to tackle it. What draws you into commissioning your own private investigation?" Delivered with cocked eyebrow and open curiosity. "We both know that 'most any P.I. is going to jump at the chance to open an account like this. Why start your own separate investigation and not use your own in-house resources?"

"Actually, this is not a local news sort of exposé. The information out there, will, I am sure, be of national importance. I'm convinced that Dantes is informed and probably directed the attack. It would be a service to the nation to get to the bottom of this and ensure that any such killings are brought to a stop." Prather was getting a grip, taking refuge in some self-righteous hyperbole, the kind of statement that went down rather well in his business.

But Zinger wasn't hooked yet. "Again, at the risk of being repetitive, there are both local and federal authorities who will be investigating…"

"Perhaps I've made a mistake in coming here. Maybe this is too big for you, might not be so comfortable for you, getting into the Feds' sandbox." Prather was now on the offensive, feeling more comfortable, in control.

Zinger noted this, as well; the raised head, the slight thrust of his jaw. "Well, as to being too big, no. And as far as conflicting with the Feds, no. But, you must understand, this will be obscenely expensive." Last attempt to scare him off.

"The money will be no problem, but I must have an outline of your approach no later than tomorrow and some initial results very quickly."

This guy is really desperate. Like most people with this kind of problem, he's not looking for the truth. When you paid the big bucks you were looking for confirmation. More to the point, you were looking for information with which to accomplish your objective, regardless of who got hurt, or worse. It's not like I'm not used to this kind of operation; just not used to doing it for private citizens. "Okay, ten grand a day, minimum of one month, paid in advance. You'll have your outline tomorrow morning and I'd expect to have something for you to start with within a week or two." Prather eased up and sat back as the tension drained out of his face. "I can't think of anything else. Perhaps it would be best if your assistant delivered the outline. I can give her your retainer then." Prather's eyes engaged, now, the expression asking, "Are we done, here?"

"That'll be fine. I'll get started."

————

The man standing in the entranceway of one of the storefronts waited until Prather's car had left, and then walked down the street in the direction Prather had gone.

Zinger stepped to the window and watched Prather drive off in his Mercedes. As he turned away toward his desk, some movement caught his eye. He froze and then saw a man move away from the building next door and walk to the street. His practiced eye noted caution in the man's movements and appearance… or else complete disregard and innocence. Knowing that it was entirely unlikely that any of his neighbors were still working at this hour, his decision was made. He locked up, went quickly down the stairs and crossed the street, going in the direction the subject had gone. He didn't forget the snub-nose .38 revolver, which he was licensed to carry.

He barely caught sight of his quarry ahead. Suddenly the stranger stopped and, Zinger could tell, pretended to tie his shoes. Then he turned about and started back, toward Zinger. This was someone who was practicing tradecraft. Thankful that he was on the opposite side of the street, Zinger backed into the small used car lot and took up position behind some trucks. He dropped to the pavement and watched from under the vehicles.

The stranger kept coming and now *crossed the street*, moving toward Zinger's position. Zinger took a chance and, staying low, moved farther back into the lot. *What? Was the guy following him?* The guy turned directly into the lot without pausing, went straight up to the Toyota Corolla Zinger was using as cover and stood there—listening? *Listening, hell! This guy was taking a piss! And I thought I was the only guy who relieved himself in parking lots!* Zinger could see only the guy's shoes from his prone position, as the guy shook himself, zipped up and got in the goddamned car. *Zinger'd avoided getting spattered, but a smallish rivulet of the guy's urine had wended its way toward him, in fits and starts. It had run into the cuff of his jacket and shirtsleeve, was dammed there and was soaking in.* As Zinger's subject opened the door, ducked into the seat and started his car—*his car!*—Zinger scuttled behind the adjacent vehicle on the off side, remaining crouched, but with the .38 in his hand. The nondescript Toyota sedan drove off, leaving a rueful P.I. in the parking lot. *I might be able to trail him, but I think I'll pass, piss, whatever. As nervous and careful as this guy was, he'd probably lose me, might catch on that he was being followed and I'd rather he not know he was observed.*

Zinger went back to his office. There he wrote down the license plate number, a Virginia tag, noted the color of the vehicle and the sticker identifying the dealer that had sold the vehicle. Before he left for the night he removed his jacket and shirt, threw the shirt into the corner of his coat closet, and put on a clean one, one of several he kept in there, if not for this particular purpose. Then he rinsed out the spot in his jacket sleeve, patted it dry, threw it on and went home.

CHAPTER 5
ANOTHER HIT

Hirsch was director of the ACLU's D.C. legislative office. His bio on "The Liberal List" summarized Josh Hirsch's life, until this morning. A graduate of Stanford Law and a Dinkelspiel Scholar there, he had been involved in grassroots activism programs and come to the ACLU via the Ford Foundation. He lobbied Congress and often testified there on criminal justice issues. He had been written up in the *Post*'s Federal Page and been a guest on several nightly news shows. Josh was openly gay.

"Yeah, well now Josh was openly dead, or would be when they found his body, he thought. It hadn't been difficult to slip up on the town house in Georgetown early, just before the papers were delivered, and then to jimmy the back door. There hadn't been any pets in the neighborhood when he'd reconnoitered and it had been a silent entry. Any random or sudden noise could be passed off as the delivery of morning papers, he'd reasoned. His timing had been spot-on and he was already at the back door when the paper delivery service passed by on the street. He took the chance that there was an alarm and slipped inside. No alarm, so either it was silent or turned off, or it was non-existent.

Walking slowly in his running shoes he was pleased to note that the floors weren't the squeaky hardwood type, but were soft carpet instead. As he'd figured, the bedrooms were upstairs. It was dark, but with some soft light coming through the windows, enough to see by as he slowly climbed the stairs.

He pressed the button on his phone to complete the call to the house phone. At 0445 in the morning, it went off like a fire alarm,

RIINNNNGGG! He'd gotten his phone using a false identity, a bogus address when he'd signed up.

"Shit, who could be calling at this hour?" One of the figures in bed rolled to a seated position on the side of the bed and grunted, "This is Josh, who's calling?" No answer, just a dial tone. Stared at the phone, cradled the receiver and then lay back down. Glared at the alarm clock and saw the time. His partner either slept through it or was trying to stay asleep. Josh, though, was fully awake. Padding across the room to the hallway, he felt his way to the spare bedroom and went straight to the phone there and hit *69, waited until the number of his last call had been spoken to him and hung up, the number not a familiar one.

Then, instead of heading straight back to bed, Josh ducked into the bath off the hall and quietly relieved himself, still in the dark. As he turned toward the bedroom, he felt a strong hand grab his mouth as his throat was cut. Losing consciousness, his struggles quieted and he was let down softly to the floor.

Panting with the effort and excitement, letting his breathing quiet, the killer listened carefully for any sounds from Josh's bed partner. There were none, so he swiftly and quietly moved downstairs and exited the house the way he'd come in. It was after he was halfway down the back alley that he saw the lights come on behind him in the townhouse he'd just vacated. He imagined he'd heard a wailing scream, but he wasn't waiting around for confirmation. In ten minutes, he covered a zigzag half-mile and came to his car, parked on another quiet street. Another thirty minutes and he was home. Throwing his clothes into the washing machine, he also methodically cleaned his knife and put it away, stood in a long, hot shower, toweled off and slipped into bed.

He was asleep in two minutes.

CHAPTER 6
THE INTERVIEW

Dance Dantes was listed in the Anne Arundel County telephone directory and had answered the phone himself. Jennings Carson found herself instantly warming to his voice as he responded pleasantly to her self-introduction. "Hello, Mr. Dantes, I'm Jennings Carson; I run the local paper, the *Anne Arundel Advocate*."

"You know, I actually subscribe to your publication—nice job you're doing with it. What can I do for you?" He chuckled, "Am I overdue in my payment?"

She had looked it up before the call, knew that he had been taking the paper for about a year. "No, I feel that *I'm* overdue in making your acquaintance; I actually have in mind an article, or series of articles I'd like to write about one of our more famous residents."

"Hmm, sounds interesting. Tell you what; I'll see how my schedule shakes out and call you back on this tomorrow."

The call came by noon the next day. "My schedule is relatively clear for the next couple of days. Why don't you come out here and we can start at my place?"

"That's nice of you, but I don't want to put you to any trouble..."

"Then it's settled. It's easier for me in my office at home than coming into town."

"Well, what time will work for you?"

"Anytime this afternoon or tomorrow afternoon."

"Great! Then I'm on my way."

———

As Jennings Crossed the Severn River Bridge, she was able to look back on the Naval Academy Chapel dominating the Academy skyline, shining in the bright sunlight. Pointing boldly skyward it seemed to her to represent the aspirations of the young men and women who chose to enter the Navy there. The drive up Ritchie Highway was pleasant and just a couple of miles later she turned off on B&A Boulevard and took Old County Rd to ultimately wend her way back toward the Severn River, she at last came out above Round Bay and drove to a sprawling ranch house sitting on the river bluff, about eighty feet above the river. The garage was open and there was a Ford F-250 pick-up truck parked in it. A note taped to the tailgate of the truck invited her to come out back to the patio.

His smile was easy, his eyes friendly as he took her hand, "Hi, Jennings, I'm Dance—it's so nice of you to have come out here."

"I appreciate the invitation, Dance; thanks for taking the time." She had dressed casually, but expensively, a nice pair of dark tan slacks and a light coffee-colored silk blouse that set off her tan and light brown eyes and hair. Dantes had taken some pains, too, wearing a clean pair of jeans, soft leather loafers and light-blue shirt that matched his eyes, now looking at her over a glass of unsweetened iced tea. They sat in lounge chairs, relaxing on the large screened patio overlooking the river.

"Nice place you have here; it's so quiet—and what a magnificent view!"

"Thanks, got lucky to find this spot still not built out. I love it here."

"I can certainly see why. So, I know that you graduated from the Naval Academy. Tell me, how important has the Academy been to you?" She gestured to the recorder. "Will this be okay?"

He nodded, "Hard to overstate how important going to school there has been in my life. It depends upon what your reasons were for going to the Academy in the first place. In my case, as a kid I always wanted to be a Navy chief, like my dad. Getting to go to the Naval Academy and be a Midshipman was a dream of mine from early on. Some Mids had a rough time, couldn't wait to get away, and said that the best view of the place was in the rearview mirror, getting smaller in the distance. Me, I ate up Plebe Year, soaked up all the tradition and couldn't wait to go out and fight my country's battles. For me the sun that rises is Navy Gold and it sets in a sea of Navy Blue."

He said this quietly, matter-of-factly, with affection. He looked directly at her as he stopped speaking. And it struck her that this man said exactly what he thought. Caught in that thought, she startled a bit when he asked, "So tell me a little bit about you."

"Oh, not too much to tell. I started out at Georgia Tech, daughter of a Florida high school principal and schoolteacher mom. Got my private pilot's license when I was sixteen, paid for it with my babysitting money. My dad always encouraged me to do the unusual and challenging things, including scuba and sky diving, kayaking. Didn't take to aero engineering at Lockheed so I took a few years off and went to Europe, instead. Got some experience in the Congo working for *Le Monde Diplomatique* before returning to the USA. Wound up finding the *Advocate* and also finding out how hard it is to make a living, publishing a weekly newspaper."

As she talked he looked at her and made up his mind. *Don't know her politics, but she's okay, understated. It's comfortable.* "I'm guessing it's the fairly recent fuss over my web site that's got you interested in writing a piece for the *Advocate*," he said.

"Yes, I caught your appearance on Jeff Prather's program—I'm interested in finding out more about you, your purposes in creating 'The Liberal List,' where you intend to go with it. Actually I thought my piece might break down into three parts, along those lines. To be honest, I think my readers will find this much more interesting than county politics and neighborhood dustups. And… I can certainly use an uptick in sales."

Over the next hour she quizzed him on his career in the Navy, at United Technologies, Lockheed (though never at the same place as Jennings) and IBM. She learned that he was fifty-two years old, had been married, been at sea on five ships and gotten divorced while in the Navy. They went over his work in the Navy's High Energy Laser Program, in Lockheed's F-22 Fighter Program, and as an executive consultant for IBM Global Services. As they talked she wrote, "extremely intelligent, lots of drive, knows what he thinks and believes and why."

She laughed; he smiled as they both heard his voice issuing from within the house as the voicemail picked up perhaps the third call during their visit. "Well, I'd better let you get back to your schedule."

"Thanks— why don't I come down to your offices to wrap this up? You could give me a call when you're ready."

"That sounds good; I'll aim for day after tomorrow, if that's okay." They parted with another handshake and she was headed back to Crabtown, eagerly anticipating another meeting with him.

———

Dantes approached the offices of the *Advocate*, located in the old port area down the street from Pusser's Landing on Compromise Street, just off Spa Creek where they served the best Maryland crab cakes. In the big glass window of the storefront there was an arc of gilt lettering across the top, edged in black, trumpeting *The Anne Arundel* with a line across the bottom, completing the semicircle that spelled out *Advocate*. Imagining a bottom semicircle to complete the sign, he chuckled as he thought of a happy face, eyes and all, with the requisite grin. That's the cost, he mused, of living in an animated Disneyesque age.

Pushing open the door he heard the tinkle of a bell and was soon greeted by the person who handled ads over the phone and the front counter, was responsible for printing and delivery, and also wrote all of the neighborhood and community pieces—Clem had been doing it for some thirty years. Jen was lucky to have him and they both knew it. Still, Clem wasn't too difficult to get along with, just had this annoying habit of butting in where he thought Jennings needed protection. To date he'd 'protected' her from three attractive males who'd made the mistake of evincing interest in Jen in front of him. "You must be that Dantes feller, in to meet with Miss Jennings."

Jennings made her appearance, coming into the front, "Commander, so nice to see you. Welcome to my humble shop." He took it all in, her hair tied back with a wisp come loose that she puffed away from the side of her mouth; her face alight with genuine pleasure, and at the same time, a sense of "Let's get down to business."

"Hey, glad to be aboard, but I think you're giving me too much credit."

"Credit?" with a bemused glance in his direction.

"Yes, I don't want to sail under false colors. In the Navy we greet lieutenant commanders as commander, but I didn't know whether you knew that nautical tidbit or not; I retired as a lieutenant commander."

Moving into her private office, with the door closed, she offered him a seat in the worn leather chair opposite her desk. "Can I get you some coffee? I'm sure it's not as good as the brew that the Navy provides."

"Sure thing, thanks." She went into the corner and stretched to secure a mug from the shelf, then drew his coffee at the coffee maker. He looked at her trim figure with her back turned, today again wearing slacks. It was obvious that she worked out.

She handed him the coffee. "Okay, let's start with the comment you made when you first walked in here." She'd realized that during their entire first interview he had not mentioned the rank he held while in the Navy, only the assignments, and they had been interesting, to say the least. She'd thought it was a sign of modesty. Maybe there was more to it than that. "So, is it a mark of non-distinction, not to make Commander?"

"Not how I think of it. For me the assignments and responsibilities are what count, not job titles or rank."

"Well, let me presume upon our relationship and venture that you are obviously one of the head and shoulders types, fast track and all that. What happened along the way toward becoming an admiral?"

Dantes looked through the wall, remembering years ago. He yanked himself back into the present. This was one very sharp interviewer. He'd known her for only a couple of days and here she was delving into stuff he had never talked about. "You're something else; I'm not so sure I want to go there."

Her eyes challenged him, said "Aw c'mon!" She waited, though, not pushing him. Dantes just didn't look like the kind that pushed well.

She had impressed him with a certain integrity and he liked her. What the hell, he thought; why not tell someone who can put it in the newspaper!

And then see if she doesn't. "It all goes back to one of my tours at sea. I was operations officer on a major combatant; we had done the full schedule, overhaul, refresher training and deployment. The ship won the Battle Efficiency E. I personally won the Seventh Fleet J.O. Shiphandling contest and was awarded my choice of duty for my next assignment. It was my fifth ship, I was in line for consideration for command, all of the boxes had been checked okay, so far." Jennings understood only about half of what he was saying, but didn't want to interrupt.

"I told you that I was married. Gloria was a beautiful, loyal Navy wife. Our wardroom was active, and the officers and their wives got together often when the ship was in port. There was something that happened at one of the parties, a dance that most of us attended. I didn't find out about it until years later, after Gloria and I had already been divorced. The skipper had made an advance, on the dance floor—a physically obvious movement that she felt—and asked if she'd meet with him. She said she was shocked, said, 'No, Captain' and nothing more was made of it. I noticed nothing at the time. My last fitness report, when I left the ship for post-graduate school, had a check in the box, "Not recommended for command."

"That's all? Just the one negative remark?"

"Yes, but it was critical. There is no more damning statement that can be made than "Not recommended for command.""

She was stunned by the rigor and harshness of the Naval service and its judgments. She was also curious about the divorce, but knew not to ask. "We covered most of your time in the Navy, assignments at both academies. Post-graduate school in Monterey, the Navy's High Energy Laser Program and service at sea. I think my readers would like to know about 'The Liberal List,' your reasons for putting it out there and perhaps your assessment of what affect it will have on society. Okay if I turn the recorder on, now?"

"Sure. The success of TLL has certainly surprised me," said Dantes. "I hadn't thought about making money with it. My reasons for putting up the web site were simple. I wanted to, in some small way, counterbalance what is undeniably an extremely liberal slant in the media and I wanted to give a voice to what I suspected were a majority of folks who felt that they had no voice. I imagined the hundreds and thousands of people waiting on the line to make comments on the call-in shows who never got to come to the plate. My thought was that there had to be a way for them to get their thoughts out. My job, then, would be to see if I could get them a hearing where it counted—with the rest of the public, like-minded or not; the so-called thought leaders and the ultra-politically correct elites that know better than the rest of us."

"The media deny that they have a liberal slant," said Jen, her eyes probing for signs of defensiveness.

"They're not competent to make the statement. Liberals, the good ones if there are any, think the normal way to be is the way they are. They don't recognize that their beliefs are anything but the way all of us should believe. Therefore, they have no label, but anyone on the right who disagrees with them does have a label, conservative."

"Are you competent to make a similar statement about yourself? Being conservative, can you make any more believable statement about your stance than the liberals can about theirs?" *Let's see how he reacts to a challenge.*

"Absolutely. I am conservative and I don't deny it. I know what I stand for and why I believe what I do. I don't fall back on statements that it's the only politically correct way to be. I haven't decided by my beliefs that I'm right and everybody else is wrong. In other words, I'm not a Sicarii."

"Sicarii?"

"Sure. In the first century, there was a band of Jews called Zealots who wanted to overthrow the Romans by force; they were less concerned with the religious aspect of Judaism than with its social aspects. A small splinter group was the Sicarii named for the small daggers they carried.

They would work themselves next to Romans and their sympathizers in crowds and then stab them, blending back into the crowd to get away. To them, the Jewish religion was evidence of their being the 'chosen' people and that, in turn, gave them the right to destroy anyone in their path who opposed them in thought or deed. I'm not like them, I feel no compunction to persuade others to my beliefs."

"And TLL? That's not an attempt to persuade others?"

"Not by me. None of the statements found there are my own."

"Isn't that a cop-out?"

"Look, I'm honest about what I intend with TLL. It is deliberately biased, yes. But I think of it as a way to dilute the steady stream of liberal intolerance of conservative views, not so much an attempt to persuade as an opportunity to be heard."

"Let's shift topics a little. TLL is raking in lots and lots of money. What will you do with it all?"

"Well, we don't know for how long the current phenomenon will last," said Dantes. "The site continues to get new participants and it's keeping most of them. I think if TLL is ultimately successful, it will put itself out of business."

"How so?"

"As more and more conservative thought is expressed and if it finally goes mainstream, the real media pros will get smart and start to offer both sides. One network already does and its ratings are going through the roof. Once that happens, TLL will lose its audience. But, to get back to what I'll do with the money, I have some ideas but not enough of them. I plan some media spots on TV and radio."

"During elections?"

"No. Specifically not during elections. For one thing, airtime cost goes up then. For another, we're not trying to elect any particular candidate. I want to detect and feed a groundswell of public opinion and emotion. I want to give voice to conservative ideas in the hope that all candidates will see some value in them. That's it. Honest. Nothing more than a modest attempt to change the entire political discourse in the country," Dantes chuckled. And, he caught himself realizing, again, how skilled Carson was. It seemed he had done all the talking. She didn't ask questions to show how smart she was, either, or to hear the sound of her own voice.

They both sat back and realized their coffee had turned cold. Dantes got up and warmed both cups. Jen could see he worked out too, but said nothing. She was reviewing the list of questions she'd prepared before the interview started.

"Okay, one last topic, then we're done."

"Saved the best for last?"

"Saved maybe the toughest for last."

"Shoot."

"There is much comment in the press, led mainly by Jeff Prather, that connects TLL with the recent murders of Senator Riggs and ACLU leader Josh Hirsch. Some are saying that you are responsible for their deaths. What would you say to my readers in response?"

"That *is* a tough one. Look, liberals believe in freedom of speech, or at least claim they do. So do conservatives. The ACLU defends the desecration of the flag as free speech. Many have been hurt; some have died in some of those protests. I've not heard any outrage in the press over the loss of those lives, just continual drumming that those who trashed the colors have the freedom to do so. I haven't noticed the ACLU rushing to the defense of conservatives being assaulted for stating their beliefs though. As for the senator, he was instrumental in denying the speech of the public, through their elected representatives, when he filibustered the president's choices for the federal bench. They never got out of committee. So what if some families got hurt? So what if some careers were ruined? Didn't matter to the senator, because he decided he knew what was best for the rest of us. He wouldn't allow any judges who didn't agree with him to move into important positions—in other words, who were not liberal. They trumpet the politically correct concept of diversity, yet they are absolutely contemptuous of diversity if it comes with a conservative tag. They want all liberal appellate, circuit and Supreme Court justices. No diversity in that."

"And the deaths, they got what was coming to them, then?"

Geez, she's aggressive. That's Neat! "I mourn for their families, as much as you would for a total stranger. The stories touch us all. My preference is for these battles to be fought in the arena of ideas. I regret the deaths and categorically disavow any participation or involvement in them."

And he talks about political correctness! "And TLL, it'll continue as before?"

"Absolutely, for as long as there is a need and there are voices to be heard."

———

The weekly edition came out on Thursdays. Jennings had stayed up all night to put the first installment to bed. It was mainly a background story, a let's take a look at one of our prominent citizens puff piece.

There were some candid photos at Dantes' house and in his office. His academy experience was covered, along with the high points of LCDR Dantes' career. His work at United Technologies, Lockheed and IBM were similarly covered. The picture given was one of an intelligent, active and dedicated man who had lived a very interesting life and settled down locally. She added a teaser for the next installment. There were some questions that were asked and some tantalizing quotes from Dantes. All in all, it was an intriguing piece that invited public comment. At the very end, she put in something she'd learned just before going to press:

> "Commander Dantes will be featured on the TV newsmagazine *Cox News Sunday,* this Sunday. He is the Power Player of the Week on this week's broadcast. If you tune in you can experience what an interview with this very accomplished gentleman is like."
>
> —J. Carson, Publisher
>
> "PS: To check this phenomenon out for yourself, go to www. theliberallist.net."

———

The phone was busier than it had ever been. By Friday, all of the copies of the *Advocate* had long since evaporated from the newsstands. It looked like a runaway hit. People were polarized, without even reading the remaining two installments.

Dantes read the piece with interest, noting as confirmation of Carson's integrity what had been left out.

Copies of the article appeared on the Internet and were forwarded to many who might be interested but who did not receive the paper. A buzz started in D.C. Network bigwigs called in producers to discuss getting Dantes on. Up 'til now the major print media had mostly ignored what was going on. Now the reactions started. Preemptive columns started popping up in the *Post* and the *Times,* both coasts. Anticipation grew. What would be next? Anne Arundel County couldn't wait to see.

And they got a chance to see at least Jennings herself. She was interviewed on local news programs in Baltimore and D.C. She was asked lots of questions, of course, about herself and her newspaper. The ones she got about Dantes she skillfully left tantalizingly unanswered. "Read next week's edition," she said.

CHAPTER 7
THE DELIVERY

Dixie came in with his first cup of coffee, early, and perched on the arm of the chair across from his desk. "So, Dick. How'd it go last night with Mr. Prather?"

"Hey, Dix, it went fine—he needs some work done and we've agreed to do it. Actually, I have the first installment here, in this sealed package; typed it up and taped it up, myself."

"Sooo, what sort of work is it that is so secretive?" she asked, eyes dancing with curiosity.

"C'mon, if I told you..."

"You'd have to shoot me," she laughed. Her mock pout looked like a supermodel's moue. "Reminds me of my brothers when I was little. They were always starting Clubs with only one rule—No. Girls. Allowed!"

"Yeah, well that all changes when little boys and girls become big boys and girls," said Zinger. "Speaking of which, I'll need someone to deliver this package to Big. Jeff. Prather. Would you like to handle that? Oh, and he'll also have a payment for you to bring back." In a more serious vein, Zinger added, "You'll need to be extremely careful, going and coming."

The smile spread dreamily across Dixie's face. "You kidding? In a heartbeat! I'll be delighted to run this little errand." She took the package and went back to her desk and made the call to Prather's office, to let them know she'd be coming over. With the visit arranged, she leaned back in her secretary's seat and her fertile imagination played with pictures of handling Jeff and going... and coming.

A quick trip to the restroom to check herself out. She had on her frilly and creamy silk blouse, the one that showed a hint of cleavage. She wore it with a business suit and she knew it was professional and attention-getting at the same time. After a critical review, she adjusted herself in her bra, more to the top, and loosened the straps, just enough so they'd move under the blouse. Didn't work! On impulse she just removed it and stuck it in her purse.

The taxi arrived and she clambered in, skirt riding up a bit as the driver looked on appreciatively through his rearview mirror. "ABS headquarters, please?"

"You got it!"

She got there fifteen minutes early and entered the twelve-story building, all of it occupied by the network. The security man at the desk in the lobby was expecting her, but he wasn't expecting *her*. She signed in and was carded into the elevator with a smile. The glass-walled elevator had only two buttons—Executive Suite and Lobby. It whisked her swiftly upward in total silence giving her a changing view of the massive atrium and ringing balconies as she rose. She could barely feel the car stop as the door hissed open and she stepped out onto the landing. She was met by an alert young aide, probably an intern, who smiled and offered, "I'm Lisa, your escort. Follow me please, Ms. DeLight. Tell me, is that French?"

What a nice thought! "Well, I do think that it may have started out that way."

"DuLumineau, or something like that?"

"Well, maybe." She was appreciating the vast atrium, the enormous planters and bright splashes of color everywhere. And a softly falling waterfall, a smooth sheet of water that fell over a huge polished granite slab. Then they were there. One more card swipe and Dixie was into the inner sanctum.

The overall impression was one of quiet bustle. Thick carpets, objets d'art. A "Wall of Fame" took up one whole side of the outer office with the various awards won by Jeff Prather and the American Broadcasting System. Two well-dressed women and a man were seated and waiting, having business there as well. The person at the desk took Dixie's name and asked her to take a seat. Mr. Prather would see her soon. She expected to wait, since she was early, but was buzzed in almost immediately.

He rose from his desk with a smile and moved graciously toward her. The walls were covered with muted TV monitors, a jumble of color and motion and it seemed they started to swirl and spin. Dixie caught herself before her jaw dropped and held her hand out to be grasped. It was almost necessary, just to steady her. "So good of you to come all the way over here and help me out!" said Prather. Actually he was somewhat used to reactions like this, happened a lot with first-time visitors, especially the girls. Dumbstruck, she watched as he actually kissed her hand and, still holding it, led her to a very comfortable leather and chrome chair, paired with an identical one at a small table close by on one side of the massive suite. With both of them seated, he asked, "An aperitif?"

"Oh, that would be just fine, Mr. Prather."

"Dixie, isn't it? Please, call me Jeff." The drinks came almost immediately and Jeff asked to see the package.

"It's right here," (next to the bra) and almost giggling, and certainly jiggling, Dixie pulled it out of her purse—the letter, not the bra.

"Please excuse me while I go over this."

"Of course." She was thinking, *what if I had grabbed the bra instead of the envelope?* As she continued her appraisal of the office, its furnishings, pictures of Jeff with U.S. presidents and a U.K. prime minister thrown in and the magnificent view behind Jeff's desk, all interspersed with surreptitious appraisals of Jeff himself. His face was more wrinkled and slimmer than on TV. He looked tanned and exuded health and animal magnetism. She'd never *seen* teeth that white! Plus, the wrinkles only added character. All in all, one of the finest looking men who'd 'bought her a drink,' yet.

Jeff noticed her glances, did a double-take and thought, "I *know* it's not that cold in here!" but concentrated for the moment on the first installment of his $300K purchase. *Hell, for that kind of money they ought to throw in the blonde.* He read through Starzinger's outlined approach, ticking off the bullets from top to bottom. Get his Navy Service Record, all of it. Examine fitness reports for anything detracting. Look for any signs of soft duty or preferential treatment. Find out why he retired as a lieutenant commander. Dantes was divorced. Get the whole story on that. Talk to former shipmates and their wives. Find out all there was to know about their break-up. Analyze all contents on "The Liberal List." Look for commonality and categorize any attack statements. Retain some Internet experts and see what could be done to actually identify some of the contributors. One of them might be Dantes himself. Do a quick background check, similar to the ones done by DOD. Agency check for arrests and any kind of criminal record and gathering statements from neighbors at every place he'd lived. Similarly, visit all of the companies where he'd worked. Look for explanations of why he'd left. It seems that Dantes hadn't stayed too long in any of the places he'd been, after the Navy.

Finally, Prather would be provided with a full report of the results, sources and methods. There'd be findings, analysis and conclusions.

"This is good," Jeff thought. *"I can call staff in and put together the media campaign once this information is in hand."* He looked up at Dixie, who returned his gaze. "Please tell Dick that this is excellent and that I will consider it a contract. I have an envelope for you to take back to him. Tell me, did you come by cab?"

"Yes, Jeff." Voice low and relaxed.

"Well, if you don't mind I'd like for you to take one of the company limos back to the office. That okay with you? I don't want to take any chances with your safety. There's a lot of money in that envelope."

"That will be fine, of course."

"Perhaps next time we can meet over lunch?"

"I'd enjoy that very much."

"Be sure to give Dick my thanks for sparing you for this important mission and tell him I look forward to our working together."

As Dixie leaned forward to put her drink on the table, cupping it with both hands and keeping her back straight, her arms perhaps not so subtly nestled her breasts together and upward, and pressed them against her blouse. She took a little extra time to place the drink on its coaster. Then gracefully and slowly she stood up, the meeting at an end. Throughout the entire performance she occupied her eyes with the coaster and looked aside for her purse and let him get a good look. He availed himself of the opportunity. She noticed. She, too, was used to reactions, though she might have characterized them with a more physically descriptive term. While her breasts had not quite popped out of her blouse, neither had Jeff's eyes popped out of their sockets. It was a close call, though, for all four orbs.

Jeff stood, too, slowly, his back not as straight. It was his turn to walk just a little haltingly and stiffly across the room, as she held his hand, being escorted out of the office. For the finale, her most wholesome smile, accompanied by a shy, "Bye…Jeff." Then she was gone and it was time for the next visitor.

Dixie DeLight, indeed! Now the pictures played and danced in *his* head.

CHAPTER 8
ZINGER

Dick Starzinger had been put on ice (terminated was too strong and suggestive a term) by the CIA. But his dismissal, because it felt like that to Zinger, had been very closely held, even within the Agency. A sealed orders packet for Zinger had been delivered to the organization for covert operations he was attached to and the person in charge there was told that Zinger was being transferred. Period. When Zinger opened his orders, he found they contained an appointment with the deputy director for operations along with a reference number and identity card to let him into the meeting place. When his old boss told him that he was being transferred, Zinger collected the few personal items he kept at his station, turned in his files, I.D.s, keys and combinations and quietly left. Zinger traveled light.

When the DDO met with him, he told Starzinger that the transfer was for his own good, and for the good of the Agency. He'd been too hot and his trail was being followed too closely. The Agency didn't like where that could lead. The Agency would continue to pay him at full pay. It was suggested that he think of it as a temporary sort of retirement. What other reasons there were, and he was sure there were other reasons, he would just have to figure out for himself, very quietly. No one at the Agency, he was told, would be told of these developments, with one exception—his "Control"—and even he would not be given Zinger's actual identity. At the end of the meeting the original packet was taken from him and he was given another packet that contained communications instructions and his new identity, along with instructions for receiving his full salary, in "retirement." Then he was escorted from the building and to his car, in the parking lot.

———

Ten years before, at the beginning, he'd filled out his resume and application forms for employment by the Agency. The information he'd received in advance told him not to indicate anywhere on the form or to tell anyone that he was applying for a covert position. That way, he went into the whole pool of applicants, being considered for employment in each of the directorates. The forms and resume were received, and he'd been invited to Langley for interviews in the Technology and Communications directorates. Just after the second interview his itinerary had been interrupted and he was directed to a small, out-of-the-way, nondescript office out in town, where he met "John," who informed him that this was his real interview and that he was from the office of the deputy director for operations.

Actually it was a personal vetting process. If John so recommended, Dick would be mailed the written psychological exam to fill out. If he passed muster with that, he'd be flown back to Langley to be fluttered— an extensive grilling with electrodes attached during which they would verify the answers he had given in his various submittals. This procedure would be repeated many times in his career; it was for all field personnel. Given a successful flutter, he'd be invited for a reception. At the reception he'd be observed and occasionally questioned by others there. The other attendees were senior persons with extensive experience in covert operations. They knew what it took to survive, if not excel, in the field. Names would not be necessary; he'd simply wear a nametag with a number on it like the other applicants. This was the last hoop through which he had to jump before he would be given employment and then would be scheduled for several months' training beginning with the next group at "The Farm."

Dick had been hired as a NOC—Not Operationally Covered. His training, for the most part, had been the standard stuff that all covert agents got. Where it differed was that he was given additional experience in the profession that he was to use as his primary cover. In the case of older inductees, they mainly used the job history they came with. For Dick, it meant actually taking a real job at an information technology firm in upper New York State.

The IT background and actual dual employment there was only one of his 'qualifications.' A Yale graduate in foreign affairs and finance, he was also familiar with the family business, which was international finance. Being not operationally covered meant that he didn't operate out of an embassy or consulate when abroad, although "covered" CIA employees assigned there coordinated and provided his logistical support. It also meant that he had no diplomatic immunity in the host or target country. If he were caught, he would never be acknowledged. There would be no flight home for him as persona non grata. In a very real sense, he would be alone, with only his information technology employment as cover.

The popular conception was true. If you were one of the Agency's best, you never retired, something like the five-star generals and admirals out of WWII. Even old Omar Bradley, two months before he died, would stand up from his wheelchair at a reception at the Fort Bliss, Texas, "O" Club, in uniform, lean forward and proclaim, "I'm ready for duty." He was on full pay until the day they played taps over him at Arlington. He was one of the legendary servants of his country.

Dick had been tapped at a relatively early point in his career as one of the great ones in his line of work. And now he was seemingly idling in place, still on full pay, sort of like the hired help, one of the contractors the Agency often employed for scut work.

He went home by a different route each day, but always passed the signal at some point to see if there was anything for him at the drop. Similarly, he could initiate contact via dead drop and "one-time pad." It was expected that he would not do so very often. And, in any case he did not know the identity of his Control. Nor did his Control know his actual identification. He had been set up with an identity that he would use to cash his checks, complete with Social Security card and credit cards. Once a month was how he received his pay, sometimes a few days early, sometimes a few days after payday, sometimes more than a month at a time and skip a month or two. You could never tell, and that was the point—not to get predictable about even something so mundane as payday. They could have established an account anywhere in the world, had him write his own checks and monitored it on-line. They preferred to do it this way. They had their reasons. He thought it was Mickey Mouse and a pain in the ass.

Today was something unusual. He was going to initiate his first message to his Control. He broke out his one-time pad and coded a short message. The pad was actually a single sheet from a palm-sized block of paper supplied by the Agency, one sheet for each day of the year, with a different code for each day, a one-for-one substitution for each letter of the alphabet. There were only two copies—one for Zinger and one for his Control. When a message was sent or received, each referred to the sheet for that particular date, then destroyed the paper. It was primitive, thought Zinger—primitive and practically impossible to break.

He coded his message to Control asking him to run down a license tag for him and give him a full dump on the individual. It was the license number he'd recorded from the Toyota Corolla. No sense in stirring up the D.C. force with this one, he'd reasoned—they gave him some work and it was a good arrangement. He'd rather not cause them any effort on his part, nor raise any curiosity there about his previous activities. He placed the coded message in the dead drop and then set the signal requesting communication, several miles away. He expected his Control personally checked for his signal every day, but he had no way of knowing. This would give him an idea of how closely they had him leashed.

To his interest and satisfaction, they had responded within twenty-four hours. The signal was there and the reply was at his drop. He decoded the message with his one-time pad for that day and sat back to read it in his office.

The subject was named David Pokorny. He did, indeed, drive the Toyota with that license number. He was a family man, wife and two kids, lived in Chantilly, Virginia, with the address provided. He was employed by a roofing contractor and made his living writing up bids for commercial jobs in the D.C. area and all along the central east coast. He was reportedly good at his job, which involved some travel.

Dick thought it was funny that they didn't ask why he wanted the information. *I know, "keep comms down to a minimum."* But it would be only natural that they'd want to know that much. Of course, he hadn't exactly volunteered the information. This retirement with nothing going on wasn't his cup of tea. But that was no excuse to get sloppy. In his mind, they had no need to know, and he didn't even know who "they" were. Dick shredded the used pad sheet and the message, after first writing down the address and phone number of the Pokorny household. This information didn't fit the rough template he'd had in mind, being a family man and so on. He had a strong suspicion that the driver of that car, that night, was following Jeff Prather, getting ready for a kill. Bad luck for Jeff if it turned out there was no connection between Pokorny as triggerman and Dantes. Even worse luck for Jeff if the real connection was going to be between killer Pokorny and victim Prather.

CHAPTER 9
THE INVESTIGATION

"This is good stuff, Mike."

"Thanks, J.D." Mike Madden had taken Jeff Prather's outline of an investigative exposé on Dantes and "The Liberal List" to J.D. Hayworth, president of the news operation at ABS, and J.D. had approved. He had named some leading liberal lights whom he wanted to use for commentary and to sharpen the focus on Dantes, all with an eye toward blurring responsibility for the attack they were about to unleash. It was the time-honored mix of lawyers, pundits, authors and entertainment celebrities. The network used them for ratings; the celebs used the network for exposure and to pitch their books.

Mike Madden had suggested perhaps including some of the people actually featured on "TLL," as they were calling it. J.D. grunted his approval and told him he wanted this to start airing quickly. As usual, they would conduct interviews and distribute pieces of them mixed with unattributed quotes from "highly placed sources" throughout the full line-up of ABS news shows.

A high point would be if they could get this Dantes back on—a sort of reality TV where the whole country could vote him off the island. Do a phone-in and web site vote and then trumpet the numbers. Timing was set to lead into the next "sweeps" period when they already used the lingerie models and "over the top" Hollywood types. This time they would solicit the most vocal opponents of President Jameson and most outrageous "thought leaders," those with wit and a popular following.

———

Tapping his $300K account, Zinger farmed out the street-work to other P.I.s and soon had several checking Dantes' old neighborhoods and neighbors, schoolteachers, ministers, employers and co-workers. They went at it, some fifteen strong, all at the same time, to gather as much information from the unguarded as possible before Dantes would know what had hit him. A P.I. with service contacts gained access to Dantes' service record.

The intense database and document search, combined with personal interviews and follow-up, had not netted very much of the sort of information that Prather had sought. Most of those with a memory of Dantes thought well of him. He had been a model, if somewhat lazy, student to whom all subjects came easily. He didn't have a lot of friends but those he had were his supporters. He seemed a quiet person, until you got him involved with an issue or problem in which he had interest. He was a go-getter, someone who got results, every time. One of his old bosses, a retired VP of test and evaluation for Lockheed Engineering & Management Services Company, when asked to sum him up, described him this way: "If you asked Dance for the Queen Mary, it would be sitting next to your office in the morning." This opinion was given at Las Cruces, New Mexico, support town to the White Sands Missile Range, where Dantes had worked many years ago.

"I don't think that Prather is going to like the results," Zinger thought. There was only one instance where prurient interest could be stimulated and that was in connection with his divorce. The team had gone to visit Gloria Workman, now living in Charleston, South Carolina. She had remarried, twice, to the same man, Jerry Workman. She was very curious about why this stranger was inquiring at all about Dance Dantes.

"Why, is he getting in trouble with that web site of his?"

"No ma'am, not that I know of, but there *is* quite a bit of interest in him because of the web site, and all," responded Jim Parker, one of the P.I.s hired by Zinger.

"And, whom do you represent?" she asked. Jim flashed one of his IDs, the one that showed he was a reporter for the *Atlanta Journal Constitution.* "You came all the way here from Atlanta?"

"We'd just like to know if you still keep in contact with Mr. Dantes."

"Why, I suppose it's been ten years since we last spoke."

"Yet, Mr. Dantes hasn't remarried..."

"Is that so? Well I certainly don't keep up with him."

"Could you tell me anything about him, what he was like when you were married, why the marriage broke up?"

"Oh, I wouldn't want to go into that."

"But he's a hard guy to get to know, in a journalistic sense. It seems that nobody has much to say about him, especially from his Navy days."

"He certainly loved the Navy; I think it meant everything to him."

"More than his marriage?"

"Well, he made it plain to me at the start that I came first, but that if I was smart I'd make sure not to make him choose between the Navy and me."

"So, how come the divorce?"

"I just think that sea duty is hard on most marriages, let's leave it at that."

"If he loved the service so much and was so dedicated, how come he got out after twenty?"

"Well, you know the Navy—or maybe you don't. It's a hard life and not necessarily fair." She turned away, eyes downcast, the interview at an end.

———

He'd also hired a small independent IT firm to do some data mining of the TLL entries. Since everyone had to give an e-mail address and other personal information in order to leave messages or correspond with TLL, it was easy to group and sort the respondees in several ways. The IT firm had written a simple software patch that flowed TLL's contents into a Microsoft Access database with fields for name, address, e-mail handle and comments. They'd quickly determined that of the thousands of visitors who had left messages, only some 1,056 used aliases or were not immediately identifiable from addresses left. Then they designed queries that sorted on various tagged attributes of interest to them, such as anger, specific threats and the like. Crews had been sent out to verify locations of D.C.-area participants. A report had been forwarded to Zinger, boiling it all down to the throwaway entries and those that were more interesting. Entries were deemed interesting if the author was local, or if the author used a false name for the address found, or if the messages were from an Internet café. The interesting list, in turn, sifted down to a smaller number, 261, of most interesting correspondents, who were believed to be local, but who had either covered up their identity or had been particularly threatening. Two hundred and sixty-one was a manageable number. One of the earlier snoop tactics they'd employed was to set up on-line to receive all inputs to TLL as TLL received them. Now that the entire contents of the database had been analyzed, it was down to tracking individual hits that fell within the most interesting list of some 261 senders. They were developing usage patterns for this list.

Of course, if the killer or killers never went to the site, or never communicated on the site, none of this was going to be of any value. Besides, it was expensive and not what Jeff was really paying him to do. Zinger thought, "Probably ought to wrap this up with the report I promised and give Jeff a refund." And he also thought about his encounter with the 'parking lot pisser' who had conducted surveillance on Prather, and what he ought to do about that.

CHAPTER 10
POWER PLAYER

Dance had been pleased and still somewhat surprised to receive the invitation from the staffers at Cox News to be interviewed for a segment of their Sunday program. It seemed they considered him worthy of being their "Power Player of the Week." A photo crew had shown up at the house and at the site where his IT staff tended to the servers and storage media. They taped some background material for voiceovers and went over their format with him. On Saturday he would meet with Riley Berry, the rising star at Cox, and they would do a walk-through of his IT facility. He was scheduled to come into the studio for the live portion of his segment. A limo would call for him at 7:00 a.m. on Sunday. They'd finish the show for that Sunday, since he'd be Riley's last guest.

Good stuff for a Navy retard, he thought as he nicked himself shaving, eying the cut in the mirror. Riley—she'd been definite about that, *not* Ms. Berry—had sounded like regular people when they'd chatted briefly over the phone. Of course he'd heard she was a beauty and he knew that she must pack a full seabag, or else she wouldn't be pulling down a seven-figure salary. Although she wasn't related to the black movie star with the same last name, on the red carpet stroll she would've been taken for the movie star's better-looking kid sister. *Yes sir, this was turning out to be one mighty interesting Saturday.*

She pulled up to the site in a Ford F-150 pickup. No kidding, a Ford pickup! And parked it right next to his. His was newer. Hers was kind of beat-up looking. Swinging out of the truck with a dazzling smile and a wave, she greeted him, "So you've got a pickumup truck, too?"

"Yep, a Ford."

"Is there any other kind?" she teased.

"Not for me." And there she was, in jeans and a colorful blouse, shaking his hand and absolutely charming him out of his socks.

"So, you gonna show me your operation?" she asked.

"Bet your boots, cowgirl…" and the TV crew set up and taped their walk through Dantes' facility. Riley was animated asking, "Can I see where you operate?" "Have you received any threats?" "How large is the infrastructure?" "How many hits do you get?" "How long have you been doing this?" and "What do you think you'll ultimately do with it?" There were three crews, one with its camera on him, another on Riley and one for the shots while they walked.

"Got what you need?" she asked her producer. She and Dantes stood together, leaning against their trucks.

"Looks good, Riley!"

When could she ever not look good" he wondered.

"Well, Dance, we all set for tomorrow morning? You know the limo will get here around seven to bring you to the studio and take you back."

"That'll work for me—I'm looking forward to it, Riley." Then she was gone and he imagined it got colder as the star power faded and the dust settled behind her noisy, rattling truck. "What a heartbreaker!" he muttered ruefully as he climbed into his truck for the ride home.

———

Sunday morning and although he knew that part of the reason for Saturday had been to allow him to adjust to Riley Berry and get himself comfortable with it all, it hadn't quite worked. His hand shook just slightly as he shaved, *twice in two days!* And he thought about it and just decided to calm down. No sense in getting another cut. But he was definitely looking forward to spending another five or ten minutes with Riley. *Jeez!* He'd honestly never, *ever* been that close to a woman who was… unvoiced thoughts, even, failed him.

Dressed in his dark-blue suit with the muted pin-stripe, a light-blue shirt and navy-blue and gold-striped tie, he was greeted by an appraising chauffeur who opened the door for him. "Morning, Mr. Dantes."

"Morning, and thanks for the ride." He had made some notes to cover his answers for the questions they'd told him to expect. Not that he didn't *know* the answers, but it wouldn't hurt to go over the stuff, just to have it on top. Riley'd said that this morning's live session would cover the causes he espoused and the uses to which he was putting the funds being generated by TLL. The rest of the material they'd taped had already been rolled into an introduction and all they needed was three and a half minutes of live action in the studio. Riley had a copy of the material he was scanning, so she'd be familiar with his answers. Looked like a piece of cake…

He sat in the Green Room while they put on the only makeup he'd ever worn and prepped and wired him for sound, setting and checking the volume. Then a producer's assistant came in and got him. They brought him onto the set and positioned him in a chair facing Riley. It was during the commercial break, after which they'd roll the intro. Like they said, the lights were bright. Didn't matter, Riley was of course still gorgeous and now was looking up from her notes at him, both barrels.

"Dance," voice soft and calm, "so good to see you. I've been looking at your notes and I've got to say I'm mighty impressed. Slightest crease between two perfectly shaped brows. These are some very important efforts you're involved in," said with an earnest and (he could swear) admiring smile.

"Thanks, Riley," gulp.

"Here, how about a mug of coffee?"

"Great."

"Okay, roll logo, cue theme, and three, two, one cue the intro." came the business-like instructions. And they sat there while the intro ran for its minute and a half.

"And now I'm so pleased to have Dance Dantes in the studio with me; welcome, Dance."

"Thanks, Riley. Good to be here."

"Dance, my viewers have sent a lot of e-mail, wondering what you're doing with the funds you're generating with TLL."

"I appreciate the question, Riley. We're funding several promotional TV spots that generally present conservative issues in a positive light. For instance, we've put together a piece that encourages young women to go ahead and have their babies, and promotes adoption as an option for single mothers. Also, we're in favor of putting Social Security on a better footing, so that there will be support for retired persons after the "Boomers" pass through. One of our ads aired in the D.C. market last week. It urges more secure borders and migrant worker programs, and English lessons for workers, funded by my group. Also, we're working on a spot in support of the F-22 Raptor Fighter and the C-130-J, both aircraft that are produced by my old company, Lockheed Martin. As you know, many in Congress are opposing these programs and the people who visit TLL are generally in favor of a strong defense."

"Dance! This often turns into a political show. I have to ask you, are you running for office?" with a definitely admiring smile.

"No, not at all. It's just that I'm carrying out my promise to the millions who visit the web site. It's their money and I've promised to use it to promote the causes they support. That's the purpose of TLL, to give a meaningful voice to the conservatives in this country. Not to knock the media, but mostly what's on is the liberal agenda—present company excepted, of course."

"But I seem to have heard of some other programs in which you're involved, programs that have nothing to do with national issues."

"Yes, we're also working with AIDS doctors in Africa and disaster relief around the world. We can't do it on a government-sized scale, but we want to do what we can to help kids and struggling parents in third-world countries."

"And some of those countries are not friendly to the United States."

"Exactly. We're helping out in Cuba and North Korea. The countries may not be friendly to the U.S. or to our policies, but the people are almost always friendly to us."

"Can't make you too popular with some conservatives in Washington… sounds liberal to me," Riley said, eyes wide open, again just a hint of a tease.

"Hey, life's not a popularity contest. I don't think either extreme viewpoint is the only way to look at an issue, Riley."

Camera tight on Riley for the close, turning smoothly to face CamOne, "And there you have our Power Player of the Week, Dance Dantes. A man who espouses conservative causes yet avoids the label! Thanks for watching and please join me on the next Cox News Sunday!"

The lights dimmed and equipment was being turned off and the producer's assistant came up to him and stood there, while they unmiked him, ready to take him back to the Green Room and out to the limo. But Riley stood next to Dance and touched him lightly at the elbow. "Dance, why don't you go back with Heather, here, and get the make-up off and then, if you've got the time, maybe we can go to lunch? We can cancel the limo and I'll drive you home in my Cowboy Cadillac…"

I've absolutely died and gone to heaven. "Riley, sure *you've* got the time…? I've definitely worked up an appetite and would really enjoy that." He was feeling like a pimply teenaged kid on his first date, at age fifty-two!

"It's a deal," she smiled. "Give me ten minutes."

CHAPTER 11
HER SECRET

She was the first-born and only child of Doretha Clemens and Chuck Berry. Doretha, a preacher's daughter, and Chuck, a guitar-playing musician, had a quiet but nice wedding presided over by the Reverend Clemens and set up housekeeping in a shotgun shack in the Houston tenements. People shook their heads at the match. Doretha was fairly straightlaced and Chuck was a hell-raiser. He stayed around long enough to name the baby and then left, splitting for another gig, as he called it. He was very fond of Irish whiskey and named the baby after Reilley's Old Famous. The birth certificate read, Riley Clemens Berry.

Times weren't easy but the minister, her grandpa, helped and Doretha and Riley gradually moved out of the shacks and into a modest rental home that Doretha could afford on her wages from waiting tables. Riley took center stage in her mother's life and delighted her no end. Early on, it was obvious that Riley was extremely smart, and a performer as well. She was well schooled by Doretha and grew up knowing that there were expectations that came with being Riley Berry, granddaughter of a minister.

Doretha eventually got a boyfriend, Rafe, who had a good-paying job with the railroad. He worked in the switchyards and owned his own car. Strong and good-looking, he pretty much had his pick. He picked Doretha and watched as Riley grew up. Riley was ten years old when Rafe started seeing Miss Doretha. He didn't move in, but he came around often. Doretha figured he was maybe seeing someone else, too, but couldn't be sure. Still, he helped them with expenses and life wasn't so bad in the Berry family. At first Doretha had wanted to get married, but when it didn't come up between them, she gradually got used to the notion, preacher's daughter or no.

Riley grew up always knowing, she thought, what others were thinking. She had received the looks from white folks that dismissed her as a nothing. She noticed when she became twelve that the women still looked at her that way but many men, white and black, looked at her differently. Riley was not only extremely smart—she was also extremely good looking. Her big eyes had a slight upward tilt at the corners, not quite oriental, but exotic, of a mixed color, a tawny combination of dark blue with a light green to yellowish-brown outer ring. She had the sort of trim nose and high cheekbones that some women get from the surgeon. Some in her school classes were black; some were "shiny black." Riley was the color of Cafe au Lait. Topping it all off was a full mouth with perfect white teeth that she showed often in her smiles.

In school she was known as "The Brain." There she was shunned by many of the black students. She didn't go along with what they were putting out. To her it wasn't cool to have bad grades. She always spoke properly, as her mother had insisted. She was respectful of her teachers and got straight As, year after year. Grandpa gave her money for her As, nothing for Bs, so she made sure to get all As. When she was fifteen, a sophomore at Wheatly High, she got a lot of attention from boys in general. She knew what their looks meant, too. When they found out that Riley wasn't to be easily had, they drifted away.

All but Jeremiah Woodley, that is. Jeremiah was also a brain. He was in many of her classes and her homeroom. He was the only competition Riley had, academically speaking. At first they sensed each other as rivals; then an easy sort of friendship grew.

Sometimes Jeremiah would walk Riley home from school. Then they were allowed to go to a movie on a Friday night, together. They'd catch the bus to the show and back. They'd hold hands and Riley could tell that Jeremiah was working up to asking for a kiss. He asked for a lot more than that. As they sat on the back-stair steps, he grabbed her and kissed her, without asking. Then his hands started moving. Riley caught her breath and said, "Oh no, you don't!"

"Come on, Riley, You know you want me to."

"I know no such thing—now you just behave, or I'm going in the house right now."

But he didn't behave and she did go into the house, after he grabbed her one more time.

It was the next year when she was a junior that she was asked out and accepted, this time from one of the older boys, a senior. He had his driver's license and could drive his parents' car and asked her to go to the drive-in. She was a little flattered by his attention and it was neat to go on an actual date, where you didn't have to take the bus or walk to get there. Her coach turned into a pumpkin at midnight, as Doretha sternly reminded her date, D'Rick. The movie was fine and the kissing was fine, too. He wanted more but Riley sweetly said no.

D'Rick said, "When?"

"Let's just be satisfied with a movie and kissing," she said.

D'Rick kept asking her out and she kept accepting. They moved to the back seat when the petting started. Riley knew better, but this was feeling really good. Finally, when she was plenty excited, D'Rick pounced and didn't ask. Riley made him stop and said, "I have to think about this."

"Think about it? My God, you've got me all excited and you're gonna just stop?"

"I never said that I'd go all the way."

"Aw, baby, *you* may not have said it, but your *body's* sure talking to me." There was moisture on his fingers and he throbbed inside his trousers where her hand had brushed him and lingered, even, he imagined, squeezed just a little.

Riley made it stick—the answer was no. She didn't intend to end up short of her goals, and she had a few.

D'Rick stopped asking her out.

———

It was only a month later, on a Saturday, when she was home, working on a project for school. Mom had picked up an additional job on Saturdays for the extra money and Riley pretty much had her Saturdays to herself. She looked up from her little desk in her room when she thought she heard something. Turning to the door, she saw Rafe. "You know my mom's not home—what are you doing here?" Seeing a look she had come to recognize she became more insistent, "You get out of here!" voice trembling and rising to the level of a scream.

"Now baby, you just quiet down, nothin' bad's going to happen." As he moved toward her she grabbed the metal coin bank she had on her desk and swung it as hard as she could, catching him square on the temple with a corner of it.

"Ahhh," he grunted and fell to the floor, stunned for the moment.

Riley ran out of the room straight to the kitchen, where she yanked the drawer open and fumbled two sharp kitchen knives out, scattering other cutlery all over the kitchen floor. They were big, for cutting the chickens and roasts her mother taught her to cook. And Momma wouldn't have a dull knife in her kitchen.

Rafe was cursing and threatening and moving into the kitchen. He had taken off his belt and doubled it over. He held it in both fists and slowly moved his hands together, then jerked them apart, making a sharp "crack" as leather hit leather. "First I'm gonna' whip you girl, and then I'm gonna' have some fun with what you're hiding under that skirt!"

Riley had a knife in each hand, and was backing around the kitchen table, keeping her eyes on Rafe, not saying anything. "Ha! You think you know how to use a knife, girl? You ain't gonna' use it on me. Don't even try or I'll make it worse on you. Now you put them knives down."

Riley went into a slight crouch, her right hand held high, the knife in her fist, ready for a downward stab. She held the other knife low with the tip pointing up. Rafe dropped the belt and came swiftly for the high blade, hands together to grab her forearm. As he grabbed her right arm he slipped on a table knife on the floor and fell heavily into Riley. Riley swept upward with her free hand, sinking the blade into Rafe, up to the hilt.

"Uhhnnhh!" The grunt from Rafe, bent over. He stood there, knees starting to buckle and they both looked at the knife in him with amazement. Amazement turned to unspeakable pain for one, horror for the other. Riley had turned loose of the knife and backed away from him. She neither screamed nor cried, but she eyed him for whatever was going to happen next. Rafe looked at Riley with a large question in his eyes, "But, but, how…?" It was a question he never got to voice.

Riley was left-handed, you see.

———

She sat on the couch in the living room and cried. That lasted for maybe ten minutes. Then she got the phone and called Doretha at work. "Yes, honey. What is it?"

"I think you'd better come home, Momma."

"What's wrong?" Can't it wait? I can be there in another two hours, sweetie."

"Come home now. Rafe came over here and…"

"Rafe! You put him on the phone. *I'll* talk to Rafe!"

"No, Momma!" she sobbed. "You don't understand, Rafe's dead in the kitchen!"

While Riley was upset, she wasn't exactly panicked. The hard part was over. She knew that there were some decisions to be made and her mother would be the person making them. She logically thought it would be best for Doretha if she had some time to get used to the notion and think things over before she got home. Doretha had all of the thoughts imaginable on her way home. She sensibly decided that Riley had to be protected. She could go to the police, but if she did, after the fuss died down, Riley's prospects would be non-existent. Doretha arrived home with her mind made up—to see if they could dispose of the body without being seen.

And that's what they did. They removed the knife and wrapped Rafe up in a blanket. Then they scrubbed the linoleum kitchen floor until it sparkled. After dark, they each took an end and put Rafe in the trunk of his car. Then they got in the car and started it, using Rafe's keys. It was an automatic and there was no trouble carefully driving to a spot within a few blocks of a bus stop, out by Buffalo Bayou. They wiped the trunk lid and the keys, doors and the steering wheel clean, walked to the bus stop and caught a bus into town. Then they called a taxi from a phone booth and went home. They were so scared they even wiped the phone and the phone booth door.

Doretha never had another boyfriend.

Neither did Riley.

———

The police came around and asked some questions. No, they hadn't seen Rafe on the night in question. Why, was something wrong? The information that he had been found dead in the trunk of his own car was received with appropriate shock. Doretha and Riley were also genuinely shocked to hear that Rafe had three other 'families' where he was a sometime visitor and overnight guest. The police also mentioned that the switchyard hadn't been Rafe's only employment and that he had been mixed up in drugs. It was assumed his death had been a drug deal gone bad.

"Thank you ladies—we probably won't need to see you again," and the police were gone.

———

She was the valedictorian of her class at Wheatly, and Jeremiah was the salutatorian. In addition to her nickname as "The Brain," she picked up another, "Ice Maiden." In her senior year she had attracted offers of help from the counseling staff. Mr. Poinsett had helped her apply for all of the scholarships and advised her on her résumés and applications for college. He was thanked sincerely and politely. She reserved her smiles, now, for those she knew very well.

She was accepted at Trinity University in San Antonio and enrolled in its department of communication's journalism program. It was only four hours from home but a galaxy away from her home life. She'd thought that her smarts and looks could take her a long way. She was determined that she was not going to be dependent upon anybody else for her livelihood. In the summers she interned with the *Houston Chronicle*, getting the chance to see close-up, if fleetingly, the life she'd chosen for herself.

At first she did office work and odd jobs. The second summer she was rotated through all of the paper's departments. The third summer she applied to intern with CNN in Atlanta and was picked up. This was more like it! She helped on the camera crews, setting up for the live shots that occasionally took place in and around Atlanta. She worked for a production assistant on all of the many details that supported the studio live performances. At CNN there wasn't much of a "star system." Everyone pitched in and the camaraderie was high. Toward the end of her summer there she was invited to join CNN after graduation as a production assistant. Senior year flew by and with high hopes she left Texas for Georgia, determined to make her name.

If not every night then certainly every week, she thought back to Rafe's attack and death and a worried expression crossed her face as she wondered if the police would come for her one day. She kept on the move and she stayed busy and she was not able to take full enjoyment in her accomplishments, wondering if it was really over.

CHAPTER 12
THE COMPANY

Nine-eleven and its aftermath of recriminations and witch hunting had brought change to the Central Intelligence Agency. A new DCI had been imposed after the much publicized intelligence failures regarding weapons of mass destruction. Congress conveniently ignored the fact that they themselves had cut funds for intelligence work, Congress that had erected the barriers to vital information flow between intelligence organs and Justice, Congress that had in all likelihood brought about the sad state of affairs within the Agency. Then it was Congress that insisted upon a 9/11 Commission and adoption of the Commission's Report, and its recommendations, in their entirety. Finally, adding insult to injury, the newly appointed Director of Central Intelligence was, you guessed it—a Congressman.

The initial influx of money and the impetus to reorganize, along with wholesale departures of senior Agency officials, provided an opportunity. CIA and the FBI were being held jointly accountable for disasters at home, regardless of their carefully carved-out and mandated separate responsibilities and areas of operations. Whereas before, there had not been a domestic role for CIA, now one was frantically being urged and demanded. Cooperation and integration of information among intelligence and enforcement organizations was suddenly required. A Homeland Security Department was hastily put together and an Intelligence Czar created.

At CIA the new DCI had not been welcomed by many. The newly promoted Deputy Director for Operations was a significant exception. He had come from heading the Counterintelligence Center Analysis Group (CIC/AG) where he had been since the 90's. He was particularly concerned that in the haste to reorganize and improve CIA's product and reputation, continuity would not be lost. A lot of old hands had been let go. In order to move forward it was necessary to break up some old and comfortable ways of operating. It was vital, however, to take care to ensure that ongoing and highly secret operations and agents not be compromised.

One such agent was Dick Starzinger. "Starz" or "Zinger" take your pick, had been a top-flight performer in more than one area of interest. He had been startlingly successful in recruiting agents and running them. He had served independently with shadowy support provided by CIA station chiefs operating within embassies around the world. And, though always successful, now for the past few years Starz' opponents had been getting closer and closer to catching up to him with each operation,. Considering the multiple identities and cutouts, extremely closely held assignments and support processes, it was concluded that someone within the Agency was supplying information to the wrong people, and endangering their best agent.

The new Director and his Deputy for Operations met to discuss this very topic. He was brought up to speed on Starz' career… His work in Bosnia, Afghanistan, Pakistan and Libya and more recently his assistance in the sudden illness and death of the Palestinian leader, Abu Amir, had been opposed by various groups, but continuing opposition had seemed to come from the Russians and Al Qaeda. Disquietingly, though there was nothing to confirm cooperation between them, it seemed that wherever Starz went, it was not long before evidence of pursuit with deadly intent had cropped up. On his last operation, in Ramallah, Starz had barely escaped with his own life after being forced to take those of several of the Al Aqsa Brigade.

"As you can see, sir, it's in our interest to put Zinger on ice and let things cool down."

"I agree. Where do you think the heat on him is coming from?"

The DDO presented in detail, the analysis that had led him to suspect one individual in CIC/AG was the source of information to enemies who were tracking Starz. "Looks very thorough—and this is your own personal analysis? No one else was involved?"

"No one else, sir. My admin assistant checked out the documents I used, along with all other materials. The information came from many different sources. Only she knows everything I've seen and I don't think even she could draw any conclusions about what I'm looking for. I absolutely trust her—she's fluttered several times a year, although why she puts up with it, I don't know. She could apply for another assignment, prefers to stay as she is. She's been my admin assistant for twelve years, now. As you can see, part of my analysis has also covered her activities and how she couldn't be, in fact, the person who might be a leak. She's clean. I am staking my life on it."

"So, what do you recommend?"

"I want to put our suspect in charge of a small task organization that will perform liaison with Homeland Security and the FBI. We'll call Zinger in and transfer him into a quiet 'retirement' that will be administered out of this new organization."

"Okay, you've got the budget and the organization change is approved."

That Friday, DDO called Control into his office and outlined his new assignment, liaison with Homeland Security and FBI. Assets from within CIC/AG were attached to his group. Additionally he was to personally administratively support an early 'retiree' in the local area. A communication system had been set up, although it wasn't expected that it would be used for much other than to pay the retiree and handle any requests he might have.

———

The new DCI believed that better communications at all levels would improve cooperation among the various elements of the intelligence community, leading to a better product. He set the example by initiating monthly updates to station chiefs. The notes generally included disposition of resources, organizational changes and various other administrative updates of general interest. Six months after Zinger's 'retirement,' a note was put into the monthly update that an agent, unnamed but known to them all, had been retired in the D.C. area.

This message was sent to station chiefs in Moscow, Tel Aviv, Kabul and Baghdad. In the Kabul station, the message was left out over lunch in the open, at the desk of the head of the logistics department. It was neither copied nor photographed, but it was quickly read by one of the foreign nationals who worked in the department. Three days later, this nugget was being analyzed in Moscow with great interest.

CHAPTER 13
THE LEAK

Control resented the changes that had been forced upon the Agency over the years. He was angry at those who attacked the CIA and weakened it, resulting in the Agency and all who toiled there being held up to ridicule. And, it only got worse. The current president had gutted the Old Guard at the Agency at the same time that his new preemptive policies were brought on line. Control felt the Agency had taken unfair hits for the administration and had been made the scapegoats for a failed foreign policy. He was convinced that those policies were wrong and that events would prove them so. Feeling betrayed by reorganizations, funding shenanigans and the daily blame game being played out in the press, he was ready to do something about it.

In counterintelligence he had had access to many reports, analyses and operations. In fact it was a thorough compilation of the sources and documents that he had checked out over the years that had yielded him up as one of the suspects under consideration. Linkages between his assumed knowledge and the turn of events in the field pointed faintly and then more strongly to him.

It had started with an offer to cooperate, phoned in to the Russian Embassy duty officer. He'd called from a phone booth and named a time when he would call again, in two weeks. On the subsequent call he was told that they wanted to meet with him. He started to suggest the place and was told that they had a place in mind. It was a seafood restaurant on Maryland's eastern shore, nothing pretentious. They had surveillance in place and used someone who, as best they could determine, was not being monitored. At the meeting he had told the Russian that he had knowledge of field operations and could provide it to them. They would be willing to examine the information, and what did he have in mind in return? He wasn't really prepared for this question. Until that exact moment he had not considered what he wanted, except to, in his own way, force changes and perhaps blunt the administration's foreign policy. He suggested that they put off any decision on payment until there were results from which to make a judgment. They considered that he might be just a flake, but decided to play along and gave him a drop location and signal to check and use and then sat back to see what would happen.

He started with notes he wrote, summaries of field objectives for specific areas. They considered the information, checked it against known or suspected activities and found that it was good intel. He got a new handler, a new drop system and a payment of $5,000. Over the years he had also become aware of the activities of an unnamed agent who had been successful in many locations. Through his reading and counterintelligence efforts he had become able to detect the signs that he was involved, or would soon be involved, and generally where. When he started giving his handler his assessments of this individual's activities his pay went up, was now pushing $10,000 a month. Then, suddenly, his Russian handlers had shut him down. They said the information had not proved as valuable as they'd hoped and informed him that there would be no further contact or payments.

Within three months he had a promotion. In his new assignment he no longer had access to information on the activities of the agent he had so assiduously followed. It had been an exciting time, though, and he missed the powerful feelings that came with imagining himself on an international stage. The more he missed it the more his thoughts turned to a new and more direct role he could create and play. He remembered an individual who lived in the D.C. area, someone who had completed a career as a Navy Seal and been turned down for Agency employment. With his own group he had autonomy, a budget and a charter of sorts and was certainly motivated to take advantage of opportunities where they might present themselves.

———

The phone rang and was picked up. "Yes, who's calling?"

"We're not acquainted, though I am familiar with your Naval service. Who I am can be left undisclosed. I have employment for someone with your skills."

"And what skills might those be?"

"I need someone who can do the types of things you did overseas. There are new enemies, within our own borders, and your help is needed."

"Not interested in dealing with someone I don't know, mister." And with that he'd hung up. *New enemies, huh? Who the hell did he think he was, calling like that?* Still, his curiosity had been aroused. He tried *69 to get the number and the recording said that Touchstar service could not be used to identify the previous caller.

Two days later came the second call. He paused before picking it up, letting it ring three times. "Yes?"

"I hope that you've had time to reconsider." Same voice.

"Let's just say that I'd like to know more."

"Excellent. There is, in your mailbox, a description of the task and method of payment. I do not intend for us ever to meet or to talk on the phone again. If you agree to my proposition I will know. I am willing to take the chance and have included your first payment in your packet of instructions." And the line went dead.

He looked up and down the street from the door. There was a car parked at the other end of the street, someone sitting in it. Nobody at his mailbox. He went out, looked in and took out an envelope, returned inside. From his window he watched as the car at the end of the street moved away from the curb and drove off. Inside the envelope he found $10,000 as well as a note.

"This must seem extremely unusual, but then I think you'll agree that these are unusual times. I know that you once sought employment at the Agency and were considered for duty as a paramilitary person. While the Agency chose not to employ you, the need for someone with your skills is now greater than ever. Our life, as we know it, is under attack by fellow Americans. Our culture is being trashed, our standards demeaned and our freedom is in danger. I'm talking about members of Congress, and judges and celebrities who are suffocating the true American way of life. I've taken the chance that you agree with me and will look at the enclosed money as a down payment. There is much money to follow, if you wish. A bank account has been opened in your name. Enclosed is the ID and password you will use to access your account on-line. Monies will be moved into the account as and if you complete your assignments. You will then be able to transfer the payments to an account of your choice."

The letter went on to describe the means by which he would receive his assignments. Interestingly it involved the web site, "The Liberal List." He was to look for the indications and take independent action to eliminate the person designated. When and if he completed his first assignment there would be a deposit of $40,000 in his account. Finally there was described an emergency means of communication, along with the statement that there would be no more telephone contacts.

He went on line, brought up TLL and read through the notes posted there. There it was! And there it was again and again, repeated twice in different messages. There was a fourth such indication and a fifth, but they didn't jibe with the three that matched. It must be the person indicated three times. But could he be sure!? He decided to try out the emergency comms system right off the bat. He went to the drop site and left the note, then to the signal site and set it.

Control sighed when he saw the indication for communication set so quickly. He retrieved the note, which said, "Riggs?" His answer put in the drop the next day said simply, "Yes."

He was faced with a choice. It had occurred to him that he could turn over all of the information he had to the CIA and maybe they could burn this guy. On the other hand this might be the Agency employment he had sought. Of course he could simply do nothing; hard to make a mistake that way. He was intrigued with the choice of his first assignment, should he attempt it. Senator Riggs had infuriated him for a long time with his inflammatory and petulant diatribes in the well of the Senate. Riggs was an obstructionist and, in his mind, was worse than useless. He started to think about the requirements for intel and resources, the means that could be employed and personal security considerations. The more he thought about it the more he started to see it as challenging work of the sort that he'd done in 'Nam those decades ago.

———

He had felt like the proverbial fish out of water when he'd hung it up and retired from active service with the SEALS at Little Creek, Virginia. He'd taken an outside job for a subcontractor, supervising construction sites and enforcing environmental rules for large projects. On one particular morning the project boss's son came around and started giving him a ration. He was short-fused and it had taken but a minute when he'd reached out and crushed the kid's cheekbone with a karate chop of the side of his hand. The kid was left lying there while someone else called for an ambulance.

Only a few minutes later his supervisor came up to him and shouted, red-faced, "Mister, you're in trouble!"

"Nah, this isn't trouble. Trouble is hanging upside down in a tree at night with fifty gooks looking for you and worrying that they're gonna' smell you! Now what's your problem?"

"Okay, calm down. Take some vacation for a few days and I'll see if I can get you back on site." And so it had gone, job to job, until he'd settled back and quit looking.

CHAPTER 14
THE REPORT

Zinger reread his report, with the appendices and exhibits, running to some fifty-five pages. An impressive document yet he knew that it wasn't what Prather was expecting. In a way, he didn't mind, at all. He'd gradually lost any initial enthusiasm he had for the task as the results came rolling in. This Dantes was just a really neat guy and Prather was trying to use him for some rotten purpose of his own. Zinger'd pushed really hard to find anything on him and had found that Dantes had led an interesting life, was a patriot and someone he'd not have minded serving with. He wrote Jeff a note, put it on top and sealed the whole bundle up, just like last time. It was getting close to closing time and he called Dixie in.

"Dixie, Dixie, Dixie!"

"What, what, what?" Standing in front of his desk and bouncing lightly on her toes, she'd noticed the taped package on his desk and hoped she knew what was coming.

"I wonder if you would be so kind as to take a package by for Mr. Prather."

"Ab-so-lutely, boss!" and out she glided to her desk to make the call.

"Why yes, Mr. Prather is in and he will wait for the package," from Nancy at the front desk. Dixie locked up her desk, bid Zinger an airy goodnight and zipped down the stairs and into her car.

Sign in, elevator to the top, no intern this time, she knew the way and the door was ajar, letting her in. "So nice to see you again, Ms. Delight," again from Nancy. Then she let Dixie into Jeff's office, poking her head in, "Guess I'll shut down, then?"

"That'll be fine, Nancy." Nancy left, closing the door softly and locking her way out onto the landing, deliberately not thinking what she was not supposed to think.

"Well! Miss Dixie… thanks for coming over with Dick's report. This is very timely."

"No problem, I wanted you to have it as soon as possible… the report, that is," both of them just standing, waiting for the next move. A faint blush had started on Dixie's throat and spread to her chest. He stood there and stared, eyes hungrily moving over her body. She felt his look as though it were his hands. The sparks started flying around the room, seeming to leave little scorch marks everywhere they touched.

He said, voice a little choked, "Dinner?"

Her color heightened even more and she said, "I'll have to make some arrangements."

He pointed, "There's the phone." While she called her friend to get her to pick up the boys, Jeff tore open the envelope.

"Oh, and would it be possible for you to stay the night with them? I could be really late. There's leftover spaghetti in the fridge and…"

"Hot date, huh?

"Well, maybe… yes, you could say so."

"Not to worry, Dix; I gotcha covered."

"Thanks, I really owe you one," and she hung up.

Jeff read Dick's note. "Jeff, I know that there isn't anything of an incriminating nature in this report, except perhaps that the investigation itself was launched at all. I think you'll find lots of information there and will agree that it's a thorough job. But you won't find it particularly useful. I've used only half of the advance you provided and I'm more than willing to return the balance, if you so instruct me. But there is one additional item of interest that may persuade you to continue to retain me. You should know that you were evidently followed that night you came to my office, and observed when you left. I am in the process of confirming the identity of the person, whom I'll call for now your stalker. I will turn over any information I develop either to the police or to you; it's up to you. Thanks and have a nice evening, Dick."

He put the note down and looked up. Dixie was leaning over, hands on his desk, supporting herself on her arms. "Where you want to go for dinner?" he asked.

"I'm easy, you choose it."

"We could always have dinner in?"

"You mean right here?"

"Well, mmmfft…" She had come around the desk, plopped herself into his lap and planted a long and passionate kiss on him.

She came up for air long enough to say, "Poor baby, you're sooo hungry…" And they stayed there, until well past three in the morning, never even thinking of food.

And the person in the old Toyota Corolla finally left at nine-thirty, figuring that he'd somehow missed Prather leaving.

CHAPTER 15
LUNCH AT THE WILLARD

Riley and Dance had relished their lunch at Willard's. The place reeked of power, money and influence. Close by Capitol Hill, it was a favorite meeting place for the lobbyists, politicians and other men and women of influence. No framed pictures on the walls because it wouldn't be politic to favor one Washington great or party over another. The furnishings were heavy oak and walnut. The menu was not French. The entrees were excellent and expensive. The bar was unrivaled in Washington, leaning heavily to bourbon and scotch along with an astonishing wine list. It had a decidedly old school, masculine feel and smelled like a mixture of crisp, new money, bourbon and prime rib.

It was a setting in which a woman stood out and a person of Riley's beauty dominated. She instinctively knew that. Today, she wore a tailored red suit. She attracted the attention that a rose would get in a winter's snowfield. Several of those there for lunch came to celebrity sightsee and on this Sunday they weren't disappointed. In addition to some House staffers there were a couple of members of the House and a senator. Compared to Riley, though, they weren't getting any attention at all. After taking in Riley and what she was wearing, many of the ladies cast curious and admiring glances Dantes' way. He didn't notice much of this as he was deeply immersed, if not drowning, in his conversation with Riley.

"So, tell me some more about Dance Dantes," she said with an engaging smile, those multicolored eyes sparkling. "Staff got a copy of the interview you did in Annapolis, so I got all that. What I want to know is what's a guy like you doing single?"

"I could ask you the same…"

"But today I'm the reporter and I get to ask the questions," with a mock serious look, head tilted to one side."

"Uh, well, it's nothing more exciting than I've stayed busy."

"Well, I'll answer the same question for you, then, 'cause the answer is the same. Sometimes I think it's too easy to just forget to have a social life."

They both sat back and appreciated what they had in common, which included the meal that the waiter was now placing before them. It was a really fine restaurant but they hadn't put it to the test. They'd started with champagne as she'd congratulated him on his fine TV performance, and continued on to ribs with applesauce and steak fries. She was charming him even as she greedily smacked the sauce from her fingers, one at a time and then the thumb, eschewing the wipes supplied with the meal.

"Man, these ribs are good!" they both said at the same time. They looked up at each other from their plates and laughed in wide-eyed delight at the ease of their connection. On the drive to Severna Park she told him about her mom and her upbringing. He told her some funny stories about his time spent in the Navy, foibles of his as a plebe at the Boat School. They rattled along as the truck rattled along and by the time they got to his place it was easy to show her around.

She loved the view and asked if they could go down to the river. They climbed down the wooden stairs he'd put in, some 80 feet, holding her arm to steady her. Again she marveled—it was so different from anything she'd grown up with. They squinted at the shimmering river, bright sun glancing into their eyes. He pointed out across the river and described the twenty-mile rows he'd taken as a lightweight oarsman, stroke of an eight-oared shell from the Weems Creek boathouse all the way to Round Bay and back. She could almost feel the sweat in the rowers' eyes, matching the painful glare as she looked where he pointed. She imagined those young athletes and future Naval officers pouring their strength and energy into the water, the river in turn strengthening them for their careers ahead. He showed her his scull, a Pocock model that was secured in a small boathouse at the base of the pier. She was a physical fitness nut, too. She told him she might like to try it out some day.

The afternoon was heading into Monday. He told her he'd always hated Sundays because of the impending crush of all that was going to happen on Monday. It was a feeling he'd gotten as the result of four years at Ma Bancroft, the dormitory that housed the entire brigade of Midshipmen, some 4,000 strong. She made admiring sounds about all of that and again offered, "Maybe you could show me that place that I know you're so proud of, some day."

"Riley, you can count on it." Back at the house he saw her off in her truck and when he went inside he found her card on the dining room table, with her cell number written on the back. He settled into a chair in the study and stared at her card. But he wasn't reading the network logo or the number written on the back. He was seeing each of the times they'd been together, so much so quickly, that he wondered if it was real.

I mean, how can it be real? he wondered. Riley couldn't be more than twenty-five or -eight. What the hell was she doing spending this kind of time with him? There had to be tons of people out there, in the entertainment industry alone, available and just waiting to lavish attention on her, spend time with her, you name it. His independent mind kicked in with the convenient reminder that not too many of those Hollywood affairs worked out so well. Yeah, he argued with himself, but most anybody who knew that would still be saying, "Please don't throws me in that briar patch!" He knew for sure that that's exactly what *he* would be saying. So something made Riley different. He knew that he liked what he saw and might as well go along for the ride. Still, he had enough pride and common sense to leave the ball in her court. He was on the verge of making a fool of himself, and he knew he'd willingly do it with her. But the next move, if there was going to be another move, would be up to her. Anyway, he reasoned, she doesn't need a dirty old man chasing after her and inconveniencing her with invitations that she'd rather not have to turn down.

Dance was that way. He figured out his part and then he figured out the other person's. He reckoned that he wasn't right all the time, just 95 percent. With a background in physics, his numbers didn't go any higher than that or lower than 5 percent. Besides, although he'd been relatively successful with women, many of them very attractive, he'd always been considerate, never assuming anything, just because he'd footed the bill for dinner, never overtly pressing his own wants or even assuming that his female companionship had any wants of her own, where he was concerned. He also never gave it enough thought to figure out that it was these qualities that had made him so different and so attractive to so many women, Riley included.

CHAPTER 16

THE DAGO EXAM AND THE INVITATION

Monday noon and Wade had called and come out to the place just to shoot the breeze. When they got together like this it had a way of bringing up in Dantes' mind the unusual way they had become friends, sort of, during their academy days. It was after Plebe Year and they were on their Youngster Cruise. Glad just to not be plebes anymore they had first run into each other at sea during the run down to Rio de Janeiro aboard the USS Intrepid (CVA 11). They'd enjoyed the embassy party within sight of Sugarloaf and the girls who had been invited to meet and dance with the Mids. Each of them had had a very exciting night with some enchanting senoritas and had rolled back aboard from the liberty launch feeling no pain. It was a fine summer cruise during which they shared the lot of the deckhand, slept in crowded compartments just like they did, stood watches in the fire rooms and engine rooms and on the bridge, in Combat and Radio Central. By the end of their cruise they had gained an appreciation for the crew and something like awe of the chief petty officers for whom they worked as they completed their journal assignments. Fast friends, they came back from summer leave to academic year and found that they were in a class together. It was Dago (the Academy term for a foreign language course); both of them were taking French. And that's where the trouble happened.

The Military Academy and the Naval Academy had similar honor codes. West Point's stated that a cadet would not lie, cheat or steal, nor tolerate those who did. The Naval Academy's midshipmen took an oath not to lie, cheat or steal. Punishment for any infraction was dismissal. Facts of the case were weighed by a Midshipman Honor Court. If the offending Mid was found to have knowingly lied, cheated or stolen he was recommended for dismissal to the administration, which carried out the sentence forthwith. At West Point it was the same sort of drill. Each body had a commissioned officer who guided the Mids or cadets in the conduct of their investigations and deliberations. The difference between the two institutions was in the part that the Naval Academy left off, the part about not tolerating those who did commit the offense. At the Point, if a cadet observed an honor violation and did not report it, the observing cadet was considered equally guilty and would receive the same punishment as the one who had committed the offense, if it all came to light. At the Naval Academy the observing midshipman had three options. He could report the offense and offender, he could personally counsel the offender, or he could do nothing.

During a Dago midterm exam, Dantes had noticed Wade Bates consulting a crib sheet that he'd hidden inside the cuff of his long-sleeved shirt. Wade had always had a problem with academics, and this was especially true in Dago, for he had no aptitude at all for foreign languages. Verbs were the key to getting by in any language; they were both vocabulary words and the main part of any written sentence. Getting the conjugation right and knowing the word itself, was more than half the battle. Dance had tutored Wade and helped him with a list of the most useful and most difficult verbs. What he saw in that moment was a small list of some of the information he'd helped Wade study and, he thought, learn.

Dance was very troubled. He felt in part responsible for Wade's action because he'd even written up a short-cheat sheet for Wade's use in preparing for the exam. He had no idea that Wade would take it to class with him and use it as a crutch. It was a clear honor violation and he had to deal with it. He had struggled with his knowledge and finally gotten an appointment with the battalion honor rep. One night after break from study hours he sat together with him and went over the whole situation, leaving out the identity of the offender. The Firstie reminded him of his options, reminded him of one of the purposes of the extremely difficult Plebe Year, to weed out those not suited for service as a commissioned officer in the Navy or Marines. He said that if he reported the incident it would be others who would evaluate it and others who would take the necessary action. Finally, the rep said that if he did nothing he, Dance, could end up being solely responsible for someone who was unsuited by character to lead men in combat if given that opportunity. The question was who deserved the consideration, the classmate or the men over whom he would have command in later life.

That was it. No easy answers. It was still up to Dance. It finally came down on the side of giving Wade a second chance. Dance couldn't simply do nothing and he wouldn't make an official report to the Honor System. On Saturday after morning classes and the p-rade at Worden field and after attending one of the varsity athletic events in the Yard that day, he'd asked Wade to take a walk out into Crabtown with him.

"Sure, Bud. What's up?"

"Just thought we could go out in town, rattle the natives and check out a drag house" (the term for a local home where Mids' dates for the weekend could stay). They'd done just that and then Dance pulled to a stop and braced himself. "Wade, I saw you using a cheat sheet during the Dago midterm." Wade said nothing. "I don't need to tell you that it is an honor offense for which you can be dismissed from the Academy." Surprise, fear and disappointment flashed by turn across Wade's face, to be swiftly replaced with the dead-pan expression that all plebes learned to employ when under harsh interrogation by an upperclassman.

He turned directly toward Dance—rigid posture, almost the position of attention, hands clenched at his sides, and said, "What will you do?"

"I am completing with this confrontation all the action I will take. I have reviewed my options with the battalion honor rep. I have decided to counsel you about this and then let it drop. Wade, what the *fuck* did you think you were doing? You ought to know by now that there are no short-cuts. Plain and simple, you've let me down and you've let the whole brigade down. Most important, you've let yourself down. How in the hell can you expect compliance from the underclass or from your men once we graduate if you don't set the example yourself?"

"Dance, you're right, absolutely right. I knew better and should never have even considered cheating."

"You took an oath, a goddamned oath! What's your word worth, now?"

"All I can say is that it will never happen again and that I appreciate the second chance you are giving me."

"There won't be any third chance."

"There won't be another offense." Then Wade did a very unusual thing. He drew himself to a proper position of attention and rendered Dance a very formal and precise salute, looking searchingly into his eyes. Dance was moved. They were equals, no seniority between them. Yet he returned the salute, holding it just a second and then cutting away. Wade dropped his salute in turn.

"Carry on," said Midshipman 3/c Dantes; they would never talk of it again.

———

Second Class year is, academically, the toughest year, at the Naval Academy. It is typically the Segundos, the second class Mids, who give the plebes the hardest time. Maybe it was because they were so stressed out by academics. Probably it was because somebody had to do it and they were the logical choice. Firsties had more liberty and were already thinking of their careers beyond the wall. The Wall surrounds the Yard, a large and imposing structure, especially in the area of the Main Gate into Crabtown. Some Firsties were making plans to be married. Others were dreaming of nothing more serious than buying their first car. Still others were having to decide whether to go Subs or Surface Navy, Naval Aviation, Marines or Marine Aviation. In a four-year course they were the elder statesmen, mostly mature enough to leave the really nasty running of the plebes to the underclass. Youngsters (third class Mids) were just glad not to be plebes anymore. They were enjoying being human again, being able to eat without being braced up, chins tucked-in and eyes in the boat. They stayed quiet and watched the nightly torture of the plebes at evening meal in the gigantic mess hall. Sometimes, when the upperclass left the table the third class would gently use the plebes to hassle a classmate, but mostly they just stayed in their place, ecstatic not to be plebes.

Wade Bates was known as the most harsh hazer of the fourth class, not just in his company, but in the battalion and probably had some reputation regiment and brigade-wide. He was imaginative, persistent and deadly earnest. Like Lincoln's pig, "He liked it." A "come around" to Wade's room was tantamount to a death sentence. Plebes feared him as no other. Wade was a genuine animal and he treated plebes as subhumans. But he left them no dignity, which was wrong.

Wade's Academy career, however, lasted for only one more year. He again got into academic trouble during his second class year. Probably one of the reasons was the amount of time he spent running plebes. He failed thermodynamics and got a re-exam, which he passed. Then, in his second semester he failed two courses, was awarded re-exams and passed only one of them. He was offered a turnback, the chance to join the class that was a year behind his. Wade declined, even though he knew the consequences. If a midshipman resigned at any time during his last two years at the Academy, he was required to complete his service obligation by serving as an enlisted man in the Navy. It was the same result if he became academically ineligible; finish out your obligation in the service, without a commission.

Instead of turning back, Wade applied for and was accepted into the Basic Underwater Demolition/SEAL (BUD/S) training. After successful completion of the highly demanding six months of basic conditioning, diving and land warfare training, he joined a SEALS unit. He served two tours in Viet Nam, running into his classmate Dance in Subic Bay on a couple of occasions. As classmates they enjoyed an easy familiarity in spite of their different stations in life. They remained friends and kept up with one another over the years.

Wade and Dance served together for one two-year period, at White Sands Missile Range in New Mexico. Dantes was the officer in charge of the Navy High Energy Laser Test program there. Bates was his senior chief petty officer. It was a small group of two officers and 21 enlisted. They were known for their excellence in that small military and civilian community in the desert, hard-by the Organ Mountains and across San Agustin Pass from Las Cruces, New Mexico.

When operations became routine, things were too dull for Wade. He took a job after hours as the night bouncer at the NCO Club on Post. The club had a reputation as a rowdy place. Wade waited eagerly for the first sign of trouble. It came in the poolroom. Three black soldiers were fighting with one white sailor. There was a mixed group of another dozen or so, looking on. Wade told them loudly to stop, right before he threw one of the soldiers into the other two. Then he turned on the sailor and decked him with one punch. There were four moaning brawlers lying on the deck with stove-in ribs and a broken arm or two when Wade pleaded with the onlookers, "Doesn't *any*body else want some of this?" Nobody did. There were no more fights. Wade quit his night job because it was too dull.

Wade did his job in the Laser Test Office perfectly. There were no problems with the men. He was extremely resourceful in coming up with jury-rigs to solve any and all problems. When an office at the Naval Surface Warfare Laboratory in White Oak, Maryland said that they could not find all of the equipment that they owed to the site at White Sands for a test series, Wade asked LCDR Dantes, his boss, to be sent back to look for it. Within 24 hours he had found it all. Perhaps it was the simple expedient of announcing that all equipment (he had a typewritten list) would be placed in the loading dock, ready for shipment, or he'd kill the first offender and drag him by the heels through the lab as an example to the rest of them—that did the trick. People generally didn't take such extravagant statements seriously until they looked Wade in the eye.

Wade had a crazy look. Everybody knew it but couldn't describe it except to say it was a "crazy look." He wasn't a giant of a man, just six-foot-one and about 200 pounds. But he had that look. He could hackle anyone with a quick move, grabbing him by the hand and bending his fingers until the person was on his knees. On his knees until Wade let him up. This was done with a joyous crazy look and a smile… even a friendly smile. Wade occasionally told his boss, Dance, and it was "Dance" because they were on first-name basis when in private, and it was only when they were in private and perhaps when both had had a little something to drink that he would make his "offer." "Dance," he would say, "you know if anyone ever gives you any trouble, any trouble at all, all you need to do is to let me know." And Dantes would make light of it, saying, "Wade, make sure I say it twice; I wouldn't want you rubbing out anyone on a casual comment made by me." And Wade would let a little of that crazy look come into his eyes and say, "Dance, just you let me know."

———

"Hey, Wade. Come on in; coffee's in the pot! How've you been?"

"Hey, Dance, doing fine, how about you?"

"Ahh, you know, same-o, same-o. Can't say there've been any problems at the site, money just keeps rolling in, life's good."

"I'll say life's good! Look, I caught you on TV yesterday. So, what about her?"

"What about who? Riley?"

"So it's Riley, is it? And any other actresses, starlets or supermodels you just happen to know by their first names, any extras that you can spare?" he said laughingly, with just a boatload of extreme envy mixed in. Wade was rolling his eyes, flapping his tongue and panting like a coyote ready to howl at the moon.

"Ah, come on, Wade. You know how it is with these TV personalities. They go where the stories are. TLL has been in the news and news is what brings the viewers and ad revenues."

"Dance, you know better than to bullshit a bullshitter. I bet that more than half of that show's audience watches just because of Ms. Riley Berry. I mean she is one fine looking and classy lady."

"Well, I guess you've got me there. She is very nice in person. Considerate, intelligent and really down to earth."

"And trustworthy, loyal, helpful, friendly, courteous, kind, cheerful, thrifty, brave, clean and reverent, too, I suppose."

"Uh-huh, and I'd forgotten that you'd been a Boy Scout, too."

"You've certainly proven that you know how to scout 'em out, buddy."

"Yeah, now if I could only have the same luck in the stock market… seriously, there's not a chance that there's anything between Riley and yours truly. Give it a week and she won't even remember my name.

Just then the phone rang. Wade looked at him as if to say, "Aren't you going to answer that?"

Dance's shrug in return said, "I'll let the recorder catch it." His recorded voice invited the caller to leave a message after the beep.

"Well, now! What's a girl to do? I mean, I left my card and here I am, pining away for a whole day and not a call, not one?" Chuckles on the phone… "Okay, if you're not there, I guess…"

"Riley, hey! Sorry it took me so long to pick up. Great to get your call. What's up?"

"I'm sitting here making out the invitation list for a party I'm throwing in a couple of weeks. Can I put your name on the list? I mean, not everyone is going to get the personal treatment. They'll just get mailed invites."

"Gee, that sounds great!"

"Does that mean you'll come?"

"Absolutely."

"Because, if you can't make it then I'm holding it when you can."

"Nah, you flatter me. I bet you say that to all the boys. I'll be there for sure. What's the occasion?"

"Oh just a soiree of the D.C., New York and L.A. glitterati, movers and shakers. I've borrowed the Georgetown house of Senator Contralves from New York. She's been most gracious to offer it. She'll be out of town and won't come, but wants us to enjoy the place."

"Okay, let me write all of this down." And she gave him the details. "Who else you got coming?" As she told him the names he repeated them, jotting them down on his notepad.

"Let's see. There's Supreme Court Justice Benton."

"Benton."

"Fanny Goldman, Howard Storm, Mark Moorer, the filmmaker…"

"Goldman, Storm and Moorer… you've got your hands full with those characters."

"Just getting started, you probably don't even know who this is, her name is Brianna. Just Brianna."

"Yeah I know who she is."

"Dance, she's a porn star!" What have you been *doing* in your spare time?" she giggled.

"Okay, I got Brianna down here. It is dawning on me that a number of these people are actually to be found on TLL. ...Or did you know that?"

"Well, Dance. Actually I did know that. I mean the lists are *not* identical, but there is some significant overlap. Will that make you uncomfortable?"

"Not me. Don't know that I can say the same for your other guests, though. Will they know that I'm going to be there?"

"Nope, just giving you the chance at an advance look. Think you can handle it?"

"Sure, I wouldn't miss this for anything."

"Great, I'm looking forward to it, then."

"Me too—bye." And he hung up.

And there was Wade, just sitting there, with this totally amazed look on his face. "Oh, I wouldn't make any big plans, Dance, she'll probably forget about it in a week... your name, even."

"Hold on, now..."

"Reckon she's invited you for the ratings?"

"Okay, I have to admit I'm surprised and pleased."

"Right. Surprised I can believe, pleased is a total understatement. Buddy, you're moving in a different world, now. Want to give me your autograph? I want to be able to prove I knew you when!"

"Okay, that's just about enough. What did you come over here for, anyway? I need to kick you out of here so I can get something done."

"You mean like getting your tux pressed, or even like maybe buying a tux? Look, I just came over to see how you and our web site were doing. Good on you. Some guys get all the luck." His expression wasn't so much envious as it was knowledgeable. As he left Dance couldn't help feeling Wade was holding something back. *And what was that, a slip of the tongue, probably. No reason to call it "our" web site. He's just genuinely pleased for my success.*

———

Riley hung up with a dreamy expression, thinking of the party and thinking of Dance. She looked in the mirror critically and saw there a strikingly attractively woman with a perfect figure and devilish eyes set in a supermodel's face. She acknowledged her interest in Dance was not just professional. He was charming and good-looking; perhaps more important he reciprocated her interest in a restrained sort of way. He had not come even close to hitting on her. She imagined him as her 'first' lover. She imagined... more. Riley was ready after all those years of wary relationships with men to engage and trust. She wanted to feel loved and appreciated. Hell, she was decidedly horny and ready for sex with a capital "S." And, she thought that just maybe she could be the one who did the choosing. She didn't want to do it with one of the importunate legion who had been so suggestive, and wind up as a notch on somebody's bedpost. This was not going to be an ego trip for anyone. Who knew? This could even be the start of something serious. She knew she wasn't looking for a one-night stand. Riley had been looking for a while now and it was Dance who had stuck in her mind, piqued her interest and stirred her heart. She had chosen Dance.

CHAPTER 17
MORE INTEREST

The Glavnoye Razvedovatel'noye Upravlenie (GRU) Headquarters is located near Moscow at the Khodinka Airfield. When the USSR dissolved at the start of 1992, and following the creation of the Russian Ministry of Defense, the GRU became Russia's military intelligence arm, a cohesive, highly efficient and professional military intelligence agency. Inside a run-down glassed-in structure known as The Aquarium, in a second-floor office, GRU Colonel Y. Kharkov and Major V.I. Gagarin were meeting. The topic of discussion was some recently acquired information of interest.

"So, Major, what have you found out about our new information? Do we think it concerns the American agent whom we've tracked so diligently, for so long?"

"Ah yes, the shadowy one, best agent of our former enemies, the Americans." Both of them pulled half smiles at the term "former enemies." While the general public was not so informed, Russian intelligence activities had greatly increased in the United States. Though their president liked to think he had a relationship with the Russian leader, it was true there had been only a pause in hostile relations between the two powers.

"The Colonel can judge for himself. After receiving the information from our Kabul source, concerning a retired agent in the Capitol area of the United States, we of course took measures to confirm and crosscheck. We have confirmed that it was not just the Kabul area which received the update, but also Tel Aviv and Baghdad." With some embarrassment he added, "Sir, we are still trying to confirm if this information was received by the Moscow station chief."

"So, you think that this is bona fide information? And that it might concern the American Agent whom we refer to as Орел (Eagle)?"

"Taken together with the total absence of any indications of his operations, I'd say that there's a good chance that this is one and the same man. The Colonel will recall that we stopped funding our source in Washington when the information on Eagle no longer panned out. That was about the same time that Eagle suspended his operations. I think that this news was sent to station chiefs who might have had an interest in Eagle, might have employed or supported him. Certainly Eagle conducted operations in their areas of responsibility."

"I need not remind you that Eagle remains a person of highest interest to us, whether retired or not."

"Indeed not. One does not know that such a resource will remain retired until one takes steps to ensure that such retirement is irreversible."

"Exactly. Eventually I will want a small team put together whose task it will be to make this retirement a permanent one."

"Eventually?"

"Yes, it has taken almost a year for this information to come to us. I do not wish to jump on it immediately. Perhaps the Americans are waiting and watching for just such a response. Tell me about the steps taken to crosscheck this message."

"As you would expect, they were subtle. For example, our inquiry in Tel Aviv was with a source that has been long in place. Also, it was part of a regular update and posed in the form of, "What's new in general?" Our source actually offered the news of the retirement as part of a general digest of recent minor developments."

"Very good. Still, I don't want any unseemly haste. If this is bait, we will let it languish for a while, say six months or more. Perhaps he will stay 'retired' for that long, at least."

"As you have directed, Colonel."

CHAPTER 18
THE MESSENGER

"Starzinger Investigations, how may I direct your call?"

"Ohhh, I need to get more sleep!"

"Jeff?" With a broad smile… "So what brings the pleasure of this call?"

"Sorry to say that it's not the pleasure of your company last night. It was rough getting in the mood for work today."

"Umm hmm, tell me about it."

"Look, I'll call you toward the end of the day, see if we might set up something for later this week."

"I'd enjoy that."

"I do need to talk to Dick, please, if I might."

"Of course, Jeff. Hold please."

———

Dick had heard a little of the tone, if not the words of the by-play between Dixie and Jeff. There was a smile in his voice when he picked up the phone. "Good morning, Jeff. So, what did you think of my report?"

"You're right; I was looking for something different on our subject. Though your report was thorough it wasn't what I expected."

"I haven't spent the entire retainer, only about half. You are entitled to a refund, which I'll gladly give you."

"Dick I really appreciate the offer but I think I'll leave the retainer with you and continue running a tab, if I might."

"That's no problem at all. Now, regarding the additional item of interest I mentioned in my report—I think that you should take up residence right where you are, for the time being. I assume that you're calling from your office."

"That's right. I have a suite here that's outfitted to cover all of my needs."

"Good, then you won't even need to go home to get clothes or the like?"

"No, I have clothes, food, and a regular place to stay."

"You'd better stay put while I see what I can do to find this guy and apprehend him. The security at ABS headquarters will be sufficient to keep him at bay. Besides, with you off the street he won't know where you are or even that you are aware of his activity. I'd suggest a review of the security procedures for the building and that you plan on laying low for a couple of weeks or so."

"I can have my schedule rearranged so it'll be no problem. Besides, I need to put in a lot of time for a campaign we're putting together."

"That'll work. Why don't I plan on sending any updates to you via Dixie, say at the end of the day, when I have them? For her safety we could use company limos?" Dick heard the smile in Jeff's voice…

"That will work out really well. Bye, and thanks, Dick."

————

Dixie heard enough to put a smile on her face, too. Dick poked his head out of his office, noted the smile and asked her to come in, close the door. He cocked an eyebrow at her and said, "Maybe it's time to let you in on some of what's going on with Mr. Jeff Prather. Or, should *you* let *me* know what's going on?"

"Well, Dick, I do find him an attractive man and he's much nicer than I thought. I certainly am not aware of anything that's…"

Holding up his hand in the universal stop sign, he said, "I'm not asking about your personal life. But, it looks like you're going to be spending more time with him than I'd thought. You will be the message carrier between us and it could place you at risk." She could tell it was serious by the look on his face. She turned fully toward him, serious herself.

"What is it, Dick?"

"Jeff was being shadowed by a stalker the night he came to the office. I was able to get a possible ID and have initiated surveillance on him to see if he makes any false moves. I wouldn't want you to get caught in any crossfire if this person were to make an attack on Jeff. In the meantime, Jeff will be living at ABS headquarters. Security ought to be good there."

"Is this connected to the project work that you're doing for Jeff?"

"Perhaps indirectly, but maybe not at all. The retainer was to cover investigative work on the background of Mr. Dance Dantes, that fellow with the web site. I don't know if you've been to the site, but one of the Top Ten Liberals listed there is my client and your friend, Jeff. One thing is for certain—there's enough money and inflamed passion to fuel a war, much less an attack on Jeff. You know, he thinks that the web site is responsible for the killings of 'Listees' that have occurred, so far. He told me that first night that he was concerned that he could be next."

Dixie was concerned enough by what she was hearing that she didn't even give the remark about 'inflamed passions' a second thought. "Thanks for telling me what's going on, Dick. I appreciate your confidence in me. I am glad that it's you who are looking out for Jeff, and for me. I'll be the messenger and be glad to help out in any way that I can."

CHAPTER 19
CONTROL'S CONFUSION

Control's first and only communication from his "retiree" had gotten his full and undivided attention. He had been given to understand that this would be strictly administrative, with the occasional, probably pedestrian request. But this was anything but routine. His interest spiked when he ran the license plate number down and realized that the owner of the plate in question was none other than his Contractor, whom he tasked through TLL. His first thought was that his 'Contractor' and the 'retiree' had to be the same person. But that was too, too coincidental. His Contractor had been turned down, not hired by The Company, hence could not be retired, and had no way of contacting him other than via the signal and dead drop he'd already used once.

So, if his retiree was genuine and was indeed retired, what was he doing asking for the identity of the owner of this particular license plate? What was this person doing, in retirement? Did the Agency already know of his use of the Contractor? Was this their way of letting him know they knew? Did they approve? Disapprove? He settled down and made some basic assumptions.

The worst case was that the Agency knew what he was doing, disapproved and was applying pressure to him through the retiree to see how he responded before rolling him up. If this were the case, he was compromised and it was only a matter of time before they picked him up.

At the other extreme was the possibility that somehow the retiree was semi-active and had been doing some freelance work on the TLL murders. If this was the case he must not have a clue that his 'Control' was involved in the TLL murders or he wouldn't have approached him with this request. If he could believe his boss, the retiree did not know his Control's identity.

Going with the more favorable scenario, he further assumed that his retiree must have been close enough to the commission of one of the Contractor's attacks or attempts to at least have noted the license plate number. In that case this request might be an innocent one. He was only trying to determine who the Contractor/killer/Toyota owner was so that he might follow him or otherwise detain him. Control's choices were to give his retiree an accurate answer or to mislead him.

He chose to mislead him. That night he went to the Contractor's home, where the Toyota was parked in the driveway, and removed the license plate. He had already entered the Virginia database, calling up Toyota Corollas that were the same color and year of the Contractor's car. He found more than three hundred. He picked one in Virginia, one that belonged to a roofer, name of Pokorny. He waited until Pokorny was at work and removed the plate from his car and put the stolen plate in its place.

As expected, the Contractor reported his plate as stolen within two days and got a replacement plate. The roofer drove around for several weeks without noticing that his plate had been changed. Control put his one-time message in the drop and set the flag for his retiree to pick it up. There was no way to sit all day for a day or two to try to identify his retiree when he made the pickup.

———

This was not entirely true. In fact, The Agency had enough resources to put surveillance in place on Control, around the clock. Had they done so they could have noted all of this activity. By now they could have placed radio beacons on both Toyotas and been tracking their movements.

But the spymasters at CIA were waiting for something overt from the Russians before they ramped up their operation. It had not crossed their minds that Control was involved in anything, much less something so close to home.

———

Zinger had gone out to the Pokorny home as soon as he'd received Control's note and verified that the car license was the same as he had written down. The color of the car was the same. His next move was to use some of Prather's money to sub out the surveillance of Pokorny to another P.I.

Reports came in daily on Pokorny's activities. He went strictly to work and home. There were no side trips to ABS headquarters or to Prather's home. On Thursday afternoon he deviated from his normal routine and visited a woman at her small home for two hours. The report contained some pictures of an incriminating nature, but not in connection with Prather or anyone else on the top ten list. Zinger filed the photos with the other reports and authorized continued surveillance for another week.

Sometimes, as he performed these routine and necessary tasks Zinger wondered why he had set himself up as a private eye. The decision to stay busy wasn't a decision; it was a necessity. Zinger actually required action. He thrived on problem solving. What he did had to matter. He wasn't built for inaction. Setting himself up as self-employed avoided most of the questions that would be posed by an employer. He was used to setting his own schedule, but he was also used to having a full dance card. He'd have gone crazy, just sitting.

CHAPTER 20
THE PANEL

At ABS headquarters Prather dove into his work with frenzied zeal. As he would later say of Dance Dantes, he had the motive, the opportunity and the capability to do the work at hand. Working nonstop at his suite in the ABS headquarters building (he did take breaks every evening) he put together a detailed indictment of Dance Dantes and TLL.

The subject of the first installment was Dantes' background. Lieutenant Commander Dantes had been found "Not recommended for command" as was evidenced in his Naval Service Record. He was given to snap judgments and ran roughshod over his contemporaries and anyone unlucky enough to have worked for him. There was a quote from a boss of his in civilian life, "There were two types of people where Dance was concerned—they either loved him or they hated him." Conveniently left out was the continuation of the Lockheed VP's remarks that he could do the impossible, even provide the Queen Mary in the desert overnight, if need be.

Prather had a panel in place for the show when he opened his attack, which he promoted as an investigative series of great importance to the nation. With him on the kickoff show were an anti-war activist, an actor who had played the part of an admiral on a popular TV series and a popular TV psychologist. Turning to the "admiral" he asked for his observations on this type of character in the Navy.

"Well, Jeff, as you know, I never served in the Navy, myself."

"Yes, Martin, but in my mind that lends even more credence to your remarks. As an actual service member you might be defensive, might color your testimony, if I might call it that, to favor your service. What my viewers and I want is your view on this type of character. After all, you have had to study the military way of life in order to star in your very successful show, 'Command at Sea.'"

"Thanks, Jeff. Yes, I have had to be familiar with all sorts of characters during my career. I must say that Mr. Dantes is one with which I am familiar. His is a classic case of what I'd call the petty tyrant. He has delusions of grandeur. His career has not turned out to be what he'd hoped."

"Yes, right on—in fact here is a copy of his fitness report that states that he is not recommended for command." The whole report was not shown, just the block with an "X" typed in, along with an illegible signature.

"Well, I have to say I'm not surprised." No, the actor wasn't surprised. In fact, he had been briefed and the "testimony" had been practiced in a dry run. Actually, the 'Admiral's' show was slipping in the ratings, as well. He hoped for a boost out of this appearance.

"Yet, this type of character is often extremely intelligent," said the actor.

"Right again. Mr. Dantes has a master's degree in physics."

"But the problem is what they do with the force of their intellect. Often they will turn it toward the undermining of the good work of others, or of groups which they hold in some way responsible for their own failures."

Turning now toward the psychologist on his panel, he introduced the popular Dr. Jackye Bothers. "Jackye, how about that? What sorts of behavior can we expect from a petty tyrant such as the Admiral has described?" Prather directed an admiring smile to the actor.

"I would certainly associate myself with his remarks, Jeff. In fact I think that there is an important point to be made along those lines. We often see anti-social behavior acted out against others. The greater the self-delusion, usually the larger the target. The added point, though, is that the acting out will become violent, if left untreated."

"Violent, you say?"

"Absolutely, in fact…"

"Thank you, Jackye. I'd like to get Jane in here. Jane, you have been protesting the violence of our military for years. Based upon your observations and the documented incidents you've testified on before Congress—a great service to the country, I might add—what do you think we might expect next, from Mr. Dantes?"

"Thank you, Jeff, for having me on. As I say in my book…"

"Right, I apologize for not mentioning that you are a best-selling author. And the title of your latest is: *Don't be the Last to Die for a Bad Idea*."

"Yes, and it goes on to describe how the military has betrayed the young men and women it uses and the country it purports to serve. Jeff, what we see, time and again, is that brainwashed men from the service will, in fact, take direct and unwarranted violent action against innocent civilians. As you said, I have taken the testimony of hundreds of servicemen and women who have explained eloquently what they were forced to do while in the military and how it has affected their lives, once they got out."

"And, Mr. Dantes; what does your experience tell you we might expect from him?"

"Well, just look at that web site of his! He is inciting many of these warped former soldiers and sailors to direct violence against the best our country has to offer."

"And that's all we have time for, but we will be coming back to this subject again, I assure you. Meanwhile we welcome your e-mails and comments. Please send them in to jeffprather@abs.com. Thank you and good evening."

Excerpts and clips of the panel's comments were cut and distributed to the producers of the rest of ABS' news, magazine and talk shows. It was a full court press, intended to stir up a response.

———

Cox News noted the panel discussion on a rival network concerning Dance Dantes, who had appeared on their network. "As you know, I had Mr. Dantes on as Power Player of the Week. We contacted him for a response. It was short and to the point. Mr. Dantes said, 'Consider the source.'"

———

On a CSPAN call in show, a lawyer for "Patriots Defending America" made news when he mentioned that his organization was initiating a lawsuit, the purpose of which was to shut down "The Liberal List."

———

At the TLL site the servers crashed and IBM was not able to keep up with the demand for storage, "on demand" or not. IBM technicians scrambled to support the largest single-day flood of hits to the site.

There was a new Number One on the Top Ten List, Mr. Jeff Prather. New to the site and debuting at Number Five was the anti-war activist, Ms. Jane Tarver. The comments were enraged and contemptuous. Many writers wrote again and again because they couldn't say it all in just 250 characters. The war was on, in earnest.

————

Dance Dantes got a call from Jennings Carson. "Dance, I want you to know that I am shocked and angry at the shoddy treatment you've received in this smear campaign launched by Jeff Prather."

"Me, too."

"Also, I hope you understand that I totally disagree with the things he's saying and I did not contribute any information to ABS News. An investigator came by the office asking questions about you, some sort of background check for a position of some sort, he said. Sounded fishy to me and I declined to discuss our interviews. I'm sorry that I didn't think to call you and tell you at the time. You could at least have had some sort of a heads-up warning that this was coming."

"Thanks, Jen. I appreciate it."

"Not to mention it. If you'll let me I'd like to do a piece that'll refute all of his innuendoes and garbage."

"Maybe when he gets down to something with more content I'll take you up on it. So far it's not anything that's too specific. What he said about my fitness report is actually fairly accurate."

"You do recall that we didn't turn on the recorder until you had already said what you had to say about all of that to me?"

He laughed. "Yes, I am human enough to have thought about all of the possibilities; including the one that maybe you had told someone everything. I know better."

"Thanks, Dance. I'll be in touch about another interview within a couple of weeks."

"Thanks, Jen. Bye."

CHAPTER 21
FIRST AMENDMENT UPHELD

It hadn't been his best day. The phone rang off the hook until he'd made a quick call to set up an answering service. The calls were all transferred to the service and he got chronological summaries faxed to him of the times, names and nature of their business. Of course there were many calls wanting to schedule him on their TV shows, their radio shows, and interview requests from newspapers. After he got the answering service going his next move was to call his lawyer and get some recommendations for a crack legal team to defend the suit that had been filed in Federal Court.

They got on it right away and confirmed that Patriots Defending America were going to try to shut him down. They had requested an order from the United States District Court for the District of Columbia to bring down his web site immediately, citing danger to the public at large. They were due in court in two days, the PDA having gotten expedited handling of their extraordinary request.

There was another note, which had gotten his attention. It was totally out of left field, totally unexpected. It was the D.C. office of the ACLU. They asked for a return call. It seems that they were interested in joining his legal team! He returned this call as soon as he'd told his attorney about the note.

"ACLU Washington, please hold. Yes, thanks for holding. How may I help?"

"Thank you, I'm Dance Dantes and I'm returning a call from…"

"Mr. Dantes, thank you for returning our call. Let me forward you to our chief legal counsel."

"Mr. Dantes, hello. I'm Terry Hamilton. Thanks so much for getting back to us."

"Yes, well it seems that there is not much time. I've got to tell you that the ACLU is the last place from which I'd have expected help. Do I understand the message you left with my answering service correctly? Have you actually offered to join my defense team?"

"Yes, that's correct. We believe that a very strong case can be made that to shut down your web site would be in violation of your First Amendment rights to free speech."

"But, I certainly don't have to remind *you* that my web site has been blamed for your colleague's death, that of Josh Hirsch."

"Not to be flippant about this, Mr. Dantes, but you don't believe everything you hear about or read, even, on that web site of yours, do you?" Dantes remained silent with speechless amazement. "Actually, we do have some experience in First Amendment cases. We also have considerable experience in arguing before the very court and likely the actual judge that will hear this case. How about it? Will you take us up on our offer…?" Finally, as Dantes still hadn't replied, he pulled out the clincher, "We here at ACLU are unanimous in our judgment that Josh wouldn't have had it any other way. Of course he also would have insisted that we not charge for representing you. This one's on him."

A choked up and astonished Dance Dantes formally thanked Chief Counsel Terry Hamilton and accepted his offer of help. He also filed one away for the liberals. Big time.

———

Two days later they went to court and it was a blow out for TLL, a no hitter for the PDA. PDA tried the shouting fire in a crowded theater argument. It didn't wash when Counsel for the Defense showed that the theater, in this case, was a virtual one and not real. There was no crowding, no immediate danger. Furthermore, anyone was free to either attend this virtual theater or not, as they chose. PDA obviously was not there to try anything having to do with the deaths of Mr. Josh Hirsch, Esquire or Senator Riggs, so no mention of them or their deaths was allowed.

The Judge, the Honorable Vernon Tuck found for the Defense and then delivered himself of a few well-chosen remarks. "There will certainly be plenty of grandstanding over this web site in the weeks and months to come. Gentlemen, none of it will be done in this Courtroom."

As he left the Court and headed down the steps, a crush of reporters and TV crews headed him off and shouted to be heard. Dantes picked out the mike that had the Cox News Logo on it and recognized the reporter. "Mr. Dantes," and the crowd quieted down so that they could all hear the question and the answer, "Mr. Dantes, give us your impression of the proceedings just concluded."

"I'll answer just this one question. It was fair. It had the wonderful quality of being swift and fair. I am greatly indebted to the American Civil Liberties Union for their most kind offer of help and for their outstanding professionalism as part of my legal team."

"One follow up?"

"Okay, just one and I'll ask it and I'll answer it. You can call this my statement, if you wish. The question is how do you square the attacks on the ACLU on your web site with the service that they have just rendered in your web site's defense? Here's the answer. Everyone is entitled to his or her own opinion. Each visitor to TLL is entitled to his or her own opinion. They are invited to write these opinions out, for the rest of us. Tonight I am going to put my own opinion, for the first time, on TLL and it'll be about the ACLU. As for what it will say, you all," and peering into each of the cameras thrust forward he addressed the American People who would be watching the news that night, "You all are invited to go to theliberallist.net to read one mighty fine compliment to the ACLU. Thank you, Chief Counsel Hamilton, thank you the American public and thank God for the U.S. Constitution."

The TLL note thanked Terry Hamilton and the ACLU for coming to the defense of free speech, even conservative speech. And, Dantes' signed note continued; "I regret not having met Mr. Josh Hirsch. For then I could say that I knew two great liberal and patriotic Americans.

CHAPTER 22
THE GUEST LIST

Sanford Benton had been born in San Francisco, California on January 14, 1963. He had been nominated as an Associate Supreme Court Justice by President Buisson, President Jameson's predecessor, and took his seat October 27, 2003. He had received an AB from Stanford University, BA from Magdalen College, Oxford; LLB from Harvard Law School. He had been assistant attorney general of California, assistant secretary for Civil Rights, U.S. Department of Education, law clerk to the Honorable Josiah Webb, of the U.S. District Court for the District of Columbia, Judge of the U.S. Court of Appeals for the D.C. Circuit Court.

He had also been a hell raiser, growing up, single-handedly trying to extend the 60's mantra of sex, drugs and rock and roll into the 80's. Mixed in with his scintillating resume were two marriages and divorces, no children. Stanford's and Sacramento's relative proximity to Hollywood presented temptations that would have felled a better man than he. Actually he fit in very well with President Buisson's friends and his name came easily to mind when the President was presented with a very late, second term opportunity to put an ultra-liberal on the Court.

The appointment didn't come quite as late as the flurry of pardons of drug dealers and scofflaw CEOs that Buisson signed in the last twenty-four hours of his Presidency. Like the bumper sticker for gun advocates said, "They can take my gun away when they pry it from my cold, dead fingers," they had had to practically pry the office out of President Buisson's grasp. Buisson liked being President, as opposed to being "not-president", in order to address what he viewed as the overriding concerns for the nation. It was a bloody Senate nomination fight, which the Democrats won on straight party line votes. The GOP was furious but helpless to prevent the nomination's passing.

Benton was young for a Supreme and he didn't figure he'd gone to the highest court in the land to shrivel up and die. He still had some buddies from his days as a defense lawyer. He'd admired some of their girlfriends. As things progressed he'd go to parties they threw where the girl friends brought girlfriends. Usually they'd go from the pool into one of the bedrooms off the pool. Always the bar was stocked with the best booze, the VCR sitting on "pause" with the best adult entertainment available. The friends changed constantly while the entertainment remained the same, his favorite flicks of "Brianna." When he went to formal dinner parties he went alone. He sparkled with the ladies, just never followed up. Brilliant, witty and with a racy background he was often invited out, seldom accepted these invitations.

The invitation from Ms. Riley Berry was a no-brainer. It looked to be fun.

———

Brianna (she'd shed her last name years ago) was thirty and had been in the business for twelve years. An extremely smart businesswoman, she occupied the top spot in a $10B industry pyramid. Being disease free had certainly contributed to her longevity. Most in the business didn't last three years but were sidelined by drug abuse or the competition. She had started with man-woman scenes and quickly moved to the woman-woman scenes and preferred them. She found that the physical effect was cumulative, that after several filmed encounters over an extended period of time with the same female partner the experience was increasingly satisfying and intense. With women she knew in this way she was always satisfied. Other than stock poses, which had become natural over the years, not much acting was required. While that was true of the entire genre, it was also true that Brianna simply didn't have to fake it.

She had won awards at the adult entertainment shindig in Las Vegas. She was getting guest shots on talk shows in LA. She had everything she could want except respectability. She was now garnering its similarly hard won yet pale and shallow substitute, celebrity. An invitation to a party in D.C. was as good as it got! She had a personal buyer out to the mansion with a trunk show of conservative travel clothes and several understated party dresses. She picked out a bra and slip that deemphasized her artificially inflated décolletage. They tried a couple of looks with minimal makeup and tame hairstyle. The bling blings were replaced with a strand of pearls and simple diamond earrings and the spike heels discarded. If not dowdy, the look bordered on something between Junior League and matronly. Nothing could dim the wattage of her powerful smile, though, as she examined herself in the mirror, anxious eyes darting, head tilted birdlike one way and then the other, adjusting her outfit for a reduced profile. She was ready, complete with camouflage for a very nice D.C. party. She was absolutely ready for something normal and wholesome in her life, even if she *had* to fake it.

———

Riley had hesitated, been undecided about this last name on her list. Perhaps it was rebellion against a strict upbringing. Maybe the enormous contrast between her own life and Brianna's had her curious. What would she be like? One thing Riley wasn't was a hypocrite. She actually had some of Brianna's films at home. Dance Dantes had noted the similar names on her list and his. She'd told him that it wasn't particularly intentional, (even though she had gotten the idea of inviting Brianna from TLL). In her heart of hearts she just felt like kicking over the traces, breaking out of the confining box she'd built for herself. This party was one way to start. She was ready to tear the tiniest corner open and start to emerge from her work-driven, self-imposed cocoon.

CHAPTER 23

GUESS WHO'S COMING TO DINNER?

Party night had arrived and all twelve guests had accepted. It was a little tight, but parking along the street was just possible. Some had come by taxi and others had been dropped off by chauffeur. The street could accommodate six or eight cars. Attending tonight were: Maisy Kearse, Chairman of the FCC and her husband, Warren; Troon O'Brien, NFL Commissioner; movie actress Fanny Goldman; Justice Benton; movie director Mark Moorer; Sir Richard Blair, billionaire owner of Blairlines; radio personality Howard Storm; Brianna; Senator Sam House, Chairman of the Senate Judiciary Committee and his wife, Dolly; Dantes and Riley. She hadn't thought of it until they'd set the table places, but counting her there were thirteen at the party.

The four piece jazz ensemble played in a corner of the large gathering room. A waiter in tux circulated taking drink orders and at the bar an attractive woman in tuxedo was mixing and pouring cocktails and wine. Howard Storm had buttonholed Maisy Kearse and was discussing satellite radio and how it compared to cable TV. He was pressing his opinion that certainly it enjoyed the same protections as cable, when it came to socially challenging content. Maisy was clearly doing some interested listening, while at the same time, in spite of herself, being charmed by Storm and his wild mane of dark, curly hair and flashing smile.

Outside a limo pulled past the residence and parked in the furthermost spot on the street. An hour later the chauffeur got out and leaned against the curbside passenger's door. Dressed in black driver's coat and billed cap he immediately took on the air of someone waiting to drive someone home. After twenty minutes or so he opened the door, placed his cap and uniform coat in the passenger seat, softly closed the door and walked away from the residence, aglow with lights and full of excited people. Dressed in tuxedo, he looked very much indeed like one of the invited partygoers inside. It was almost time to crash the party.

Dantes was seated across from Mark Moorer, the controversial movie director. He found him to be very charming, in person. Fanny Goldman congratulated him on the success of his latest documentary and asked what he had in mind for his next project. With a wry smile at Dantes, "Why I've been thinking of doing a piece on political uses of the internet."

"Bloggers, you mean? said Dantes.

"Actually something a lot closer to home…" with a twinkle in his eye.

Dance's ears perked up, "Ah, maybe the Democrats' use of the internet in fund raising? They were particularly effective in the last Presidential campaign."

"Actually I hadn't planned to announce this early, but, no, I'm thinking of doing a film on your web site, "The Liberal List," Dance.

"I'm certainly flattered to think that you even know about TLL."

"Not to get into business at a social gathering, but would you be willing to grant me access to your operation, and to do interviews?"

"Michael, you could contact my lawyer on Monday. I'm sure he'll have a nice way of politely declining," said Dance with a smile.

"Sure thing, know his number?"

"It's in the book."

"And his name, that's in the book, too?"

"No one ever accused you of being slow on the uptake, Mike."

———

Dessert had been served and Cognac and cigars for those who wanted them. The musicians who had taken a short break to graze on a buffet set up for them were sitting down to play some dance tunes. It was then that Sanford Benton got around to introducing himself to Brianna.

"Hi, I'm Sanford Benton. It's certainly a beautiful night, made more so by your presence, here."

"Why, thank you Sanford. Yes it is a wonderful evening and nice to be included by Riley."

"Brianna, would you like to dance?"

"That would be very nice," with a pleased smile. They stepped to the dance floor and moved easily into a foxtrot. Others were joining them as the music swelled and the couples floated in glittering patterns across the floor."

"Do you get to D.C. often?" he asked.

"Not me, how about you?"

"Actually, I work here, he said."

"Oh, and what do you do? making conversation.

"Ah, I'm in the legal profession."

"Hmm, then I guess Washington is the place for that, for sure." Alarm bells were going off and she anticipated his next comment.

"Yes. And you, you're from where? California?"

"Originally from Arkansas, but I make my residence there, it's true." With some feigned modesty she allowed as how she was able to monitor her investments from there, liked the California lifestyle. Then, as the music stopped she thanked him for the dance and moved off in Riley's direction.

————

"Brianna, we haven't had the chance to chat! Thank you so much for coming!" Others noticed her approach to Brianna and the happy welcome.

Riley's sincerity was obvious. They both smiled and immediately were talking like old girl friends. Brianna felt the tension in her shoulders ease. That lawyer, Sanford seemed like he was going somewhere with his comments. "You have so many nice friends, she said."

"Well, you work in this town and eventually you run into a lot of people." They were joined by Maisy, Dolly and Fanny and the conversation turned to politics, movies, upcoming judicial nominations and the life of Washington in general. …Oh I *saw* that movie! I thought it was sooo funny. Did you see it, Brianna?"

"Yes, it was hilarious, and did you see the one with Fanny, here? I just absolutely loved it." Brianna had a catch in her throat and her eyes filled as she realized what was happening, what they were <u>not</u> talking about. The girls had circled the wagons and were protecting a sister. She had made the effort to fit in, dressing the part. It was not an attempt to hide, but a silent cry for something resembling acceptance. The ladies took her in and her spirits took flight in the sanctuary they provided. When discussion turned to the economy and the market she ventured some remarks. "I like Cisco's market penetration and the target for them my broker has for the next year. I'm also into the health segment. We've picked companies with new patents and a relatively young portfolio of products." Shrewd looks of admiration came from these women who admired independence, talent in the stock market and financial success.

———

The men had similarly drifted into a loosely knit group in the study and were enjoying their cognac and cigars. Sir Richard was enthusiastically discussing the possibilities of a cricket league in the US with Troon O'Brien. "For sure you're kidding," Troon said. "How do you think baseball would go over in the UK?"

Dantes and Storm were laughing, comparing some of the outlandish statements made on TLL with similar comments made by Storm on his radio show. "Hey, I agree that maybe each of us is outlandish in our own way, but no one compares to you, Howard."

"I certainly appreciate that as a compliment. Just promise me that you're not going to take up radio. I don't think I could stand the competition!"

Sanford Benton had his eyes on Brianna, a smile playing across his lips.

No one noticed when a gentleman, dressed as they were, slipped from the garden area into one of the bedrooms with garden bath that opened out onto the beautiful grounds.

———

He had come around to the back of the house, which was bordered by a ten-foot brick wall. He stretched and jumped, securing a hold on the edge of the wall, then pulled himself up until his elbows rested on top. A quick scan showed him that no one was outside. He flipped up and over, coming to land in a crouch at the base of the wall. Then he moved quickly to the side of the house. He had his eye on the garden bath. He approached it quietly and quickly went in.

———

The party was winding down. Both groups had dissolved and there were expectant looks exchanged between Maisy and her husband, and the Senator and his wife.

Brianna had spotted the pretty bath that led into the garden. She headed toward it for a visit before taking her leave.

Sanford watched Brianna going to the bathroom and moved in the same direction.

———

Dance sidled up to Riley, who was just standing, appreciating her guests. "Hey, Riley I think it's about time to head for home. It's been great. The Glitterati, as you call them have all been fun."

"Dance, you don't need to go already, do you?"

"I think it's going to be breaking up soon; why don't I give you a call sometime tomorrow. Probably you'd like to spend time with your other guests as they take their leave."

"Probably you've got it backward."

"What backward?"

" I'd hoped that you might stay and help me say goodbye, after which…"

"After?"

"I thought you might like some dessert," kaleidoscopic eyes dancing.

"Riley? Dessert? What dessert?"

"It's special."

"I'm sure it is. I'll bite, what's for dessert?" still not ready to believe this.

"Well if you bite I hope you'll be careful."

He flushed. "And the dessert is…?"

"berry…"

Now he was playing dumb. "What kind of berry?"

She grasped his arm and leaned close to him and whispered, "It's a new kind, me-berry… me, Dance.

"Oh my God?!!" the unspoken words filling his inflamed imagination.

CHAPTER 24
THE ASSAULT

"Oh my God?!" The spoken words filling the hallway, the rooms, the whole house. Dolly House, the senator's wife, was screaming and screaming.

———

As Brianna entered the spacious bathroom, Sanford had come up quickly behind her, said her name, "Brianna" and placed his arm around her waist. She'd turned around, totally startled, disappointment registering on her face. She'd been having such a good time…

"Brianna I thought maybe…"

"I know what you thought. I know what you're thinking. Now you'd better listen to what *I* think."

"All I want to do is party…"

"Sanford, that's what I've been doing, partying. What you want to do I call <u>work</u>! Now, I suggest you get out of here before I embarrass you and let me finish what I came in here for without you watching."

"I watch you, often, at home."

"Get out!" and shoving him aside she slammed the door shut and locked it. Afterward they said that's what had saved her life.

———

Sanford reeled backward from her push and was brought up short against something behind him. A karate chop crushed his larynx. Another blow whistled in from the side, snapping his neck. His assailant's hand covered his mouth and nose as he let him down to the floor. A quick slash across the immobilized Justice's jugular and his still beating heart was pumping blood onto the tile floor.

The attack was over in less than 20 seconds. He wasn't dead yet, but would be so in another minute or less. The attacker left through the garden, retracing his steps. He scaled the wall and ran down the block and around the corner to his waiting limousine. He drove off and headed for the car lot where he'd rented the limo the week before, using an assumed identity. He wiped the limo down and left it in the rear of the lot, dropped the keys in the slot in the door and then jumped in the Toyota parked down the street. He was home in another thirty minutes.

———

Dolly House had come into the bath area from the house to powder her nose before leaving. When she saw the Justice's body on the floor she screamed. Brianna came immediately through the toilet door and saw the body. She felt for the pulse and found none. She pulled out her cell phone and called 911. She wore a flinty expression as she decided not to try CPR.

Nobody could leave. The police were on the scene within ten minutes. The street was barricaded. The house was being protected as a crime scene. The media had not caught any of the transmissions and for the time being were not there. In the house all of the guests and servants wore drawn and haggard expressions. Riley felt like apologizing to them but there was nothing she could say. In ones and twos they came up to Riley with puffy eyes and sad expressions and comforted her. There had been a buzz of urgent conversation when it was realized what had happened. Now everything seemed deflated as if all of the air had been taken out of the room and the people in it. They waited for the detectives to take their statements.

In spite of themselves some of the guests were casting furtive looks at Dance. The ones who were on TLL's Top Ten of course knew that fact. Howard Storm took a sip from his glass, "You know, Mike, I think I saw Dantes talking to Riley when the screaming started."

"Yeah, but that doesn't mean that he couldn't have done it before that. I mean, can you recall specifically where he was during the time the Justice was here?"

"Actually, yes. He was yanking my chain about who had the most outrageous content, my show or his web site." They warily scanned the partygoers, waiting for their turn with the detectives, and then sat down at the table, each with their own thoughts and perhaps suspicions.

Everybody was interviewed individually with a recorder taking it all down. All of them were accorded their rights, none of them asked for a lawyer. It took until midnight to complete taking the statements. One of the detectives came in and whispered something to the one in charge. He asked for attention and asked them all, "Has anybody been outside this evening? Has anybody been in the back yard?" Universal shaking of heads, murmured no's, no, they hadn't been outside. "Well, would anybody object to giving us a DNA sample?" Sir Richard spoke up and said he'd be glad to do so. Everyone else concurred. The detectives used cotton swabs to obtain samples from inside the mouths of all of the guests. Then the swabs were put into Ziploc bags and labeled by a detective wearing latex gloves.

The detective had found disturbed earth next to the garden wall where evidently the assailant had jumped the wall. He had also found a swipe of blood on the wall where someone had, it seemed, badly scraped a knee; probably on the way back over the wall, on the way out. It could have been blood from the victim, they didn't know. Of course they had the victim's blood and they would soon have the answer as to whose blood it wasn't. Maybe, if they were lucky they'd even know whose blood it was. None of the party guests were given this information.

Riley asked permission to call the Senator's office and leave at least a voice mail about the incident. The police asked that she not do that and said that they would make all of the proper notifications. Finally they were all admonished not to talk about this evening's murder to the press or to anyone else. They were free to go. Dance and Riley were asked not to leave town as they might be needed for further questioning.

CHAPTER 25
DESSERT

Dance and Riley stood outside the house. Whereas it had earlier blazed with light, excitement and fun it was now closed and dark and festooned not with party decorations, but with yellow "Crime Scene" plastic tape, yellow knife wounds that slashed across the front of the house and disfigured the lawn and cut deeply into her confidence. She had thought that she might be staying in the house tonight with company. *Oh, her thoughts and plans!* Now her expression mirrored that of the inanimate house. She too was locked up, with her feelings dying inside like a guttering flame. Her playfulness had been wholly displaced with fear and dread. She felt foolish to have ever thought of a party, a "coming out" party at that. What had started with so much promise now lay in wreckage at her feet. Dance looked at her with concern, "How can I help, Riley?"

"Ohhh, Dance. I feel so bad."

"I know. I'm feeling pretty rotten, too."

"Take me home?"

"Sure, got my truck. You'll have to navigate. I don't know where you live."

"No, home to your house. I don't want to stay at my place tonight. I don't want to be by myself."

"C'mon, I've got room." His mind was spinning with the possibilities. This was the worst time for considering what he was considering... still, Riley'd brought it up, hadn't she? It was better not to assume anything and maybe another time...

———

It had been a slow drive around the beltway out US 50 and into Annapolis. Neither of them talked much. She slid over to his side of the seat and nestled her head on his shoulder. He put an arm around her and just kept driving. She dozed off and he drove carefully, not to wake her up. He checked his rear view frequently to see if anyone was following. He remembered the joke, "Just because you're paranoid doesn't mean they're not out to get you." He felt protective and anxious for her wellbeing.

They pulled up in the drive, headlights shining on the house, the shadow of the tree out front speeding across the front of the house as he swung past the tree and into the garage. She woke up and he held the door of the truck and steadied her to the kitchen door as she awoke fully and he let them inside. He turned on a couple of soft lamps and showed her where the bathroom was, off the master bedroom. When she came out there was a pair of his pajamas lying on the bed along with a big fuzzy bath towel and a large terry robe.

"Take a shower if you want," he called from the kitchen. "You've got some PJs there and a robe." There was no reply, but he heard the water running. He heated up some milk and made hot chocolate, set it out on the table. While she showered he went into the bedroom and got himself some PJs, which he normally didn't wear and a robe for himself. He ducked into the shower stall in the hall bath, got clean and stood under the hot, almost scalding water until the mirrors had all fogged over and the hot water was running out. He dried off, put on the PJs and robe and went into the kitchen.

"Hey, good chocolate!" She struggled with a tremulous smile, her chin wiggling and jumping.

He smiled with concern and sat down across the table and took a sip. "You're right. It's cathartic to let that hot water run and then treat the insides with the hot chocolate. Sorta' cauterizes the wounds. There have been more than enough of those for one evening. Look, you take the bed room and I'll bunk down in one of the spare rooms."

"Thanks, Dance, for everything."

"Not a problem. I'll leave the night light on and not to worry, I'll set the alarm and lock down. Goodnight, now; see you in the morning."

"God, what am I going to tell them at work?" She wasn't ready to let him go and she didn't have it all thought out. He was rushing just a bit trying not to take advantage of the situation.

"Time enough for all of that tomorrow. They can put in a substitute for you for the next month or more if they need to. I imagine it'll all be automatic. In any case it's not something you need to think about now."

Now was when he would have given her a kiss on the cheek and tucked her in. Instead he squeezed her shoulder and went to his room. His thoughts were running riot and he didn't want to do anything to cause her problems.

"Good night, Dance."

———

A hand was shaking him awake. He really wasn't used to that. Instantly awake he restrained his immediate reflex to strike out. It was three o'clock in the morning. "Yes?" She was standing there with just enough light to see that there were tears running down her cheeks.

"Dance, I haven't been able to get to sleep... Hold me?"

Now he was really awake. "Aw it's been a tough night."

He rolled out of his bed and stood up. She came into his arms and he just held her, like he had in the truck. Well, not quite as he had in the truck. He was excited and she rubbed up against him and neither of them pulled back. She raised her arms and hugged him around the neck, so he lifted her and carried her back into her bedroom. He set her down and pulled the covers back and got into bed with her. She lay on her side with her back to him and he spooned next to her and put his left arm over her and hugged her.

After a few minutes of this she wiggled closer, nestling even deeper. He didn't pull back and he was sure she could feel him, because he was caught between her legs and running out of space. She adjusted her pillow and resettled herself, even closer against him. She gently moved with slow, rhythmic motions pushing back against him. He took his hand from her waist and moved it up inside her pajama top. She sighed and placed his hand inside her pajama bottoms.

"Riley, are you sure about this?" he choked out, one last time before he was over the brink.

She turned to face him. "I'm not sure about anything *but* this. Maybe you should know that you are my first."

He was astonished. "You're a virgin? But, why me?!"

"Dance, I found that I wanted you to be the one. Now it's need as well as want and I need you now." And her look seemed to him to say, well are you up to it?

It was probably too late, but he'd give it one last try. "Ahhh, I don't know. I'm not sure I'm the one you've been saving yourself for."

"Dance!" And with that she rolled on top of him and initiated their first kiss. It was a long, long kiss. "Any more 'buts?'" she asked with a husky voice."

He didn't answer. It was past time for talking. He unbuttoned her pajama top and she shrugged it off. She lay down as he took her in his hands and kissed her passionately. She raised her hips and he pulled her bottoms off. And she shone softly in the dim light and her eyes were on him. She sat up and gently pushed him down. He arched and she pulled his PJs off, catching on him before they pulled loose. He lay there taking in her startling, heart-breaking beauty. Both of them were breathing hard when she straddled him and took matters into her own hands, so to speak.

He noticed the slight resistance as she came down on him. She hurt a little at first but not bad. A few minutes later she panted, "So how was dessert?"

"Felt like seconds to me!" And it was his turn and he took a long time. Her soft cries came again and again. It was close to dawn when they finally got to sleep. And sleep they did until almost noon. This time it was his turn to wake her, with a kiss.

"Ummm…"

"You know what they say…"

A smile tugged at the corners of her mouth as he cupped her and gently squeezed. "What, Dance? What do they say?" said with a teasing and her sweetest voice.

"They say that some things, desserts even, taste better the second day!"

"Ohhhh, Dance!" And finally he tasted his me-berry. And had his fill. And it was good; and she was sweet, indeed.

CHAPTER 26
FALLOUT

The aftermath could best be described as brutal and universal. In no particular order a lot happened. Riley called in to work and confirmed that the network had subbed for her on her Cox News Sunday program. She had been sleeping or sharing dessert when it had aired. She was placed on administrative leave, with pay until things could get sorted out.

News of Justice Benton's murder had preempted all other news. The papers were full of it. There was a hue and cry to get the murderer. The president, himself, had appeared before the nation and promised that all resources would be applied to find this killer.

Magazines rushed to the public provided analysis that connected all three murders; Senator Riggs, Josh Hirsch and Justice Benton, with "The Liberal List." Everyone except Cox News called for the site to be shut down.

ABS News and Jeff Prather invited several of the Top Ten Liberals from TLL to his program and discussed their situations. They were sometimes defiant, often frightened and always in agreement that TLL was 'dangerous' and just plain un-American.

Cox News was the only network to feature as news several articles written by the liberal left that called for elimination, by force if necessary, of conservative institutions; conservative thought and anyone who was not politically correct. They showed clips of movie stars using bleeped obscene language, spewing hate of President Jameson at an award show. And there was the outrageous statement of one actor that the president's children should be killed and eaten. It seemed to work to calm down the one sided and extreme coverage.

Overseas the pundits had a field day. US news outlets with a liberal bias (all of them except Cox) interviewed them endlessly. The general gist of this was that a "cowboy country" with a "cowboy president" was getting what it deserved.

And at GRU Headquarters in "The Aquarium" next to Khodinka Airfield Colonel Y. Kharkov and Major V.I. Gagarin were meeting. "So, it would seem that there is a firestorm in America."

"Yes, Colonel, they go through these periods of intense media activity from time to time."

"I think more and more frequently and with increasing intensity."

"I agree, Colonel. And I see where President Jameson has vowed to catch this killer and to use all resources."

"Yes and therein may lay our opportunity. With their police and intelligence apparatchiks occupied in this investigation perhaps our Operation Aerie can go forward unnoticed.

"Would the Colonel like to move up the time table?

"Yes, Major, I would.

CHAPTER 27
RUSSIAN PREPS

Within a month the weapons and communications equipment that their agent would need had been collected at the Mount Alto facility in Washington. All had been delivered to a safe house set up for use by the agent in his interrogation and disposition of Eagle. The Agent, code-named Aerie, was given a German passport and identity. His papers identified him as Kurt Pfennig, an industrialist from Stuttgart. Herr Pfennig had, in fact, been sent to spend a week in Stuttgart in order to familiarize himself with the area and make his cover that much more convincing. Of course his German was perfect and his English nearly so. The American informer had been located, but not contacted. He had a new assignment. So, it was possible that he might have no recent information on the whereabouts of Eagle. The informer's Russian handler was still assigned to the Embassy and was standing by in readiness to support Aerie.

———

"Colonel, all is in readiness. Our agent, Aerie, has been briefed and is ready to commence this operation. He knows that we want to first interrogate Eagle, if at all possible, but that the ultimate objective is the elimination of Eagle. Do we have your authorization to proceed?"

"Yes, Major. By all means let us bring the American Eagle to his nest."

———

Mount Alto, in Washington, D.C. at 350 feet of altitude was the third highest point in the area, with a direct line of sight to many strategically important U.S. government facilities, including the Pentagon. It was widely assumed that it had been an American mistake to cede this site to the Russians for their use as a new embassy, since it afforded them a great opportunity to intercept American communications. Overlooked was the fact that the Americans had the same, or reciprocal, line of sight opportunity to intercept Russian communications.

In fact, the Defense Intelligence Agency (DIA) and a little-known military intelligence organization within the Pentagon jointly operated a listening and recording facility which monitored all Russian Embassy communications. Most traffic was encoded, but not all of it. A digest of these communications was then passed to the CIA. The term "Aerie" had come in the clear, without explanation and was provided to CIA. CIA ignored it.

CHAPTER 28
CONTROL

"Dick, it's a call for you on line one; sounds like one of your subs."

"Thanks, Dixie. Starzinger here."

"Hey, Dick." His sub went on to tell him that their person of interest, "the roofer" had been at home at the time of the Benton murder.

"No way he could have been at the Contralves' house?"

"None. We had him under direct surveillance, pictures, even, taken that night. We didn't discontinue until after we'd heard about the Benton murder."

"Thanks a bunch. I think it's safe to terminate surveillance on Pokorny. Good job. Send me your bill."

It wasn't adding up. He went back over the sequence of events. His Control had identified Pokorny for him. Now, surveillance had revealed that Pokorny had nothing to do with at least the Benton murder. He could be somehow involved but he doubted it. Maybe Pokorny could still be of some use..." He picked up the phone and called the D.C. police.

"Zinger! What can I do for you?" It was Detective Pat O'Brien, his contact...

"Oh, I don't know; maybe I have a lead for you. Interested?"

"Shoot yeah, gimme the rundown on him."

"I've had surveillance on him as a suspected stalker of one of the TLL top ten, a client of mine. Could be a dead end." And Zinger gave him the full boat on Pokorny: name, address, occupation and phone number.

"Thanks, Zinger. Anything I can do for you?"

"Wellll, since you ask, it's come out in the press that you took DNA samples from everybody who attended the party that night."

"Yeah, we tried to keep a lid on it; you know how those things go."

"Speculation is that you must have a sample with which you're trying to match it…"

"And if that's so, a certain PI might just like a copy of the report?"

"Any chance?"

"My butt is going to be in a crack if it gets around…"

"No chance of that, at all Pat."

"Okay, Zinger. Just keep it locked up and don't let on where you got it."

"And if I come across anything else…?"

"…Get in contact with me, right away."

———

Zinger sat in his office, feet up on the desk while he considered the latest intel he'd received. The D.C. police contact said that Pokorny had been cooperative, even anxious to help out. It was almost as though he had been relieved to find out that they wanted a DNA sample for their investigation in the latest D.C. murder. The DNA checked out negative. Zinger smiled as he thought of the pictures of Pokorny he had in his file. You bet he was relieved that it was *only* a murderer they were after.

So at least he had a copy of the report on the killer's DNA. Great! He was in the same boat with the cops. They had the killer's DNA but they didn't have a match. Without a match you had nothing.

As long as he had a lead he felt he could justify spending Prather's money. After all he was advising the Number One Liberal and helping him to stay alive. But, if he had no clue whom to watch, it seemed he was just throwing his money away. Prather seemed to be loosening up. Zinger grinned as he thought of the late night breaks he was most certainly enjoying with Dixie, based on the tired but happy looks she had when she came to work most days. Prather had made another request. He wanted Dick to check into the accidental death of one Richard "Knucks" Halloran. He had died in a single car accident awhile back. Zinger checked and was able to confirm that an alarming amount of alcohol had been found in Knucks' blood and that death resulted from trauma to the head received in the collision of his car with a tree. It certainly didn't look like foul play.

———

It was lunchtime and he was just about to go out when Dixie had a call for him. It was his detective friend. He wanted to tell Zinger just one last bit of information on Pokorny. When they'd gone to the house they'd routinely checked his license plate and found that he was not using his own plate. Pokorny seemed genuinely nonplussed by this development, but got a ticket, anyway. Zinger laughed at his picture of Pokorny. This guy was like the coyote in a Roadrunner cartoon. Couldn't win for losing. Pat agreed.

————

Zinger got up and started out for lunch again. He remembered his shirt in the corner of the closet and decided to take it to the cleaners, yellow stain and all. He pulled in at the cleaners and got in line to drop off the shirt and some trousers. Something was bouncing around in his head and wouldn't let go of him.

The license plate! Okay, so, it was the wrong one. But it *was* the one he'd seen on the car at the parking lot. Control had identified Pokorny as the owner of that plate. But surveillance—and now DNA—had shown that Pokorny wasn't the guy.

If Pokorny wasn't the guy, how'd he get that license plate on his car? Now, as Zinger pictured Pokorny's car when he checked it that night he could recall that there was no dealer's sticker on the car… It was coming together swiftly, now. It was the wrong car but the right plate! His Control, whom he'd asked for the plate number rundown, had misled him, fingering Pokorny. The only logical explanation was that his own Control had lied about the plate's owner and then switched the plates in order to protect the probable TLL killer, the guy who staked out Prather that night in the parking lot. Maybe he was also "controlling" the TLL assassin. Whether using someone else to do the killings or, and this was unlikely, doing them himself; the person who had sent him up a blind alley had to be the same person who tried to cover it up by transferring the license plate. No one else would have had the knowledge or the motivation. That person was his own Control.

As it was his turn at the counter he filled out the laundry slip and tossed it all into the bag. He turned to go and stopped. It hit him like a ton of bricks.

"Ma'am, could I have that bag back?"

She handed it to him and he retrieved the shirt with the urine stain.

————

Actually, he retrieved the shirt with the DNA sample.

CHAPTER 29
BRINDING FRASHES

In three days Zinger had his report back from the lab. Urine samples were being increasingly used with blood samples of athletes to confirm that the urine samples came from the athletes who submitted them. The stain from Zinger's shirt had barely yielded up enough of a sample to support a finding. Zinger had commissioned the Lab's work with his own funds. He didn't yet know where it was going to lead him, but he was certain it was going to get personal.

In his office he laid out the familiar DNA chart of line segments that was the police's version. Holding his breath he put the one he'd just received from the lab next to it. Although the scale was different, stretched on the one compared to the other, the lines were in the same relative positions. To him it looked like an exact match! He now knew that the person who contaminated his shirt in the used car lot that night was the same person who left behind a blood sample at Senator Contralves' home.

What he *didn't* know was the identity of the person with this DNA. He went over to the station and dropped in to do some politicking. Apologizing to O'Brien that he'd sent him on a wild goose chase, he dropped off a dozen doughnuts, had a cup of his coffee and left. He went out via the police garage, slipped into one of the cruisers parked there and brought up the laptop in the car.

Using the patrolman's computer, he quickly found the proprietary license plate database and entered the number he'd written down. It came up as stolen. The original owner of the plate had been one Wade Bates. His home address and phone number were also given.

As he drove back to his office Zinger thought the name was familiar. In his office he checked the stack of documents and transcripts that supported his report to Prather, the investigation of Dance Dantes. Ah, yes. Here it was. Subject Wade Bates, retired Senior Chief Petty Officer, USN. He read the transcript of the interview.

Investigator: "We're doing some background work on a friend of yours, Mr. Dance Dantes."

"It's true; I'm a friend of Dance's. Let's see some ID and maybe I'll talk to you."

"Here you go."

"Okay, so why are you doing this investigation?"

"Well, maybe you know that Mr. Dantes runs a web site?"

"Yes."

"Well, we think that his site is a departure from the usual, a real innovation in political communication."

"And…?"

"And, before we do an investigative series we naturally want to get to know him better. What better way to do that than through his friends? Tell me, do you know Mr. Dantes through the Navy?"

"Listen, Dance is as good as they come. I don't trust the media to do anything with the information they get except promote their own agenda. Our interview is over."

The report closed with the observation that Bates seemed nervous and hostile. He did not, however, reflect unfavorably on Dance Dantes. Zinger closed the report and put it back in the file drawer. He knew that he had enough to nail Bates. All he had to do was turn him in to the police, along with the DNA report and his report and they'd have him.

But they wouldn't have the goods on Control. That's why he gave them Pokorny; he already knew it would be a blind alley for them, as it had been for him. He wasn't ready to turn the killer in without first catching his control with him. If his Control had tried to cover up Bates' identity it was a sure thing that he was somehow involved in the TLL murders. Maybe as much as Bates. Knowing how careful his Control was with him, it was likely that Bates couldn't identify his Control any more than Zinger could. They likely both had the same sort of relationship with the same man, a secretive one.

Zinger made one of those snap decisions he was known for, in the field. They all came out of his appreciation for what was likely, given his total knowledge. He had a great deal of confidence in these "blinding flashes" as he called them. Actually he liked to swap the 'Ls' and the 'Rs' ever since he'd spent some time in Japan. He thought of them as his "brinding frashes'. They had saved him from a false step many a time. They had also led him to various spectacular successes. His next stop would be with Dance Dantes. It was time for some straight talk. He felt like he knew him. He thought he liked him.

CHAPTER 30

REACTIVATION OF CONTROL

Control definitely was having an effect, he knew that. His ordered assassinations were receiving worldwide attention. But under the crush of media attention, he was having nervous thoughts. Again and again he went over his situation and his options. He believed that his bosses at Langley knew nothing about his activities with Bates. Surely they would have rolled him up by now, if they did. It worried him that his "retiree" evidently knew something about Bates' activities. He didn't know what the retiree knew. But he knew that if and when the retiree found out about the plate switch it could get dicey, especially if he went directly to the Agency with his suspicions.

The system he was employing with Bates was working. Further, if Bates were caught he would not be able to identify his Control to anyone. They would be far more interested in Bates' connection to Dantes, who ran the web site. He considered the possibility of anonymously turning Bates in himself. Then another whole range of possibilities opened up to him.

The phone rang at home. He picked it up and was surprised to hear a voice from out of his past.

"Sir, it has been some time since we last met. Do you recall the nature of our business at that time?"

"Yes, I remember your voice."

"Good. We would like to meet with you. We believe you might be able to help us. We are prepared to make it very worth your while if you are able to provide the information we seek."

"As you might imagine, this takes me quite by surprise."

"Yes, we anticipated that. We are prepared to call again in a day or two to get your answer. If we decide to proceed we would suggest meeting in the same place where we first met. You remember it?"

"Yes, I do. I think that I may not be able to help you. My job has changed and…"

"Yes, we're aware of that, as well. We still want to meet."

"Well, as I said, I need to think this over."

"Very good. You will hear from us again."

————

His mind was settled; he would meet with the Russians again. *"If it's in connection with the activities in the field I used to report on, they should know that I'm not plugged in to that anymore. I can't see where I'm going to be of any use to them."*

CHAPTER 31
THE CONNECTION

"So, Mr. Starzinger? What can I do for you?" It had not been easy to get a meeting set up. First, Dantes had had to get past the answering service. He'd left a message asking for a meeting to discuss a vital issue. Answering service came back with, "Gag order from the police, can't answer any questions about the Benton murder." Then he'd tried again, with, "I have no questions, just vital information for you." This time no answer, so he sent one last voicemail, "I'll take my chances and camp on your doorstep, Thanks."

The scull, a George Pocock wooden model, arced toward the finger pier that projected out from the landing. It had a healthy amount of way on and the oarsman had dropped his port oar into the water to bring her around, lying to just next to the pier. He shipped his pierside oar, keeping the other oar flat on the surface for balance and reached out to the pier to steady the boat. Slipping his feet out of the shoes on the stretcher he was careful not to place them on the fragile wooden skin of his boat. He flipped the catch on the outboard oarlock. Swiftly but with practiced care he levered himself from the boat to the pier, using the reinforced space between the rails to place one foot and his hand on the pier to support his weight as he shifted over to the pier. Then he reached down and retrieved the oars and seat and put them aside. Finally he reached down and grabbed the scull by both outriggers and lifted it from the water. Dantes carried it over his head and carefully placed it, hull up, on the rack he had for it within the small boathouse.

He grabbed a towel and began to wipe his boat down. It glistened a bright brown peppered with gold. A beautiful, if anachronistic, machine. Then he acknowledged the man sitting on the steps that came down from his house.

"So, Mr. Starzinger? What can I do for you?"

"I apologize for intruding like this; it seemed the only way to see you anytime quickly."

"Fair enough, you're here. What's this all about?"

"I believe that I know who the TLL killer is."

"So, tell the police."

"I'm a private investigator; I have good relations with the D.C. police. I could do that. I have chosen instead to see if it might be possible to catch all of the people involved."

"How many do you think are directly involved?"

"I think two."

"I think that we should go up to the house and hear what you have to say." Hanging the towel across the rack to dry and retrieving the oars and seat he locked his boathouse and they headed up the steps.

———

"Pardon me for asking, but have you had your house swept for electronics?"

"You mean bugs, that sort of thing?" A nod from Zinger. "No, I haven't. I get your point. This is going to be a highly classified sort of conversation, isn't it?"

"Yes. I doubt very much if any bugs have been placed on these steps down to the river."

———

"So, you took a chance coming out here."

"Meaning I might not catch you at home?"

"No, meaning what if I am the one who did these murders. Ah, but you did say that you know who the killer is. Are you ready to tell me who?"

"Yes. You're not going to like hearing what I have to say." He sat there, curious, waiting.

"I can prove that the killer is your friend, Wade Bates." Shock, disbelief and anger crossed his face. It was fully a minute before Dance trusted himself to talk. He thought about this man's motives, his ability to know, what he was trying to accomplish and what it would all mean if it were true. He gestured, "More, tell me more."

"I have a copy of a DNA printout from a sample that was retrieved from Senator Contralves' garden wall. I have another DNA report from a sample that was recovered from the man who drove Mr. Bates' car.

They are identical. The same man who drove Bates' car, stalking Mr. Jeff Prather, I might add, climbed that garden wall and left his DNA behind."

"You say there are two men involved. How can you be sure that the other is not me, Wade's best friend?" asked Dance.

"That's complicated, but I am sure," said Zinger. "That suspicion would naturally fall on you and it's one of the reasons I'm here. I've got a confession to make. Jeff Prather hired me to dig up anything I could on your background. I did a very thorough job. I couldn't find anything bad and my report to him said so. I offered him the bulk of his retainer back. He kept me on for protection against the stalker I observed tracking him when I didn't know who the stalker was. I only confirmed it recently. You are the sole person with whom I have shared this information. I want to get both people involved, Bates and his Controller."

"Knowing Wade as I do, I am sure he wouldn't be doing something like this on his own hook. Wade's a guy who will do anything for his country but he's not someone who goes about deciding who the country's enemies are, all on his own. Tell me again, why are *you* so sure that it's not a one man show?"

"Until I finally got the correct identity of the original owner of the Toyota's license plates, I had no idea that Bates was involved. What I did know was that I had been deliberately lied to by the person to whom I went for that identity, a contact of mine in the CIA. I knew fairly early on that this CIA person was involved, at least in a cover up. And why would he be willing to risk himself to accomplish that cover up? Either he was the killer, himself, or he was connected with him. With Bates' identity known, and I knew he was a friend of yours from my investigation, it was plain that he was not my CIA contact. With Bates' skills as a former Navy Seal it's a no-brainer that he's the killer. That leaves my CIA contact probably acting as Bates' Control. He's the logical one to be giving Bates his assignments."

"I can see that this is going to take a long time, to get me up to speed," said Dance. "Why don't you stay for dinner? Maybe we could continue the debrief in your office?"

"I've got to say that I've never seen anyone come up to speed so quickly. I could not do what you just did, taking the information so calmly and getting right down to brass tacks without missing a beat."

"Who says I believe you? For now this is all about getting to know *you.* Your motives, penchant for overstatement, how you think, more about the evidence and then I'll know what to believe."

"How'm I doing so far?"

"You already know the answer to that, or else you wouldn't have asked the question."

———

At the house Zinger was introduced to the most gorgeous woman he'd ever seen in person. It was obvious to Zinger, as he watched the meal preparations and Riley moving about the kitchen, that she wasn't familiar with where things were. Dantes got up from time to time to find something for her. Still, she produced a serviceable meal on no notice and did it enthusiastically. Of course he knew who she was. While she put together the meal he put together their likely scenario.

Dinner was served and they all sat at the table, everyone being polite and nobody asking any questions. Until, "Dick, I assume that you're somehow involved in the investigation of the unfortunate murder of Justice Benton that occurred at my party,"

Dick admired her straightforward manner and directness. He exchanged glances with Dance, who nodded and looked at Riley and placed his finger against his lips. He got up from the table and brought back paper and pencil. He wrote a note and handed it to her.

Riley, we don't know that the house isn't bugged. We'll have to wait until we're sure before we talk about this, here. She read it, nodded at both and handed the note to Zinger, so that he could read it, too. Riley retrieved the note and pencil and wrote, on the back.

"Dick, thank you for coming, I'm sure, to help." She gave him a warm and grateful smile as she handed the note to him. Zinger knew better than ever that this was the right approach. "*Chalk one up for the brinding frash.*" He was glad that they would be helping each other in the days and weeks to come.

CHAPTER 32
THE MEET

"We have reason to believe that the agent we pursued with your help is retired. We also think he's residing in the local area. Do you think that you can be of some help in locating him?"

They were meeting at the seafood restaurant on the Eastern Shore. The place had been thoroughly checked out and monitored for the past two days. A perimeter had been set and was manned by an armed person who commanded the approach to the restaurant. They were ready for any developments.

The request didn't surprise Control. In fact he was ready to say that he couldn't help them at all. But he was astonished at the rest of the news in that the agent was believed in retirement in the local area. Stifling his reaction at that part of the news he took some time to think before replying. *"If the agent they want is my retiree… Even if he's not the one, they could prove useful. I've got to slow this down and think it through."*

"It is just possible that I will be able to identify him to you."

"Just possible?"

"Yes."

"What do you propose?"

"Let's meet tomorrow and I will have a proposition. If we agree and this is the man you seek, what will be my 'salary' for this information?"

The two Russians exchanged glances. Money had not been the object when they'd worked together before and it had made them uncomfortable. Sitting back with a small smile his handler said, "If you can put this agent in our hands it will be worth one hundred thousand dollars to us."

"To do this will place me in some risk… after all this will take place in Washington, not in some faraway place."

Another glance and the second Russian nodded slightly. "For the correct lead, one quarter of a million dollars."

"Agreed. I will require half in advance. Two days ought to be enough time for me to set up an account to receive the money. Let's meet here again in another two days."

They sat and appraised him. He seemed confident enough. If it didn't all work out he would not hold on to any of their money. Besides, they hadn't made up their own minds whether to let him live, after he was no longer useful to them. Truth be told if he'd asked for a million they would have agreed, at this point. He was inexperienced at this game, a small man with small aspirations. "Agreed, say the day after tomorrow at noon, then."

———

Control needed an afternoon to sort it all out and make his plans. Assuming that his retiree had not yet discovered the license plate switch it was possible that their communication system was not compromised. Whether or not the retiree was the Russians' agent, he did not know. What he did know was that in either case he needed him removed. He planned to use the Russians to accomplish that. That still left the Russians as a danger to him. *I'm running out of options. Maybe my Contractor could help in that department.*

This could get complicated and in any case would depend upon a clear understanding with his Contractor. *If I want to use him to clean up I'm going to have to contact him. The emergency comms system is not going to work quickly enough.* He picked up the phone and violating his own rule placed a call to Mr. Bates.

CHAPTER 33

PLANNING FOR CONTROL

It was past closing time and Dixie had locked up. Zinger started a pot and they sat in his office. Dantes had plenty of questions but waited for Zinger to start.

Firstly, I am, or was, a CIA agent for more than ten years. About a year ago I was placed on retirement, full pay. I consider that this is a permanent situation. Truly, if it is not then this may be one of those situations where now that I've told you I have to kill you." Delivered with a rueful grin. Dantes raised an eyebrow but didn't reply. Zinger poured two cups and set one down in front of Dantes.

It seemed a screwy set up, but he'd been told it was for his own protection at the time. His masters at CIA had essentially put in a cut-out between them and himself. They were using a CIA control to pay him while not letting either know the identity of the other. There were lots of ways they could've managed the pay, but they'd chosen to do it by having his Control deliver his checks to a dead drop.

He went over the initial contact with the person who was stalking Prather, stood up and pointed out the window to the parking lot where it had happened. "I contacted my Control and asked for a rundown on the plate. It came back describing a guy named Pokorny

"You put surveillance on him?"

"I did and he turned out not to be our TLL killer. It also turned out that he did not own the plate on his car, which was the same plate I'd identified in the parking lot." I found that out from the D.C. police. It meant that my controller had deliberately misled me. It must have also meant that my controller was also controlling the killer. Oh yeah. The original owner of the plate was one Wade Bates."

"I think I know the answer, but I'll ask anyway. Why not just go straight to your bosses at CIA and turn in Bates and Control?"

"Not sure that I can trust anyone at CIA. It's a CIA man who is responsible for the TLL murders. I'm used to operating on my own, and I like to do the whole job when I get the chance."

Dantes nodded, as though he'd figured. "So, now you need to roll up Control to go with Bates. How you going to do that?"

———

"The only chance I have of getting Control is if our communications system still works."

"Yes—your comms system, the way he pays you?"

"Right." And he went on to explain the use of a signal and dead drop and one-time pad sheets for passing messages. "This is all very basic and primitive stuff. It's been around so long because it still works."

"So, you'll use it to try to set up a meeting and grab him?"

"More or less. That's where you come in."

"How so?"

"I think if he comes he won't come alone. If he comes at all it's because he thinks I haven't tumbled to his involvement in the plate switching. If he thinks I know he won't even come. But if, and this is a very big if, he thinks he's safe he'll come to the site with the thought of eliminating me. To do that I think he'd naturally fall back on the guy he's using, Wade Bates."

"And my part in all of this?"

"I'll give you a copy of all of the evidence I have that proves the TLL killer is Bates. If I get Control you'll know, right away. Then we can figure out how to handle turning any survivors over to the D.C. police. If it doesn't go the way I plan, you'll have what you need to put Bates away for good and maybe his Control as well. Since you are a natural lightning rod for suspicion for anything involving TLL I think it appropriate that you be able to bring these killings to a close.

"By the way, I am starting to believe that Wade has committed these murders. I can't believe that this is his own idea, though."

"No, I think that his Control probably contacted him."

"I still think that you could use some real help on this."

"Actually I've found that sometimes it's the 'help' that screws things up. I haven't told you about any of my operations, and I won't. Then I'd *really* have to kill you. Trust me, if Control shows up, with Bates, even, I should not have a problem handling the situation. There will be two copies of the package, yours and one in my safe. My admin assistant knows that in the event of my disappearance for one week to go into the safe for any instructions I may have left for her. Any questions, and are you willing to play your part?"

"Yes, of course. I'll stand ready to deliver the package, if necessary. When do you think this will go down?"

I'll take a little time to ensure that Bates is in town and when I'm ready I'll let you know. Do you want to go through some of the "What ifs?"

"For instance…."

"For instance what if Bates gets me instead of the other way around? One could assume that he'd pry your involvement out of me. You and Riley might be in some danger."

"Wade and I have been pretty close over the years. I do believe that he's capable of doing the TLL killings. I don't think he could kill either me or Riley."

They looked at each other, each nodded and they stood and shook hands. Showing him out, Zinger said, "By the way, I'll have someone out to your place tomorrow to sweep it, no charge."

"Thanks, Zinger."

CHAPTER 34

THE COUNTER PLANNING

"Yes." Picking the phone up on the first ring, Wade Bates, the Contractor, waited for his caller to identify himself. He didn't get many calls.

"This is…"

"Actually I know who this is."

"I need to meet with you, urgently."

"We have a communication system that you insisted you would always use. Why are you varying from our policy?"

"I appreciate your strictness in complying with our policy, but…"

"That's right, our policy. It protects me as well as you."

"Listen, I can't continue to talk on your phone about this. Would you consider going to the public phone booth at the end of your street, the one at…"

"I know where it is. Yes, I'll be there in five minutes."

"Thank you."

———

"Hello, I'm less concerned now that we're both on public phones. Uh, and I thank you for agreeing to this breach of our communications protocol."

"What is it that is so urgent?"

"Actually I am in the black Ford that you can see if you look toward the street corner. If at all possible I want to take five minutes of your time. In person. Perhaps in your car or in mine."

"Drive up here where I can see you. We'll use your car."

Bates peered into the car and saw a rather smallish and bookish man, mid-forties. If he was armed it didn't show. He got in and agreed to a short drive around the block. I assume that it would be fruitless to ask your name, so I'll call you Mr. Blackford."

"That will be fine," smiled Control. He pulled up alongside the curb in a quiet neighborhood. Bates looked up and down the street and saw no vehicles parked at the curb, looked questioningly at Blackford.

"There is another opportunity, another use for your skills. The work you have been doing is nothing short of spectacular. How you manage to find your targets and make your escape is nothing short of amazing to me."

"What targets do you have in mind?"

"There are two Russians, an agent of the GRU and his handler who are here and who plan an espionage operation against the United States."

"How do you know this?"

"My assignment is in Homeland Security. We receive tips all of the time. This one is confirmed. In fact I will have the opportunity to point them out to you."

"I would think that Homeland Security has the assets to deal with something like this."

"You would think so, but in fact we may be penetrated by the Russians and not have the capability to respond with assets that are too readily connected with the CIA or FBI. It has occurred to us that you could do the job most efficiently and most surely."

"I'm interested. How much?"

"Fifty thousand each."

"Two of them?"

"Two, three at the most."

"Okay, how will I know them and know where to find them?"

I will be meeting with them at…" and he described the restaurant and its location. "They will set an observer there, I don't think you will be able to come into the restaurant."

"I'll handle that."

"Well, then, the idea is that you identify the men meeting with me. Then you follow them to their safe house. I want them to be taken out when they are in the safe house, the next day. Not as soon as you first see them at the house. The next day."

"Expecting somebody to join them?"

"Quite possibly. That's why I was not precise about the number of targets for you."

"Put $200K in my account tonight. I'll do it." And he stared at Mr. Blackford like he was a fly he would like to swat.

"Very well." And he took his Contractor back to his car. Before shaking hands, Bates placed the magnetic GPS beacon under his seat. It would run for at least a week. They exchanged grim looks and Control said, "I'll be in touch."

––––––

Bates rented a nondescript Chevy Cavalier with another assumed identification and took it that night out to the restaurant on the Eastern Shore. He had in the back his night vision equipment and he'd dressed in black and had serviceable boots on. He stopped a half-mile short of the place and pulled over into some trees. This place was out in the country. He took a hike through the woods and came up on the place with 200 yards to go.

He sat down against a tree and waited and watched. He saw cars coming and going. After a while he saw him, the guy they'd placed overlooking the road into the place. He picked him up easily, especially since he was smoking. The restaurant closed and the help would be leaving soon. He looked over at the sentinel. He guessed he'd be waiting for the employees to leave and then he'd follow them out. He picked up and swiftly returned to his car.

Backed into the woods and turned around to observe traffic as it passed, Bates watched and counted vehicles. When the four that were parked in the parking lot had passed, he looked closely for one more. Sure enough it came, five minutes later. He noted the taillight pattern and gave it a one-minute head start.

The guy wasn't being too careful. Bates skillfully kept a safe distance while following him. After only ten minutes he saw the driver pull into a carport of a small country house sitting on what looked like five acres of land. It was set well off the road. No light was coming from the windows, but Bates stayed and observed for another hour. He sketched the terrain and the house and any openings he could see. Finally he left and returned home, taking multiple precautions in his route lest he was being followed. As a double precaution he parked the Chevy two blocks from his house and walked the rest of the way.

He spent two hours examining the sketches he made and where they would put their sentinels. There was a draw that led into the area of the house from the rear that he thought he could use for ingress. Next he selected his gear and weapons and thought about how it would go. Tomorrow he would again go to the restaurant and take advantage of the opportunity, in broad daylight, to identify his quarry. As long as they headed toward the safe house he'd identified; he would be able to 'wave off' before getting so close as to raise suspicions. Finally he turned on the GPs receiver keyed to the beacon and launched the navigation software application. Shown on the screen was the location of Control's car and directions to get to it. He recorded Control's location.

Satisfied that he was prepared, he showered and turned in. The excitement of the hunt and action that would take place over the next two days kept him awake for an extra ten minutes.

———

That night one hundred and twenty five thousand dollars was wired into Control's Cayman Islands account. Shortly thereafter two hundred thousand went into the account that Bates was able to access.

CHAPTER 35
THE CONFESSION

Dantes showed the technicians to the door. "Thanks, guys, it's good to know we're clean." While they were out there he'd had them install motion sensing IR gear all around the house, along with cameras in the visible and IR segments of the spectrum. The feeds went to the master bedroom where a monitor was set up with a split screen to show whatever the detectors 'saw'. He laughed to himself. "*The way I'm feeling now I'd like some triple concertina and a couple of .50 cal. machine gun towers, too, and maybe some tripwire flares and a couple of claymores.*" Thinking these thoughts he figured it might be time to talk to Riley.

"Well, they all done turning our happy home into a fortress?"

He reacted to her tone, which was just a little proprietary. It had the sound of someone talking about her own place. "Actually, I was going to talk to you about that…"

"UmmHmm, what you got on your mind?"

"Sweetie Pie, you *know* what's been on my mind."

"Yes I do and it's been practically all I've thought about, too. In fact if you'd like to postpone this lil' discussion for an hour or so…"

"I never thought I'd hear myself say, not just now, but I am saying could I take a thirty minute rain check?"

She patted the couch next to her and smiled. After enough kisses to totally change his mind about the rain check she pulled back and with a straight face said, "Okay, now let's get down to business. He gazed at her in total amazement. She had a way of doing that to him, all the time.

"Riley, let's talk about things."

"Uh-huh, I *knew* this was coming."

"You did."

"Of course. We women have a sense about this sort of thing."

Chickening out he said, "Okay, then you tell me."

"Nope, ain't letting you off the hook. Something you gotta' say then you gotta' say it, not me."

He took a big breath…

"You're going to tell me something along the lines like what about our age difference and what about your career and I want you to be safe, Riley and everything except the real truth, which you would rather *die* than tell."

"Which is?"

"Which is it's nearly worn down to a nub and you don't know where you'll get the energy to go another night, much less another week or two." Delivered with wicked look of glee and delight at her own prescience.

He thought of that song from the sixties, "Chantilly Lace" by the Big Bopper, and he sang it for her, "*Aw baby, you know what I like!*"

They dissolved into laughter and hugs and kisses. "We going to get serious, now?" They both said it at the exact same time. It was spooky, this connection of theirs.

"Okay. Are you saying you're afraid I'm going to take seriously something that was poked at me in fun? And that you feel like a lecher, deflowering me and being a dirty old man, and all that? Is that what you're thinking? Never mind, I know it is. And I'll do your favorite trick. I'll ask the question and also give the answer."

"This is getting interesting. Go ahead. You're doing just fine."

"That's true. I am doing just fine, just really fine and I don't want you to go screwing it up with a bunch of crazy protective thoughts. You do that, you know." Said with an accusing look and pointing her finger at him. "You figure out what's best for everybody but Dance. And Dance comes last!" And some honest tears suddenly filled her eyes and overflowed and ran down her cheeks. And they both knew they were tears of affection, at least and her protective feelings for him.

He just sat and held her for a couple of minutes.

"I say, just let's not mess this up with too many words. I mean, if we've got to use words let's just say we're in lust." Said against his chest, eyes wide open and staring into some sort of future as he held her. And she pulled away and looked into his soul, parts of his soul that he didn't know he had and said with that tiniest wrinkle between her perfect brows, so sincere and with the question in her voice, "We are, aren't we? We are in lust, at least?"

Thinking back to their first night, she had been too ready, too inexperienced to think twice about protection. She had thought about it in the weeks since, considered the pill and just hadn't followed through. At times like this she had fleeting thoughts about the risk, but not enough to bring them up or to do anything about it. She hadn't figured out whether this was carelessness or by design.

But then they were at it for the hour promised and most of another one to boot. As he called it, "flinging laundry." She continued to call it dessert. How much he loved her. And it scared him and he was relieved he didn't have to say it.

It was settled then and there that she was not moving back to her place. He'd told her about the dangers that were possible. He told her not everything but he told her enough so that she knew there were things he had to do. When it came down to cases, even though he hadn't done anything to those poor victims, he felt responsible. And if there was anything that the Academy did, it taught responsibility. She shivered as she pictured Tecumseh Court and the Virgin Cannons and the vast sweeping entrance of Bancroft Hall, where young men and women were fed into the maw of discipline and accountability and survivors emerged, upon whom a nation could depend. And she held him and would have suckled him at her magnificent breast but he slept.

And as he slept and she lay there she conceived, though she did not know it. She had opened to him as never before. Her feelings had been acknowledged and not trashed. She had become a proper vessel of love with which to nurture the baby that would become theirs. Even as the cells started to split and multiply the distress she sometimes felt dissolved. And the feelings she seldom acknowledged grew, with the tiny spark of life there, deep within.

CHAPTER 36
THE REALIZATION

"Hey, it works!" Seeing Zinger's puzzled look Dantes explained. "My new system, you were plain as day, coming up to the house."

"The guys I sent over did a good job for you?"

"Very good job. So, you all set for your encounter with Wade, if he shows?"

"Well it wouldn't hurt if I had a description of him."

"I can do better than that. I got out some pictures of him. Here's one of us on the beach in Subic. It's kind of old. Then here's one that's more recent, taken when we took in a Redskins game, couple of years ago."

"He looks to be fit…?"

"Very. He has an insane regimen of running and weights. I know he keeps up practice at gunnery ranges. Something else you might not know; he worked with arms dealers for a year or two. It would not surprise me to find out that he can get his hands on some pretty powerful and sophisticated weapons systems."

"Plastiques, grenades, that sort of stuff?"

"And claymores, stun grenades, I would expect him to have it all, knowing Wade. He has a code, a core set of beliefs. Wade believes in winning at all costs. And he does not skimp on preparation. So, you're going to set the trap and see who shows up?"

"Yes. If it's Wade, I'll try to pass. If it's anybody else I'll nab him."

"On the assumption that he'll be your Control?"

"Yes."

"And if Wade shows up, as you expect?"

"I'll tackle him only if I have to and only if he's with Control. Our objective is to nab Control, not Bates. We can always pull Bates in. It's Control whom we can't identify."

"This all goes down sometime tomorrow?"

"Yep, probably towards late afternoon. I'll keep a watch on the drop site. I figure they'll be more confident then. Anyway, here's your package. You got a good place to keep it?"

"That I do. Don't you worry about me! Good luck, Zinger."

"Thanks, and please give my regards to Riley."

———

"Riley? Hey, babe."

"Right here, sugar."

"Hey, look, I'm going over to visit with a buddy of mine. You've heard me speak of him, Wade Bates. I'll be back for supper. Let's make it something easy so it won't spoil if I'm late. I don't know exactly when I'll be back."

She was catching some undercurrents, here. Her expression said "should I be worried about this?"

"Nah, no big deal. Us guys gotta' come up for air, *some*times!'

"Well, I don't mind admitting I've been more than a little sore, myself."

"Get in the tub and soak for an hour or so. I'll be back before you know it."

She waved him off with a kiss and a smile at the front door. When she turned toward the dining room she saw the note. "Riley." It was clipped to a typed sheet. It was a shocker. Dance had written out a will, essentially giving everything he had to her, and signed it. She ran to the door with a lump in her throat but he was already headed down the road. Looking back at the note she turned it over. "Don't go getting alarmed. I'm not planning for you to have to use this. Just taking precautions."

But Riley felt dread that was not easily dismissed. It seemed a pattern of violence was showing in her life. It started with Rafe, in her home in Houston, was repeated at Senator Contralves' home in Georgetown. She devoutly hoped she would not be swept up again in the horror of death suddenly visited upon a friend… or a lover. Oh, and what a lover, what a tender and considerate yet wild and passionately imaginative lover he was. True, she had no one with whom she could compare him. Yet, even if it were only lust, she felt totally appreciated, worshipped, even. *"My life is finally starting,"* she thought. And, Minister's granddaughter that she was she said a heartfelt prayer for Dance's protection. She said thanks for what she had. And she couldn't prevent the notion from creeping in that it was too much and she didn't deserve this much happiness.

CHAPTER 37

SHOWING OUR CARDS

"Dance! How about a brew? I got some of your favorite kind. At least it was your preference in WestPac.

"You've got Kirin?"

Setting it on the table before him, "What else? Only the best for you, Dance." This was laying it on a little thick, even for Wade. His look gave it away. He wasn't just curious, he was worried.

"Yeah, it's business, Wade."

"What kind of business, boss?" looking with studied concentration at the drops of condensation working their way across the golden dragon on the label, tilting his head this way and that.

"Maybe I ought to cut to the chase. You've been receiving instructions, probably through "The Liberal List" for each of the killings of Top Ten Liberals. That includes Riggs, Hirsch and Benton. You killed them all. Wade, I know that you are the TLL killer."

And with those words both of them were slammed back in time, more than thirty years. No, they weren't Mids any longer. But the feeling was as fresh and raw as it was on that day when Dance first confronted him. Wade's response was the same: "What are you going to do about it, Dance? No Honor Rep to go to, is there?"

"I don't know, yet."

"Is it really your job to go around finding offenses to your Code of Honor? These killings—as you call them—are CIA sanctioned assassinations."

Dantes smarted at the reference to his Code. "I'm aware that your Control probably works for the CIA. I strongly doubt that the CIA has anything to do with the killings. I think that your Control has ordered another hit, this one not on the TLL list. I think that you have been asked—probably paid—to kill Dick Starzinger. And you should know, he is prepared to defend himself. I'm here to see that neither of you kills the other."

Bates stared at him intensely. "You want the straight skinny? No bullshit? Yes, I do have instructions. And the targets are *not* on your Top Ten List. CIA wants me to do two or three Russians, in two days. I don't know anything about any Starzinger."

"Where's this supposed to happen?"

"I've scouted out a safe house and I am to go there in two nights and nail two or three Russian agents."

"Two or three? Why the uncertainty?"

"I'm told that there might be an additional target."

————

"What if the third man happens to be Starzinger?"

"If he's not a Russian, linked to espionage work against the US, he's not a target of mine."

"Wade, I want your commitment that you'll not attack Starzinger."

"What's this, the flip side of my 'offer'… only I'm promising to protect somebody instead of making him disappear?"

"You could think of it that way."

"What about you? You come in here talking about killings. I ask what you intend to do about it and all I get is you don't know. If there's one thing you know about me it's that I take care of ol' Watash, first. You know I killed more than a few in 'Nam. The way I figure it whenever I've done it, it was done in the service of my country."

"Wade, I'm positive that the D.C. police and the FBI will not look at it the same way. I have some ideas. Let's plan how we're going after the Russians, *and* Control." They both eased back, opened another Kirin and together laid it all out.

————

There was a lot to do, especially as they'd decided to move up the timetable by a day.

CHAPTER 38
PHONING AHEAD

"Dance Dantes' service. May I take a message?"

"Oh, I forgot. I haven't called my number since I started this with you. This is Dance Dantes and I'd like to be connected to the house."

"I can do that, but if you don't mind I'll stay on the line for long enough to ensure that it is you—and not someone else—calling, Mr. Dantes."

"That'll be fine."

"This is Riley," picked up on the first ring.

"Ms. Dantes, I have a call from Mr. Dantes. Go ahead, please."

"Oh, I'm so glad you called." And her voice conjured up pictures, pictures…

"I just didn't want you worrying." Click. "Hey, I just thought I'd hear your voice before it got too late to call."

"Gonna be tied up, huh?"

"Yes, looks like it. I don't know when I'll be getting home so don't wait supper on me. No sense in staying up, either."

"I'll be fine. You just take care of yourself."

"You sound fine… I must be crazy to be running around this time of day. I miss you already."

"Miss you too."

"Bye."

"Bye." He looked to see if Wade was getting ready to make some remarks. Nope, no smirks and no funny remarks. Wade had his game face on, camouflaged the same as his. It struck home. This was all business.

CHAPTER 39
A TRAP IS SET

"Ah! Glad to see you. You're always on time!" Control's Handler rose to make the introductions. "Let me introduce Herr Pfennig. He is leading our operation. Herr Pfennig, this is our trusted and very valuable American source."

"Very good to meet you." smiled Pfennig. "As you see, I've brought with me one additional person, Vladimir." Vladimir, Herr Pfennig and Control's handler all shook hands with Control. "Sir, I shall think of you as Eagle's Control because I hope that is what you are."

"Herr Pfennig, I believe that is what I am, as well." Control's expression was hopeful yet reserved.

"*Believe*?" said with a look of concern and mild suspicion in his voice.

"Yes, I can't be certain. Before I received my new assignment I never knew the identity of the man whom you call Eagle. You were able to form your own opinion of the information I gave you; perhaps you even came close to an identification. I never did. When I received my new assignment I was also given a collateral duty. In addition to acting as liaison to Homeland Security I was given the responsibility of supporting a 'retired' operative, in the local area. I do not know his identity."

"Very interesting. What sorts of contact have you had with your retiree?"

"Only to pay him," he lied. "We use a dead-drop system. In the event of the need to communicate we use the one-time pad system."

"And, have you had occasion to communicate with him other than to pay him?"

"No," and he hoped that he was convincing.

"So, you do this at the same time of the month, every pay day?" asked with searching look as he examined Control for any signs of dissembling.

"No, I have purposely varied it. He must monitor the flag frequently. I expect that he checks it daily." Control knew what was happening here and deliberately kept his manner matter-of-fact. He projected a confident air and a steady gaze, looking directly into Pfennig's eyes.

"Is this a usual means of paying a retiree in your country?"

"I would certainly expect not. It has seemed very unusual, though not difficult."

"And your superiors assigning you, personally, does this not seem— shall we say coincidental?" Pfennig was boring in, now, trying to shake Control's calm demeanor.

"It could be, or it could also be that he is being used as bait, in order to find and draw you in." Control was scoring points with up-front candor. Of course Pfennig knew all the tricks and it would take a lot to convince him.

"Or maybe to expose you, Control?" was his quick rejoinder, sprawled back in his chair, a small smile playing about his lips.

"Of course, there's always that possibility," he replied. "Look, this was your idea. I'm telling it to you warts and all. If you don't want to go with this, I certainly understand your decision.

The Russians all shifted in their seats, clearly uncomfortable with these developments. Pfennig continued the grilling. "Tell me, what is your thinking on this matter?"

He was amused at the notion of any catering to an "employee's" wishes. "But this method of payment—unusual, no?"

"Yes, but it is also not unusual given that the Agency wants to take extraordinary measures to protect a top agent. Eagle's identity was never known within the Agency except at the top-most level. From recruitment on he has used different aliases. I am sure that the name on the checks is also an alias."

"Control, I appreciate your candor. Let me confer with my colleague."

Control excused himself and went to the restroom.

"Vladimir, go into the restroom and make certain our Control does not leave or attempt any communication," said Pfennig.

Turning toward Handler, he held his hands out, palms raised, an expression of some disbelief on his face. "We have come very far on something so shaky."

"We could stop the operation now, Herr Pfennig. I would hasten to add that he has proved reliable in the past. He has been a very careful man."

"Have you also monitored him in the past?"

"No, we wanted to protect him as he was a good source. Other than the usual caution at the beginning we did nothing out of the ordinary that could have attracted attention to him or to us."

"It is possible he is being monitored by CIA, is it not?"

"It is possible. For that reason, if we go forward with our plan we must exercise extreme care."

"I agree. I also think that at this point Control has almost outlived his usefulness. Whether we go forward or not we will eliminate Control. Tell me, you have additional resources."

"Certainly."

"I want a different safe house, suited to our plans. Also, I want additional men placed at the original safe house, as a decoy. If the Americans have been tracking us they will be aware of this location."

"Very good, it can be arranged." They discussed options, settled on one and Handler gave Pfennig directions to the safe house, another place out in the Virginia countryside.

"We will proceed."

Control and Vladimir were waved over to the table and sat down. Control, as you see we have a small team on hand. We would like to enlist your help in the interrogation of Eagle."

"I suppose I can do that. Should I call my office and alert them that I will be out for a day or two?"

"I think that will not be necessary. We won't wait for Eagle for more than a day or so. If we need to, you can call in tomorrow." Your firsthand knowledge and my field experience combined with sodium pentothal should make any of Eagle's efforts to dissemble futile. You agree?" Control nodded and they handed out the assignments. Control and his Handler would ride in Control's car and lead Pfennig and Vladimir in the other car to the drop site. Then Control and his Handler would go to the safe house and await developments.

———

Handler got into the black Ford and accompanied Control to the drop site where they secreted Eagle's check, which Control had brought with him. Pfennig and Vladimir followed in their own car. They all went to the signal location where they turned a metal label on a telephone pole to the vertical position, setting the flag. At that point the two cars parted company. Control and his handler drove to the safe house, following the Russian's directions and parked behind the building. Control was frisked; he had no weapon, and was given a bedroom where he could stretch out while they waited. Herr Pfennig and Vladimir returned to the drop site and took up stations where they could monitor the drop site, a park bench.

CHAPTER 40
THE ALLIANCE HAS SHIFTED

Wade's car was still parked at his house. He and Dantes loaded all of their equipment into the rental car and drove out to the place from which Wade had monitored the restaurant, figuring that this was as good a place as any, close to the safe house. They pulled into the cover afforded by the woods and sat there, checking Control's position. The car had moved, was en route to the restaurant. They took up a position where they could view the observer they expected the Russians to station at the approach to the restaurant. Just before noon they observed the arrival of the black Ford. Through binoculars they could clearly see everyone who went into and out of the restaurant. After an hour or so they noted the departure of four persons in two cars, the black Ford and one other car. As these vehicles pulled away they followed at a distance while tracking the black Ford. As the two cars slowed and stopped at the park they kept moving, stopping several blocks away. Wade turned to Dantes, "I thought your buddy was going to set the trap."

"He was."

"Well, that's not what happened. Their first stop was at the drop site, their second at the flag. It looked to me like they're setting up Zinger instead of the other way around."

"We need to shuffle the deck, just a touch, here, Wade."

"What do you have in mind?"

"Well, we were going to be available to Zinger as backup even he didn't know about. He was setting the trap and probably wouldn't need any help bagging Control, especially since you wouldn't be along with Control for muscle. Now it looks like it'll be the Russians he'll have to deal with and they're waiting for him, instead of the other way around.

We've got no way to tell Zinger about this."

"Here's another wrinkle. The black Ford isn't headed to the safe house I've already scouted out." Looking at the handheld Nextel GPS navigation package presentation he showed it to Dantes. "See, they're headed out toward hunt country. That's not where I expected them to go. What do you want to do? This is your operation."

"We can always find Control, as long as the beacon holds out or they don't discover it. Zinger is up against two guys and they are fully qualified or they wouldn't be handling this end of it. He doesn't have a clue. I say we sit well back from the park bench and set up a watch for the attempted grab."

"What are you gonna do if they grab him?"

"I say we move in and get the drop on them while they're busy with Zinger."

"You still any good with a firearm?"

"I needn't remind you that I qualified Expert Rifle with the M1 and Expert Pistol with the .45 the first day on the range during Plebe Summer."

"Yeah, but it's different when you're firing at live people and not some paper target 200 yards away. This is going to be close-in and not some exercise where they say, 'Cease fire and run 'em up and disc 'em.'"

"I'll be fine. I just think it's taking too big a chance to let them get away with Zinger. We don't know what'll happen after that. Even if all we do is get Control we're doing good. And you even know where he lives, right?"

Wade nodded, "You da boss." And they went back to the park, sitting in the car well back where they could observe the park bench with binoculars. They weren't sure, but they also thought they could see the two Russians, up closer to the bench. This could be a long night. They settled in to wait.

———

Zinger donned his bulletproof vest, checked and loaded his .38 revolver, grabbed his binoculars and drove straight to the signal flag site. He had decided not to leave any note this time. It was to be a simple exercise of setting the flag and waiting to see who showed up at the drop site. As he approached the pole he noticed that the flag had already been set!" He sped up and went past the site. Already his plan was being affected. Either his Control was innocently leaving his check for the next month, *too much of a coincidence and I don't believe in coincidences,* or he was being invited into the trap that he had hoped to set for Control. *"It's a no brainer! I've no choice but to expect that it's a trap for me. The system is compromised and it's up to me whether or not I intend to take the bait."* Adrenaline having upped his pulse by forty beats per minute, he came back to the flag and reset it to the horizontal. Then he headed for the drop site.

CHAPTER 41
AVOIDING THE TRAP

"Don't move! Not one eyelash! I have a weapon trained on you and I can't miss from this distance." They hadn't heard anything, and they'd been listening. They hadn't seen anything and they'd been looking.

Both of you put your hands on the dash, where I can see them." He came around toward the front and Dantes said, "Zinger!"

"I'll be damned. Dance, what in hell are you doing here? And who's this with you? I told you I worked alone. And how in hell did you find this place? Do you piss people off naturally, or do you work on it in your spare time?" Zinger was shaken. He'd come within an eyelash of making a terrible mistake. He'd *told* Dantes he worked alone!

"Zinger, this is my friend, Wade Bates. Control is not coming here tonight. He has been taken to a safe house by the Russians."

"Russians!" How would you go about finding something like that out?" He was still very irritated but had regained control of his emotions.

"Zinger, it's a long story."

"I've got time."

"Just trust me that we know where Control is and we know that there are two bad guys down there, waiting for you. We have a beacon on Control's car so we can get to him. It's now your call."

Zinger shot an appraising glance at Dance. "Getting just a little big for those britches, aren't you?" Then he looked steadily at Wade, who still had his hands on the dash. "You can stand easy, Mr. Bates. I don't think anybody here is going to shoot anybody else, at least not for the time being. You pose some interesting opportunities, Dance. Are you suggesting that we just go up there and try to overcome two (maybe that's all) Russian agents, have to kill them, maybe, without any ID or cause, just because you think they're Russian agents?"

"You didn't exactly know who we were when you snuck up on us, did you? And yet you came after us.

"No, but I thought it might be Control and Mr. Bates here. I did take the precaution of identifying you or you wouldn't be alive to be talking about it. Okay. Let's figure this out. Bates, can you show me where Control is?" Bates showed him Control's location. I'd like you to go out there and stop about a half-mile this side of the house and wait for us. Can do?" Bates nodded.

"Dance and I will see about the pesky former Soviets and then come down to join you. Just in case they manage to get to us first, you need to be aware that it could be the Russkies and not us that show up at this safe house location you'll stake out. Got that?"

Dance spoke up. "Got time for a little input?" Zinger nodded. "Maybe if it were me they were after I'd take it more personally. But I think that the Russians whom we haven't positively identified are number ten on a list of three. It's much more important that we bag Control. You've been chasing Control in order to catch the TLL killer."

"Yeah, and my former bosses seem to have set me out as bait to either catch the Russians…"

"Or to get Control, themselves. Anyway you cut it we need to roll up Control. The Russians are less important, secondary targets." Zinger looked at Dance with new respect.

"I didn't know you could be so devious, Dance."

"Yeah, well I've been around the block a time or two, myself. Here's an alternative plan. We go down to the safe house—by the way it's the second one they've used in the last three days—and we pick up Control. Then we wait at the safe house for the Russians to show up. We turn the tables on them and maybe, just maybe get them all."

"How about it Bates, you got any input to this?"

"To be honest, I'm less worried about how the immediate problems get sorted out than I am about the aftermath."

Zinger looked at him and said to Dance, "Well, you got your classmate's problems figured out, too?"

"Actually, I think I do. Why don't we talk about that when we count up the living and the dead? We may just not have a problem, at all."

"Meaning I might not be around to worry about?" Wade was more than a little nervous about the whole thing.

"Not at all. Meaning I think that with Zinger's help, here, it'll all work out. Let's go play some cowboys and Indians."

"Roger that!"

"Wade, you lead us to the safe house. I'm going to ride with Zinger and we'll follow. That okay with you, Zinger?"

"Sounds good. You'll pull up well short of the safe house?" Zinger asked, looking at Wade.

"Here's where we're going. Here's where I'll pull up," said Wade. And they quietly—and unnoticed by the pesky former Soviets—drew away and headed for the safe house.

CHAPTER 42
ADJUSTING THE SIGHT LINE

"Zinger, Wade's been doing these killings and calling them assassinations."

"Doesn't matter what you call them, the same people wind up dead."

"True, but there's a big difference between murder by an individual and a sanctioned removal by a State."

"Who's going to believe that the US of A would order the killings of, among others, a Supreme Court Justice?"

"Who's also going to believe that the CIA would leave one of their own hanging out to dry?"

Zinger grunted. "You're working up to something; what is it?"

"Wade was led to believe that Control was CIA. It's also true that maybe he thought they needed killing. We'll get to my idea, but first I'd like your take on what was really going down with Control and you."

"The deal that he would pay me and the way it was supposed to happen never sat well with me. Also, it was squirrelly the way they handled letting me go. I was retired, or I was dismissed or I was just in the cooler. I was never comfortable about any of it. I'm used to running my own show, (sideways glance) as I told you before you up and decided to come to my rescue."

"I asked if you didn't need some backup. I felt this whole thing was my responsibility, regardless of what I say to reporters. If TLL wasn't out there... you know."

"I know. Anyway, this was like no other lash up I'd ever heard of, just like somebody at the top who didn't know from nothing about a real field operation had dreamed it up. It was amateurish. I figured fairly early on that they were probably trying to ferret out whoever was selling info that enabled several of my opponents to get close to me. They probably had an idea it was this guy we're calling Control."

"Well, Zinger, its Control who fouls things up."

"How so?"

"If he gets turned over to the Agency what'll they do to him? Does he get silenced or does he get a trial?

"Dance, to tell you the truth, I don't know anymore."

"More specifically, how do we handle him and the CIA without endangering Wade? Okay, here's my plan…"

CHAPTER 43
END OF CONTROL

"Wade, has there been any activity since you got here?"

"Nope. I can see the black Ford parked around back. Two's all I think are in there."

"Well, neither Zinger nor I can tell one from the other. To tell the truth we think both are being paid by the Russians. In fact it's highly likely that the Russkies are going to do Control in as soon as they figure out they have no further use for him."

"Are you thinking what I'm thinking?

"Probably."

"Kill 'em all and let God sort 'em out?"

"You borrowed that from the Green Berets, didn't you? Yeah, that's just about it. Oh, one more thing…"

And they described the rest of the night's planned activities.

———

Vladimir was restive, "Herr Pfennig, it is very late, I think, for Eagle to pay us a visit."

"Vladimir, I have not been too impressed with this operation from the start. Too much depends upon this amateurish communications system. I suspect that the CIA is most likely monitoring Control."

"It was wise to switch safe houses and a good idea to put some people in the first house."

"Maybe. I think it is time to bring this attempt to an end. Let's wrap up here." They decided to head for the safe house. They already knew how this night would end for the person they called Control.

———

Wade swept the area with his night vision binocs. "It's clear, no one between us and the house."

Zinger took a look, expanding his search to include behind them and well out to each side. All he turned up was a rabbit. "Yep, looks clear. Let's go and let's keep it quiet." The three of them started up the long drive toward the house. Wade had a shovel and he busied himself in the drive in two places, tossed the shovel in the brush and caught up with the others. They fanned out, Dance taking the back, Wade the side door and Zinger the front. All three tried their doors, very carefully. As it happened, the back door was locked and the other two were not. Bam, bam, bam! Dance knocked loudly on the back door.

The Handler looked up, drew his pistol and went to let Pfennig and Vladimir in. As he approached the door Zinger and Wade burst through. Handler hesitated just a split second and spun around. As he was readying for a shot at Wade at the side door Zinger got off a shot, hitting him in the left side, the bullet traversing across his chest and through his heart. He fell to the floor, twitched and lay still. Zinger let Dance in and they went into the bedrooms.

Wade ran into the furthest bedroom, threw open the door and swept the room with his pistol gripped in both hands. He moved suddenly inside and scraped along the wall against his back in a crouch, trying to look and point everywhere at the same time. He dropped to a sitting position, leaned to his side and scanned under the bed. No one there. That left the closet and the bath.

Zinger and Dance had similarly cleared the other rooms in the house. They came up to Wade's room and looked inside. Wade signaled them, Dance to cover and Zinger to take the bath while he took the closet. Zinger and Wade hit both doors simultaneously. "I've got him; he's here in the closet," said Wade. He pulled him out and frisked him. Control was dazed and scared and relieved.

"Thank goodness you're here! I didn't expect you until tomorrow," he said to Wade, eyes then darting to all three of them. This didn't look like a rescue squad. Zinger came up to him and looked him over.

"I don't believe we've met. I'm Dick Starzinger. You've been one very busy boy, haven't you? I don't think you have too much to tell us and we don't have a lot of time to listen. You're the traitor who gave information to the Russians that had me in hot water several times over the last eight years, or so." Looking at Wade, "He's also the contact who signed you up to do sanctioned CIA killings, isn't that right, Wade?"

"He's the one."

"What do you think we ought to do with him, Dance?"

"I think he has two options. Option A is we give him the Russkie's pistol with one round in it and shut him back in his closet."

"What's option B?"

"Option B is we take turns knocking off his knee caps and balls and various other body parts until he finally expires in a very painful death." Wade went into the other room and retrieved the Handler's side arm. He chambered one round, ejected the magazine and thumbed the safety on.

"Here's how you take the safety off." Holding the weapon where Control could see. "Personally I hope you take Option B. I'm the one who's gonna shoot you in the crotch." Wade looked at Zinger with the question, "Okay?"

Zinger nodded. "Yeah and make sure you wipe your prints off of it." Wade wiped it down while they all looked at Control. He was sweating profusely as he took the pistol into his hands.

He stammered, "Wh—why not an Option C?"

"There is no Option C," said Zinger.

"But I am willing to tell everything that I did with the Russians!"

"We already know what you did. Why do you think this whole lash up was put in place? You have no bargaining position. We don't need you telling a police or CIA interrogation team about your TLL ops with Wade, here. Now, are you going to use that smoke wagon or are we going to do it for you?"

"Wait a minute, Zinger." Turning to Control, Dance said, "I think the price for a painless death just went up. Before we'll let you use the pistol, and avoid an excruciating death, I'd like to know the location of your account where you put the money the Russians gave you. And, I want to know how you withdraw the money." As Control hesitated, Wade shot him in the foot. Control screamed and fell to the floor, writhing and holding his foot.

"Think how much more it'll hurt in the knee or the balls," Wade said.

"Ahhhh," he was moaning and his eyes were squeezed shut in pain. He was past hope that there was any way out. "It's all in a folder in my closet at home, the passkeys, everything… It's all in a bank account in the Caymans."

"No way to know for sure if he's telling the truth. I'm thinking it might be nice to give Uncle Sam a rebate, could come in handy when we go in and talk to them," Said Dantes.

"Let me take out a knee, just to see if his story changes." And Wade took studied aim, first at the knee, then at his crotch." Control yanked the pistol to his head, flipped the safety off and pulled the trigger, knocking himself to the floor and leaving bloody spray on the closet door.

Zinger had a camera and they took several pictures of the Russian and Control. There were shots of the Russian with his pistol in sight, and some close-ups of Control. As it happened he actually had his identification on him. They weren't supposed to wear their badges when out of their facility and he hadn't. But he did have his driver's license and they got some close-ups with his license, picture side up, just beneath his chin.

They tidied up, leaving the Handler where he'd fallen. Closing and locking the doors and leaving a light on they rolled Control up in a blanket and Zinger and Wade carried him out to the road. They put him in Wade's rental car along with the shovel. Then they drove both cars down past the safe house about two miles so as to not occupy the approach to the safe house that they figured the two Russians would use.

"Good work, Wade."

"Thanks, Zinger, if I may call you that..."

"Yes it turned out pretty good so far. My guess is that it won't be too long, now." From Dantes.

"I'm gonna take a nap, if you don't mind."

"Okay, Wade. Help yourself."

———

CRUMP! CRUMP! Both Claymores going off, almost at once, in the drive up to the safe house. As the car went into the air, ripping it and its two occupants apart the Russian's best Agent had no time to realize what had happened. Without opening his eyes, Wade smiled.

"You guys ready to go home?" asked Zinger.

"Sounds good to me." Looking at Zinger, Dance said, "I told you he had a bunch of stuff, a regular armory!"

They took off with both cars, Wade going to a place two blocks from his home, Zinger dropping Dance to retrieve his car and go home himself. It had been a very productive night.

———

Dance crept into bed. It reminded him of the first time they had been there, together. He put his arm over her and lied to himself that he hoped she didn't wake. She backed into him and they were both awake... until dawn.

CHAPTER 44
LOOSE ENDS

"Oh, Dance! Good morning or good afternoon…"

"I think its afternoon, but just barely." Large and long yawn in bed…

"Dance, I apologize for my remark about a 'nub'… in fact, maybe something's growing, again?"

"Riles, you are the most stunningly beautiful, wonderful woman." And he, too, looked at 'the nub' as if it had a mind of its own.

"Well is he going to just stand there or are we going to do something with it?"

"What, approximately, do you have in mind? Oh, Riley!" And there was no coherent conversation for a while, just occasional sounds. Her mother had always told her not to talk with her mouth full and he wasn't thinking of anything but what she was doing to him. She took an occasional peek and he seemed to be enjoying himself. At long last he seemed to float above the scene as all of his senses became tuned to what she looked like, what she felt like, what it sounded like and the smell and the joy and it all fused and went on and on and he didn't want it to end.

———

"What's that you're reading in the paper, lover?"

"Oh it says here that they found a car blown up out in Virginia Hunt country along with a couple of bodies. Big holes in the road, a drive back to where another body was found."

"Ummm, hmmm. And you wouldn't know anything about that Dance, would you?"

"Riley, after what you did to me I wouldn't know my own name."

———

At Mount Alto in the station chief's office the decoys had checked in with a report of no activity at their safe house. Nothing had been heard from Herr Pfennig or Handler or Vladimir. An aide to the chief came into the office with some amplifying news. "It's in the afternoon papers. They found a blown up car in the driveway of Herr Pfennig's safe house. Two bodies in the wreckage and another in the house."

"That would seem to leave at least one body unaccounted for. I suppose that the Americans will call in the ambassador to tell him that they've found some people they've already identified and ask that we send somebody to identify them, before they release the identities to the news media."

"This will be most embarrassing for the ambassador."

"I must compose a message to Colonel Kharkov. The Aquarium is not going to like this, either."

———

"Office of the Deputy Director for Operations. Please hold. Yes?"

"Forwarding your call."

"DDO."

"Sir, I regret to report that Harold Harbrace, head of the Agency's Liaison Office to HSD has not shown up for work for the past two days. He doesn't answer calls at home or on his cell. No one appears to be at home. He seems to have just disappeared."

———

"Hello, sir. DDO here." The DCI listened keenly with an impatient look on his face. "He's been missing for two days and his car has been found. It's not been in the news, they're keeping it out, but I'm told that a GPS bug was found in the car. Preliminary identification of the three bodies at the scene is in hand. One of them was a really bad actor, one of GRU's very best. The other two are runners out of Mount Alto. State knows this and is having the Russian ambassador over to sweat him some."

DCI grunted, "Maybe it's time to get Starz in here and find out the rest of the story. Do we think *he's* okay?"

"Sir, I'd never bet against him. We'll locate him and ask him to come in."

"Ask him?" The DCI's voice was gaining in volume and exasperation.

"Sir, he is, ah retired."

"Get him in here! The DCI's secretary looked up at the vehemence in her boss' voice. He could be heard through the glass wall separating their offices. We don't know anything about Harbrace and we need to wrap that up. We're going to look dull when we have to say to Homeland Security that we don't know where our Liaison Officer is. I wasn't aware that this was going down. Were you?"

"No Sir."

"Well, why the fuck not?"

"Sir… no excuse."

"And we could have lost Zinger in this, too?"

"Sir, it's always a possibility when you…"

"At this point I'm not dealing in possibilities. I'm ready for some certainties. I want a meeting with Zinger or I want a body. That's all." And he slammed the phone down.

———

Wade Bates waited until sunset and walked the two blocks to his rental car. He got in and drove carefully, observing all traffic signs out to the seafood restaurant on the Eastern Shore. It was dark when he got to his observation point overlooking the restaurant from the woods. Using the same shovel with which he'd buried the claymores he buried Harold Harbrace in a blanket from the safe house. He carefully spread humus from the forest floor about the gravesite, smoothing it as best he could so that one really had to be looking to notice a slight hump above where the body was buried.

———

At the Aquarium GRU Colonel Y. Kharkov and Major V.I. Gagarin were meeting.

"You have heard?"

"Yes, Colonel."

"What went wrong?"

"Reports won't be complete for a while, but it seems as though our small task unit met with better intelligence and superior force and organization."

"Pfennig was our best."

"Yes Sir. It appears that their best is better than our best."

"It was worth the gamble, was it not?"

"Yes. Colonel."

"We underestimated Eagle."

"Yes Sir. I think we are at least equal to our counterparts at Langley. But Eagle, this is truly a special man." Both men looked down at their shoes and mourned their best. Then the Colonel turned back to his desk and the Major saluted, did an about face and left the office, closing the door quietly behind him.

CHAPTER 45

SWEATING THE AMBASSADOR

"Starzinger Investigations, how may I direct your call?

"I'd like to talk to Mr. Starzinger, please. Let's just say it's about setting up a new pay system. He'll understand."

"Hello."

"DCI wants a meeting."

"Himself?"

"Well, along with me."

"I have someone I'd like to be there, as well."

"I'm not so sure about that."

"Tell you what. When you are sure, you can get back to me."

"Questions about clearance, need to know…"

"This guy knows it all. I've cleared him. He comes or you can read our report in the press."

"Can you make a meeting at noon?" It embarrassed him to act as though he couldn't clear someone to a meeting.

"Yes. I need to be sure that Dance is available. Give me a number where I can let you know if we have to reschedule. We'll be at the front entrance at 1155. That's Dance Dantes and yours truly."

"Thanks, Zinger." His voice lowered, filled with emotion. "I'm glad you're okay." Zinger hung up. *"No thanks to you,"* he thought.

———

"He's coming to meet with us at noon and is bringing along a Mr. Dance Dantes."

"That guy with the web site?"

"Not sure but I believe so."

"Our business isn't with him. We only need to get what Zinger has and close out our investigation into the leak in Counterintelligence. Then, since he's had almost a year off, I suppose Zinger will be available for reassignment." DDO thought about that for a moment. This meeting with Zinger ought to be interesting.

————

"Hey, Dance. You recovered?" Dantes wondered if Zinger had done a camera installation of his own, in their bedroom.

"Recovered from what?" Zinger smiled and didn't say what he thought.

"If you're back in battery I've got a meeting set with my boss' boss. It's time to go in and wrap this up. Can you meet me at the front entrance to Langley? They'll have your name at the gate. Just show them your driver's license and they'll let you in to visitor's parking. I'll see you at the front. We're meeting at noon so be there at 1155."

"Will do. Thanks, Zinger."

————

"Mr. Ambassador, this sort of thing was supposed to have gone the way of the Berlin Wall!" It was another meeting in Washington officialdom. The Russian ambassador had been summoned to the Department of State for a 0730 meeting. At 0800 Secretary of State Harlan Major came in to the room. It was the photo op room with the fireplace and beautiful and comfortable furniture.

"Dmitri, so good of you to come. Have you been here long? Ahhh, I see that the meeting was for 0730. Please forgive the oversight." SecState sat in an overstuffed chair and rang for one coffee.

Dmitri was standing, as he had been since the secretary entered the room. "No, Mr. Secretary. My time is of no consequence. Of course I am here at your pleasure and that of President Jameson."

"You bet your sweet ass, you are! We know the identities of your people that were found out in the countryside. I'm asking you straight out why we should not declare you persona non grata!"

"If that is the way that the Administration feels then of course…"

"I want your explanation. I want your Government's apology for the hostile acts it has attempted on our soil. ON OUR SOIL!"

The ambassador was sweating, soaking through his collar and into the knot of his tie. He was decidedly uncomfortable and he wished he could sit down. "Mr. Secretary, you mean how did those three individuals happen to be there and what were they doing?"

Mimicking his strained voice, the Secretary repeated the ambassador's words, "You mean how did those three individuals happen to be there and what were they doing?- Well what the fuck do you *think* I mean, Dmitri?" SecState had worked up a good one for this meeting.

"I understand, Mr. Secretary. I apologize profusely..."

"Your personal apology is not what is needed, Dmitri, as you well know. We want your Government to know that we know exactly what you were doing over here and we want the apology of the Russian Government as well as assurances that this will not happen again, between friends."

"Between friends?" His suddenly realized possible release from purgatory was palpable on his face. His shoulders dropped. He was so grateful that his voice shook when he said, "Mr. Secretary you will have that apology."

"Dmitri, sit down. Have a cup of coffee. Some vodka maybe?" And he looked at his watch and the ambassador instead excused himself, bowing and backing out of the room.

Well it was good to know that he hadn't lost that nasty edge he'd picked up in Platoon Leader's Class in the U.S. Marine Corps those many years ago. Who did these fucking Russians think they were, anyway?

CHAPTER 46

AFTER ACTION CONFERENCE

"Good of you to come, Starzinger. We've got a lot to catch up on."

"Director, an honor to meet you. Congratulations on your appointment. My friend, Dance Dantes. Dance, the Director of Central Intelligence and his Deputy for Operations."

"Mr. Dantes."

"Director, Sir."

With the introductions out of the way the DCI, Harry "Pete" Peterson, former thirteen term Congressman from the 14th Congressional District in Texas waved them all to comfortable chairs at a table in his large office. Coffee was poured. Putting down his cup after an appreciative sip, the former Congressman who called Galveston, Texas home and was now DCI did what came naturally. He did a little politicking. "Zinger, if I may call you that?" Zinger's nod acknowledged that he could call him anything he liked. He, on the other hand had something related to the Congressman's lineage in mind for him. "Zinger, I've heard a lot about you."

"Sir, that's not necessarily good."

"Oh, it's all good."

"But, in my line of work it's better that people don't hear about you. The less the better, as the Director knows."

The bonhomie and easy nature left the DCI's face like a curtain falling. *So this is how it was going to go.* "Of course, of course. Tell me exactly what happened between you and your Contact, here at the Agency."

"I think I would rather, if the Director doesn't mind, start at the beginning. By that I mean I'd like to know what the Director had in mind when he set this lash-up in motion." The DCI looked at his DDO, a questioning look.

"Well, we ordinarily wouldn't discuss Agency matters in a setting like this, said the DDO." looking in Dantes' direction.

"Let me help, then. I was cut adrift on the end of a very short tether with a crazy and amateurish method of payment and communications. I was used as bait to see if the Russians would bite. I suppose that my Control was the person who had been the leak, the reason for my narrow escapes in places that will remain unmentioned… in the present setting."

"I told you he would figure it out." DDO to the DCI.

"Gentlemen, it is the first time I have been sent out without a clue as to what was going down."

"I can see that this upsets you," said the man who had called the meeting.

"Sir, in Congress you make the appropriations that buy the bullets. Out there we get in the line of fire. It's…" He stopped as though it was useless to go over something so basic.

"Zinger, I'm going to admit my inexperience in your line of work. I made a bad call when I failed to bring you fully on board. I sincerely, if not abjectly, apologize."

Zinger sat back in his seat, with that. He'd never had such a complete and total apology. One was warranted, yes. And this one had drawn his poison. He cocked an eye in the DCI's direction. "Sir, I forget my manners. How may I be of assistance?"

DCI and his Deputy leaned forward. "Tell us what happened," they said. "How did you tumble to the fact that Harbrace and the Russians were coming for you?"

"It's really complex, and a lot of luck was involved. I, in my capacity as a Private Investigator had witnessed a stalker who might be planning an attack on a client of mine. This client is one of the Top Ten Liberals on Dance's web site. I was fortunate enough to obtain a sample of his DNA as well as his license plate number. I stepped out of character and asked my control, Harbrace, to run it down for me. I took the information he gave me and put surveillance on the subject. Later it was proven that the identity given to me by Harbrace was intentionally misleading. I was trying to catch the TLL killer and had been given a bum steer by my own Control. I became convinced that Harbrace was involved in the TLL murders, either directly which I doubted or through another person who did the actual killings."

"What would the motivation be, for Harbrace to accomplish these killings?" said the DCI.

Ops spoke up. "Sir, we'd need to go back to his motivation for the earlier betrayals Harbrace accomplished. Because the Russians contacted him, falling into the trap we'd set for him, we now know that Harbrace was the informer. We've proven that, I think. By the way, do you know what happened to Harbrace, where he is, now?"

"I know." Dantes spoke up for the first time. The DCI turned and looked at him with some interest, for the first time.

DDO continued, "I believe that Harbrace had a hard time with what he perceived as the rough treatment the Agency had received at the hands of Congress." He looked at DCI as he said this and got no reaction. "He probably didn't agree with the current Administration's policies. I think he saw himself as a player on the world stage. The Russians exploited this. If all of this is true, and I think it is, then Harbrace would not have had an easy time once he moved off-stage and into his new billet. I can see Harbrace as a person in revolt against the society that he once wanted to protect. I can see him wanting to be the big man, make the big moves, once again."

Dance spoke up. "Zinger and I finally got together because of our joint desire to catch the TLL killer. We analyzed what each of us thought we knew and came up with the following scenario. Control, Harbrace if you will, was using another person to accomplish the killings that furthered his notion of a better American society. He knew he had misled Zinger and was worried that he'd be revealed for his involvement in the TLL killings. When the Russians fell into your trap and contacted him, he hatched a grand scheme. We think he planned to use the Russians to kill Zinger and the TLL killer to clean up the Russians. Probably the Russians were going after Zinger and were going to also eliminate Harbrace. The Russians never knew of the involvement of the TLL killer or Harbrace's role in those killings."

———

They took a break and let that all soak in. The director asked his secretary to cancel the rest of his appointments for the afternoon. With sodas, some sandwiches and iced tea they continued.

"I'd like to know how you handled your end of it," said Zinger.

"Very badly, I'm afraid," said DCI.

"Actually we set it up pretty well," said DDO. "We let some station chiefs know that an Agent whom they knew had been retired in the

D.C. area. We left that information out for a foreign national to see and it got back to the Russians. We were waiting for any indication that they were going to take the bait. I think that what happened is that we lost our focus when Justice Benton was killed and a lot of our resources were siphoned off to pursue that investigation. Simply put, we failed to cover our bases and Zinger almost paid the price."

"So, now what can you tell us about Harbrace? Is he alive?" asked DCI.

"He's dead. There was not much opportunity to question him," said Dance.

"Do you have proof of that?" said DDO. Dance broke out the pictures they'd taken at the safe house. They all looked at the pictures, without comment. "Can we have these pictures, all copies?"

DCI, who had been watching and listening to the conversation, took over. "Dance, you have something we want, absolute assurance that Harbrace will not come back to haunt us. The Russians took a very severe tongue-lashing today over at State. We have to be certain that they don't have a card to play politically, such as Harcourt suddenly showing up dead in Russia, for instance. It's true that I spent twenty-six years on the Hill. And, I'd like to think that I learned a thing or two about negotiations. I can recognize someone who wants to sell. You know what we want. Now, I'd like to know what you want. What's it gonna cost us?"

"We'd like to pin the TLL murders on Harbrace, who actually directed them, or with your assistance on anybody else of your choice," said Dance.

"Easier said than done," said DDO. "We can make up a disappeared person, paper trail, only. Untraceable. But without a body..."

"We can provide the real killer's DNA."

"Hmm. Yes that will work." The DDO was actually an extremely quick study.

And Zinger spoke up, "Oh, and I want the information to be given to a police contact of mine. I'll deliver it."

"Anything else?" asked DCI.

"Yes, we have a candidate for your NOC program," said Zinger. "You do?"

"Yes, he was instrumental in Harbrace's capture."

"You vouch for him, Zinger?"

"Absolutely. He doesn't do the social circle vetting and he comes on my recommendation in the next starting class on The Farm. He's an ex-SEAL."

"Got it. Now then we'll get back to you…" from DDO.

"One more thing," from Dantes. "We have pictures of Harbrace with one of the Russian at the safe house. Both dead. We also have the body. I want one last thing."

DCI looked like a man who wasn't sure he wasn't buying a blind horse. He sighed. "Yes?"

"You never retire your best, do you? Zinger's your best. He will be retired and he will draw full pay … the normal way."

Zinger looked at him in surprise. The DCI and DDO looked at him with curiosity. "You got it," they both said.

"Fine. And you get a bonus. We did have enough time to ask Harbrace where he hid the money he'd received from the Russians, before he committed suicide. What he told us was that he kept it in an account in the Caymans. There's supposed to be a folder with complete instructions in his closet at home. We thought that money ought to go to the Agency. Also, that's the address of a Russian safe house." He pointed to the writing on a sheet of paper he handed over.

At that the DCI and DDO looked at each other and shook their heads. With approving grins and absolute respect they ushered Dance and Zinger from the office.

———

"So, Dance. Would it have killed you to ask me first whether I wanted retirement?

"If you want back in all you have to do is tell them. You can go ahead and work for some amateurs who will leave your butt hanging out if you want. At least I got your pay straightened out!"

"Pay straightened out…" he was laughing and laughing. They both were. "Let's go tell Wade about his career move… Pay straightened out!"

CHAPTER 47
THE STORY

"Pay straightened out?" It was Wade, roaring with tears in his eyes. This was too funny! They were out at Dance's place, the three of them and Riley. She was in the next room, smiling. This was the loosest she'd seen Dance be.

"Yeah, well wait 'til you hear about your career move, Wade; he's fixed you up, too!" Wade turned to Dance, "Well, buddy, what gives?"

"Remember when you applied to The Company for a job as a military contractor and they turned you down?"

"Dance, I try to forget insults like that, else I'd just have to do something about it." It was a weak attempt at humor and they all knew it. He was still looking at Dance, his eyes pleading now.

"Wade, Zinger got you into the next course at The Farm. You're going to be a NOC and I'll lay money the best they've ever had, present company excepted." Dance would later say it was the only time he'd seen Wade cry. His face crumpled up and he covered it in his hands, not trusting himself to speak. His shoulders shook with the silent sobs of a very tough man letting go of years of shame. Zinger and Dance sat and watched, understanding what it meant to him.

Finally Wade looked up, "Zinger, thank you. Thanks to you I can be proud of what I do for my country. There is no dishonor in this. Thank you."

"Wade, it wasn't me. I just spoke the words. It was your classmate, here. He had the idea and the moxie to go in there and negotiate for you. At the highest levels."

Wade swallowed hard, sniffled and swallowed again. There wasn't a dry eye in the room. "Boss, I got just one thing to say… If anybody ever bothers you…" And all three erupted in laughter and affection. If only it could always be just like this; in the company of two good friends whom you'd trust with your life. Hell, they'd already *done* that!

In the next room Riley silently wept, too. She shed tears of happiness for the men in there. She also shed a few for the young girl who had been forced to kill and forced to think about it ever since. She wept for her own lost honor and dreaded the day she might have to tell Dance.

———

"Open some more Kirins and let's figure out how we're gonna catch the TLL killer," said Zinger.

"Knowing Dance, he's already got that figured out." Finally with dry eyes, Wade was warming up to the task. They both turned to Dance.

"Okay, you clowns. Let's play twenty questions. Do we need a body?"

"Yes!" in chorus.

"Nope, that's the last thing we need. No body we could come up with would match the DNA we need."

"What DNA do we need?"

"Yours, Wade. We need some of your blood to prove that we have, or the D.C. cops have, found the real TLL killer. They already have some of your blood that they got from the garden wall at the Contralves' house. Zinger has some of your DNA that you left in the parking lot across from his office."

Wade looked really confused, turning from one to the other.

"You're saying that they have already identified my DNA and anyone we try to stick with this must have DNA that matches mine?"

"Exactly. So the last thing we need the police to find is a body. It won't have the DNA they need unless it's your body. What we'll do is give them some of your blood and no body with which to contradict your DNA. In other words, we'll steer them to the supposed death site, but there will only be your blood there, no body. Now, how do we make this convincing? CIA will give us a fictitious identity to assign to the non-existent body. Wade will donate the blood that will identify this non-person as the killer. What excuse do we have for the fact that the body is missing?"

Zinger had looked on with pleasure at the unrelenting logic. "I've got one. Mr. X is turned in by an anonymous caller, me. I say that someone stalking my client took a shot at him. My client fired back. This person escaped. I suspected that he was hit. After a week of looking around I found blood and animal signs in a wooded copse near where the attack had taken place. It looks to me like the stalker had died of his wound in the woods. Then he was eaten or carried off by animals that frequent that wooded area."

They both looked at him and thought, I think he's got it!

———

"Hey, Pat. I think I may have something for you on the TLL killer."

"Again, huh?"

"Well, you decide for yourself. Remember the guy that was stalking my client? I mentioned it before. Well evidently he made another run at him. My client got off a return shot and thought he'd maybe hit him. They both scattered and my client told me about it. It took me a week, but, sure enough, I think I've found the place where he croaked."

"Croaked?"

"Yeah, there's no body there, just some blood marks on the ground and trees. It's out in the woods. I figure that the guy went in there to hide and died, instead."

"No body… so you figure…"

"That wild animals ate the corpse or carried it off. It's a big area; I doubt there'll be any remains to be found."

"Except the blood."

"Except the blood."

"Did you take a sample, do a lab test, anything like that?"

"Nope. I'm thinking I'd rather just remain anonymous, and so would my client. Oh, and by the way, if there's a reward for an anonymous tip, I'd like that to go to the Police Patrolmen's Association; get 'em some vests and some money for the widow's fund. I'd be glad to take you out there and show you what I found. You can get your own sample and decide for yourself."

"Thanks, Zinger. What say we go out there and check it out?"

"Yeah, I figure what's to lose?" They went together and found Wade's blood that Zinger had copiously placed there. There was the spot where he fell and the animals ate. There were a couple of trees where blood had stuck to the bark. O'Brien took some samples and taped off the area as a crime scene.

"If this turns out to be the guy, you're gonna' look pretty good."

"If this turns out to be the right sample, I've got my career made."

"Then could I ask a favor, in addition to my total anonymity?"

"Shoot."

"I'd appreciate it if you'd give the exclusive first leak of the news to the publisher of the *Anne Arundel Advocate*. They publish on Thursdays. If the results come back positive, it'll just mesh with their schedule…"

He got a curious look but a promise, too. That was a nice touch by Dance, a nice touch.

———

Jennings got a very nice call from Officer Pat O'Brien a "highly placed source at the D.C. police department." He said that they had positively identified the remains (blood only) of the TLL killer. The word would be getting out to the rest of the world by the day after tomorrow. "My anonymous source asked that your publication get to break the news. We never had this conversation, but you can take it to the bank." Jennings called back as soon as the call had ended and was intrigued when the answer was "D.C. Police." She went with it.

The blockbuster issue of the *Advocate* forced a press conference by the D.C. police chief. He got questions including: Do you have an identity? Do you have a body?

"All that was left of the body we collected and analyzed for DNA. We have a match." The identity and background supplied by the Agency was released. The photo op went on for another thirty minutes, asking and answering the same questions and then shut down.

Press investigators weren't satisfied with there being no body and they kept up the investigation for another week. A schoolteacher was interviewed and said the usual things. A neighbor likewise chimed in with the usual statements, "Nice guy. We'd have never suspected." CIA had been good about supplying the needed backup personnel to strengthen the story. If needed they had, in addition to the schoolteacher and neighbor a childhood friend and a co-worker waiting in the wings. They generally tended to use a light touch with these 'extras', not wanting to use too many in order to keep their exposure down. The less complicated the better, they thought. Finally it died down and the press had to find another hot story. This one was stone cold.

———

CIA was shown the gravesite where they recovered the body and identified it. All of the photographs were delivered to them. In gratitude a certain 'retiree' was given a promotion and a raise. The new course started at The Farm and the class included one Wade Bates, under an assumed name.

———

The Agency allowed the Russian Embassy to pick up their dead. They also included an item in the DCI's monthly missive to station chiefs mentioning the unfortunate death of an operative whom they all knew.

————

At the Aquarium the Colonel and the Major sat together. "It would seem that Herr Pfennig accomplished his mission before he was, himself, lost in action."

"Sir, I devoutly hope so."

"Major, I believe so." And together they silently saluted both agents, Pfennig and Eagle.

————

"Well, if we are going to retire Starz, we ought to at least try to ensure he lives to enjoy it, or until we need him again."

"Sir, it worked once; maybe it'll work again. I know that they will want to believe." That month's DCI-gram to station chiefs with the note in the personnel section was read aloud where a foreign national could overhear.

"Zinger got the promotion and raise?"

"Yes sir."

"They never revealed the identity of the so-called TLL killer."

"No sir and we never asked."

"Figure we just hired him?"

"Sir, I'm counting on it."

"What did you think of Dantes?"

"My assessment? A cool customer that I'd want on my side every time. He hasn't been through the course at The Farm but you'd never know it. I was particularly impressed with his integrity."

"Yeah. One tough smart son of a bitch, too!"

CHAPTER 48
A NEW ANTAGONIST

"Jeff, this is Dick Starzinger."

"Dick, this is good news, I suppose; the TLL killer being killed. I mean was my stalker the same person who did the Top Ten Killings?"

"Yes, Jeff I am absolutely certain that your stalker and the TLL killer were one and the same person." Dixie was getting the gist of the call in her office. "And, I wanted to let you know that there is thirty thousand left in my retainer. I'll send Dixie over with your refund."

"That won't be necessary. You can keep the change. Oh, and tell Dixie thanks for everything, too, will you?" And with that he hung up. Zinger cradled the receivr and stared at it with distaste. It was with distaste that he did the next thing that he had to do.

"Dix, can you please come in here?" She popped too quickly into his office, a look of hesitation and anticipation written all over her face.

"Yes, Dick?" He looked really unhappy. "Anything wrong? Anything I can do?"

"I just talked to Jeff Prather." She stood, very still, face starting to fall. "...And his business and mine is concluded." He registered the confusion and hurt feelings starting to gather in her expression. "He asked me to tell you thanks for everything." She looked down, flushing with the embarrassment.

"That's all he said?"

"Yes, Dix; that's all." She turned and started back to her office. "Uh, hold on just a sec, Dixie. Look, you haven't had a vacation, have you?"

"Boss, you know I don't get vacation time, not one of the bennies."

"Yeah, well I think it's time and I also think that the firm can afford it. I want you to close out the Prather account; I believe there's thirty thousand in it. Write yourself a check for the balance and use it to go to the Bahamas, or something. Take two or three weeks off and go have a good time." She almost sobbed and instead rushed over and kissed him on the cheek. The look said she knew he knew and thanked him. She didn't trust herself to say anything.

———

Prather evidently had lots of money to spend on investigations. "Tonight's segment of ABS' ongoing TLL expose covers one of Dantes' friends and a former competitor of mine, Ms. Riley Berry."

Prather faced the camera with a sheaf of papers in his hands and employed that 'look,' the one that said hard-working reporter defending the public's interest.

"The latest buzz in the winding down of the Contralves' house killings involves the hostess, Ms. Riley Berry and her friend, Dance Dantes, who ABS learns also attended the party. Viewers may recall that Dantes was a guest on Ms. Berry's program; that is the program she once had. We've learned that her program has been dropped and her status is uncertain, to say the least.

"Our investigators have uncovered another messy murder case in Houston that involved Ms. Berry. So it seems that bad things follow Mr. Dantes and his associates. Dantes and Berry have been seen about Washington, evidently very much an item.

"While the TLL killer has been himself killed (and all Americans are glad of that) this reporter wonders if the person who may have directed the killer is still loose, in public. ABS and many others continue to call for TLL to be shut down, and for Mr. Dantes to explain himself to a Congressional investigation."

———

"Hey, Pat."

"Yeah, Zinger, what can I do for you?"

"Congratulations on your promotion; looks good on you."

"Thanks buddy; couldn't have happened without you."

"Look, Pat I wonder if you have any police contacts outside Washington."

"You mean like in Houston, for instance?"

"Yeah, would you mind?"

"Gotcha covered. Personally I hate the son of a bitch, too."

———

Though Dantes wasn't taking any calls, of course Zinger was welcome. They sat out on the patio, the three of them at Dantes' house in Severna Park. Riley had produced some iced tea and they sat there in a world-weary and tired sort of way.

"Riley, Dance, I took the liberty of asking a senior contact at the D.C. police force to connect up with his peers in Houston. He was told that an unsolved killing of a Rafe Johnson occurred there some ten years ago. The Clemens household was part of the investigation, as were several other households and individuals. They were not charged with any crime. The case is closed. That doesn't mean that any reporter can't and won't dig up the same information I just gave you. Also, if push comes to shove, I believe it will be easy to keep the case closed. My buddy, Chief D.C. Detective Pat O'Brien owes me big time. This probably will cause a fuss for a couple of weeks, that's all. I wanted you to know and be ready."

"Zinger, thanks for your concern. We appreciate your checking into it for us."

"No sweat. Anything I can do just let me know." Dance showed him to the door and came back to the patio.

"You know, I think we're both due for a vacation. Whaddyathink?" with a concerned smile.

"Not in the mood for a vacation."

"What kind of mood *are* you in?"

"Not that kind of mood."

"Look, I know how you feel…"

"You have *no idea* how I feel. About this. About Houston." Her eyes filled with tears that refused to fall.

"What do you want for supper? I'll fix it."

"You're going to just sit there? You have no questions for me?"

"Nope."

————

Things sort of rocked along in the Dantes household, but not as before. Riley was not her excited and exuberant self. She was getting sick and vomiting, had a pale look a lot of the time. She wasn't as interested as she had been. She had checked the calendar and knew. She'd missed her second period and had gotten a pregnancy test kit. Dance figured she was upset with the continuing occasional news items and kept his own counsel. Finally, two weeks after Zinger's visit, she had her mind made up.

"Dance, honey. Let's talk."

"Sure, babe. What's on your mind?"

"What's on my mind is what happened in Houston."

"Oh, you mean that trash that's in the news? I don't pay any attention to it."

"Dance you're going to not talk and just listen or I may not be able to say this." Fear struck a cold feeling into his heart. He was anticipating this. He didn't want to hear that she was leaving. If she wanted to go of course he wanted what was best for her, he loved her so. The blood drained out of his face and he set his jaw, ready for the worst.

"I'm not at all worried about anything that happened in Houston. But if you have something to say, here I am."

CHAPTER 49

CONFESSION – GOOD FOR THE SOUL

"Dance, I killed Rafe Johnson!" Riley looked at Dance with a terrible expression on her face. "I have no honor. I lied. He tried to rape me and I killed him."

Dance looked relieved, as if to say, "Is that all?"

"Didn't you hear me? I'm a killer! Not only have I dishonored myself, I've dragged your name in the dirt, too. I feel so guilty and it's killing me. I've let you down and I can't stand it. Now you know—I'm not the person you think I am. I know how important honor is to you. I don't deserve you or any happiness at all." And now the tears came. She sobbed and he wondered what to do. "I'll move out…"

Dance interrupted. "Is it my turn, now?" Riley nodded, her head bobbing up and down rapidly and her eyes tightly shut. "You're not moving anywhere." And he took her into his arms and let her sobs continue until they died down to sniffles and convulsive inhalations almost like hiccups and her sniffles turned into a snuffling kind of snoring. She had exhausted herself with her confession. She slept the first innocent and easy sleep she'd had in ten years, in his arms.

———

It was the next morning and they'd had some coffee when what he'd wanted was some dessert. He was horny and he didn't care who knew it. They sat at the kitchen table and eyed one another, each waiting for the other to speak, about something that mattered. It was obvious that inanities wouldn't do.

"Okay, let's talk." They'd done it again, saying the same thing at the same moment. It brought only a small smile. "You first." A new record, two times in a row. This time a couple of real smiles popped out. They sat back in their chairs.

"You ready to tell me what happened, ten years ago in Houston? You were just a kid."

Her face darkened as she thought back. She took a deep breath. "I was home alone on a Saturday. He was Mother's boyfriend. He came into the house while she was gone and threatened to rape me. He came after me in my room and I ran to the kitchen and got a couple of knives. It didn't make him stop. When he grabbed me I stabbed him. Mother and I moved the body where it could be found, in his car." She took a big breath and let it all out. It relieved her to tell someone.

"But Riley, this is a case of self-defense, not premeditated murder!"

"I know what I'm going to do. I'm going to Houston and turn myself in. I'm going to have a trial and I want a public one."

"You know that Zinger said that this is a closed case and he can make sure it will stay that way."

"That's just the point. I don't want it to remain a closed case. I want it to be reopened and dealt with. I can't live with life on hold, waiting for the next Jeff Prather to expose me."

"Okay, but let's just look into what options you may have. Perhaps a finding of justifiable homicide or self-defense can be made. It's one thing to throw yourself on the mercy of the court. It's another to first look into this whole thing before going to Houston."

They called Zinger.

"Hey, bud. We could use your help some more with this Houston thing." They explained what had happened in Houston, ten years ago. The threats, the confrontation and killing and the cover-up. "Do you think that you could find out, hypothetically, what Riley's options and her mom's might be?"

Once again Zinger approached Chief Detective O'Brien. He outlined Riley's case as a hypothetical and asked if he could find out from the Houston police how this would likely be handled.

"I know how we'd handle it here," Pat said. He made the call to Houston and described the hypothetical in relation to the Rafe Johnson case. In Houston they broke out all of the documentation they had on the case and on the victim. The DA said he'd like to hear the whole story, but that it looked like a case of self-defense and not a case he'd likely prosecute. If this hypothetical person were to show up he thought it could be settled quietly in the judge's office.

Riley made her decision. She was going to Houston, without a lawyer. There'd be time for getting legal representation if it came to that. She couldn't get it done fast enough. They left for Houston the next day.

CHAPTER 50
JUSTICE IS SERVED

"Doretha, I'm so glad to meet you."

"Well, I wish it could've been under different circumstances. Glad to meet you, too, Dance." They were sitting in the Berry household kitchen. Doretha had set out some brownies and milk.

"Momma, you're looking good."

"Well, child, I have to say I've seen you looking better. This thing with Rafe has been hanging over both of us for years and years, now." She looked at her daughter with obvious love and concern.

Turning to Dance she said, "It would have been better if we had faced it when it happened. I thought I needed to protect Riley at the time. It's never better to lie and then have to swear to it."

No question, he liked her mom. "Look, we're going down to the court house. We have an appointment with the judge." Pat O'Brien had set up the appointment. It was no longer a hypothetical. The district attorney was prepared and would also attend.

"If you don't mind, I need to go, too." So they all three (not counting the littlest one of them all) went downtown to face the music.

———

They were invited into Judge Harlan's offices. His Honor was known for his no-nonsense but fair approach to the cases that landed in his court. Also attending was the Harris County district attorney, Sam Walker. Around these parts he was known as 'Hangin' Sam' Walker. The judge offered coffee and invited them to sit in chairs arranged around his massive oak desk. It wasn't the bench, but it might as well have been.

The desk had been an intimidating sight for many a wayward youth and petty criminal in the making.

"Thank you all for coming; Mrs. Berry, Miss Berry, Mr. Dantes. We appreciate you both coming forward and helping us to properly close this matter. Strictly speaking, this is not a judicial matter. It actually falls in the bailiwick of the district attorney. I'd rather call it drive-through justice, a sort of abbreviated one-stop shopping for the right answers. I've been in consultation with the district attorney and he is prepared to proceed."

"Your Honor, the possible charges in the Rafe Johnson murder case include making false statements to a police officer in an investigation, conspiracy to obstruct an investigation, and wrongful death of Rafe Johnson."

"And have you found any information that would be shared with Miss Berry and her mother, or their attorney if they had retained one?"

"Yes, Your Honor, we have. In the interest of fairness we have discovered that Mr. Johnson had been accused in several rape cases, none of which went to court. Mr. Johnson also had an extensive rap sheet. He had also been involved in the sale and distribution of drugs."

"Miss Berry, Mrs. Berry does this information come as a surprise to you?"

"Well I certainly had no idea; until he did what he did to my daughter."

"Miss Berry I would like for you to be sworn, if you please." It felt like going into the voting booth, or serving on the jury. She was a trustworthy citizen! It was acknowledgement that she could be asked questions and it was expected that she would tell the truth. And they would believe her! She *felt* honorable as she stood and placed her hand on the Bible that the judge kept there for this very purpose. "Miss Berry, now why don't you tell us what happened?"

———

"Your Honor, I was only seventeen. I had never engaged in sexual relations. Of course there were boys who asked, but I'd always said no. I think I felt, like many young girls, that it would be something joyous when it finally happened, a choice that two would make. I think I also felt the shock of how inappropriate it was that my mother's boyfriend would betray her and try to steal something from me. I know that when he came after me I was scared and I didn't know where it would stop. I hit him with a coin bank when he tried to grab me. I screamed for him to get out. He cursed and came at me."

And here her eyes filled as she relived the whole experience. "He had stripped off his belt and was cracking it and swinging it at me. He backed me into the kitchen where I was cornered. I grabbed two knives and he laughed. He told me I didn't know how to use the knives and if I didn't put them down it would go worse for me…"

She stopped to regain some composure; dabbed at her eyes with a tissue the judge gave her. She looked at him gratefully.

"At the time I was not able to reflect in this manner. I can't accurately describe all of my feelings at the time. I know I was frightened but I didn't think I was helpless. Your Honor, I was determined to at least cut him up and make him stop. It went further than that. He grabbed one arm and tripped into me and I stabbed with the other. It was a horrible choice to be forced on a girl, so young. Your Honor, I have lived in fear of being discovered for ten years. I have sincerely regretted the taking of another person's life. Although I feel I did it in self-defense, I know it was wrong to not come forward at the time. I can only say in my defense that I was in some fear for my life and only a young girl at the time."

"Ms. Berry, thank you for your testimony." The judge was also affected by the story. Everyone in the room was.

"Your Honor, I have more to say, if I might."

"Certainly, Ms. Berry."

"I've tried to describe my actions and the feelings I might have had as a young girl, so many years ago. In honesty, I can't be sure of my thoughts or feelings at that time. But I am absolutely sure of my thoughts and feelings now, about attempted rape and assaults on women. It is a much more serious offense than I think society realizes when the powerful prey upon the defenseless. It is not necessarily about just a physical assault. It is also about profound betrayal of a young life, about causing fears that can last a lifetime. It can also be about an unwanted pregnancy, about ruined lives as well as fearful ones. It can be about sexually transmitted diseases and lost health as well as lost hopes and aspirations.

"Of course it was not even remotely possible that I could threaten my attacker. Nor, I suppose, was it possible for the law to protect a young girl in her home from such an imposition, such unfairness. However we all live in the country of the second chance. As I see it, justice has a second chance to right a wrong and mend a life, here in this court today. Thank you for giving us your time and considering all that I have been privileged to say."

Riley looked at them all and finally in the judge's direction and nodded, with a prim and expectant expression.

"Ms. Berry, it has been a privilege to listen to your story. Thank you. Mrs. Doretha Clemens, do you have anything to add to these proceedings?"

"Your Honor, the decision to not come forward and to lie was mine. I told Riley what to do. I, too, have lived with my lie. I apologize, Your Honor." And Doretha sobbed quietly and her face scrunched up and she took some deep breaths as she took refuge in another tissue from Judge Harlan.

"Mrs. Berry, I thank you for your statement, too. I bet it feels good to tell it." He nodded in her direction.

"Yes, Your Honor, it does."

"Sam, how will you proceed?"

"Your Honor, we believe that the 'defendants,' if we wish to call them that, have been punished far beyond the power of any earthly court." *Sam always* did *have a religious bent to him,* an admiring Judge Harlan thought. "Your honor, no purpose would be served in prosecuting a case against either Mrs. Berry or Miss Berry. It would be a waste of the taxpayer's money. The people intend to close this case as justifiable homicide and this result will be so entered in the court and county records."

"I have an additional statement, if I may."

"Go right ahead, Miss Riley."

"I retained an investigator for the purpose of identifying any children Rafe Johnson may have fathered. He also did his best to determine the identities of any other girls who may have been raped. So far it has come to three children and four rape victims. I have taken the liberty of setting up a fund to be used for counseling services for these women and others and for the education of Rafe's children, in the amount of five hundred thousand dollars. Please understand that this was not an attempt to buy any result, one way or the other. I purposely withheld this information until the district attorney's decision had been rendered. I would be so grateful if the court would arrange for proper administration of these funds. As my guilt was covered up, so I would like for the source of these funds to be anonymous."

The judge nodded, with an expression of wonderment at the true majesty of justice. This was what made him come to work each day—

the rare occasion when everything worked out the way it should. It was corny, but Harlan even kept a gavel in his desk drawer with which to impress the juvenile offenders he often had in his drive-through court. He rapped it on his desk and said, "Ladies and gentlemen, justice has been done. Thank you all. This court is closed."

At that everyone just stood up and hugged one another.

———

RILEY BERRY CONFESSES! The rest of the story in the *Anne Arundel Advocate* detailed the entire case and the Harris County DA's action, taken in Harris County, Texas. The editorial, also written by the publisher, Jennings Carson, extolled the willingness of Ms. Berry to come forward with the truth. It was a feel good story and one that Jennings was happy to print. Her editorial ended, "Now it is time for the persecution of Ms. Berry to stop. Now is the time for civility and perhaps kindness, even, to be reintroduced into our public discourse."

———

The rest of the D.C. and national media scrambled to catch up. Frustrated at once again being scooped by the *Advocate*, they tried to come at it from new angles. Everyone realized that Riley had come forward, not merely with the Houston police, but also with the media. The *Advocate* had an exclusive story because she had come forward. Stories tended to emphasize that aspect; along with how difficult it must have been, keeping it to oneself for so long.

For her part, Riley knew the media. They loved nothing so much as a cover-up. She had determined to beat the next sharp reporter to the punch. The result could be found in Harris County court records by anyone who chose to look. She was besieged with requests for interviews. She accepted them all.

Except for one. She did not agree to appear with or talk to ABS. Jeff Prather's approach had been to crow over the Harris County decision and to attempt to take credit for it all as a result of his aggressive reporting. Strangely enough, not many were particularly aware of Prather's preening and posturing. Most viewers were tuning him out. His numbers had taken a hit and were still declining.

CHAPTER 51
THE HAMMER FALLS

"Sorry, Mike. You know how this works. Your numbers have taken a nosedive. We're dead last in network news and last by twenty points. We need a general shake up and some new blood, some new ideas. I'm bringing in some new execs we've been able to lure from Cox News. I've recommended to the Board that we adopt a more evenhanded approach to the news, something along the lines of the shop they run over at Cox. They've approved my recommendation and have given me three months to stanch the bleeding, six months to get our numbers on the upswing.

Mike Madden was surprised, but not shocked. "J.D. I know you don't have any choice…"

"Glad you can see it my way. The new guys will need the office space tomorrow, this afternoon, actually."

"Sure, boss. Do I need to talk to…?"

"No, no need to talk to anybody else. Thanks Mike."

———

Nancy came into Jeff Prather's office with some office papers and placed them in his basket. "Hi, Nancy."

"Hi, Jeff. I just got a call from Mr. Hayworth's office. They want you up there on the first Eastern shuttle you can catch."

"Tomorrow?"

"No, they said this morning."

"This morning? Well, I'm not sure I can make the round trip that quickly."

"They mentioned that and said to schedule one of your colleagues to sit in for you for this evening's broadcast." Jeff sat back in his seat with a frown.

"Okay, please call in Dan… no, I'll do it. Thanks, Nancy."

"Dan, something's come up and I need to go to the head shed in NY. I'm wondering could you stand in for me tonight?"

"No problem, Jeff. Say, did you get the word that they've let Mike Madden go?"

"No, this is the first I've heard."

"Maybe JD is looking for a new VP to replace him?"

"Wellll, you never know, Dan. Hearing anything about his replacement?"

"Nothing yet, but I'll let you know when I hear anything."

———

Jeff caught the shuttle that left for New York every hour. He skipped the cocktails and twitched and jerked at his tie, thinking over the possibilities, staring into the reflection in his shoes. Although he preferred working before the cameras he supposed that maybe it was time to move on up in the head shed.

"JD, good to see you."

"Jeff, appreciate your getting up here so quickly."

"Sure thing, JD; what's up? Anything I can do?"

"Things are moving rather quickly and I needed to get with you personally, Jeff."

"Yes?" Jeff was sitting forward eagerly, a look of anticipation on his face.

"We've appreciated your contributions over the years. Your broadcast has represented ABS to the world for a long time."

"It's been my honor, JD. As you know, I stand ready to serve the corporation in any capacity."

"The board knows that, Jeff. However due to our plummeting market share and lost advertising revenues we have decided to take a new tack." Jeff started to wilt in his seat. The color drained from his face and he dreaded the next words. "We're letting you go, Jeff."

Jeff uttered a choked cough and with a shaky voice asked, "What's your schedule for this? Do I finish out the month or the week?"

"No, actually you've done your last broadcast for ABS. We'll be bringing in new broadcast talent from Cox. We'll fill your seat on the evening news with interim anchors until we can get a full time replacement. Sorry it came to this. I know you saw it coming. The numbers don't lie. Actually I think it was that campaign of yours against that Dantes guy that really hurt. We haven't bottomed out, yet. Have you seen the coverage his girlfriend Riley Berry is getting? We were the only ones who couldn't get her on. She has been everywhere on the tube and it's all friendly—adulatory, actually."

Jeff's head was spinning. He was now flushed a bright red, the embarrassment having taken hold. JD looked down at his desk and then at his phone console as his administrative assistant, following his earlier instructions buzzed him. "JD, I have two calls holding and your next appointment is waiting…"

"Thanks, Heather. Just a second before you connect the first call. Jeff, we will of course buy out your contract; the terms will be generous. Our lawyers will get together to draw it up."

"Jeff…" he said, with an apologetic smile and hands outstretched, palms up, rising from his desk, "Jeff, I gotta go. Thanks for coming in. We'll be in touch with arrangements for an office get-together." He grasped Jeff's hand, shook it heartily and steered him out the door. Jeff knew not to let it hit him in the ass on the way out.

———

Jeff was into his third cocktail on the shuttle ride back to D.C. It's a short flight and that many drinks a person really has to gulp to get them all down before the flight attendants shut down cabin service. He hadn't called the office to ask for the limo. All he was carrying was his briefcase. He was getting a taxi home. After they landed, he called Dixie on his cell phone. The recording said leave a message.

"Dix, Dixie! It's been awhile. Uhh, really sorry not to have called! Are you there? Well, that's right. You're probably at the office. I'll try to get you there."

"Starzinger Investigations. This is Dick Starzinger."

"Dick! You surprised me! I expected to get Dixie."

"Who's calling, please?" Zinger knew full well who was calling.

"Oh! Sorry Dick, it's Jeff, Jeff Prather."

"What can I do for you?" *You inconsiderate little prick.*

"Ah, Dick, I was actually calling Dixie."

"Did you try calling her house? You could leave her a message there."

"Why, are you telling me that she no longer works for you?"

"Nothing of the kind; she's actually out of the office and away from home. She's taken the boys and gone on some well-earned vacation."

"Ahhh," and he burped into the phone… "'scuse me Dick."

"You okay, Jeff? You're not sounding too well." *Maybe it had something to do with getting sacked by ABS. The word was already out.*

"Hey, look Dick. I *really* need to talk to Dixie."

"Well, I can appreciate that; but it's just possible that Dixie might not want to talk to you… vacation and all. Not to mention your very shabby treatment of her when our business was finished…"

Hiccup, "You know how busy it gets."

"Sure, but it's never too busy to treat someone nicely. Face it, Jeff. Ahhh, look, it's against my better judgment, but Dixie did leave me a number where she can be reached. Look, I'll give her a call and see if she wants me to give you her number. And you might ease up on the sauce, just a thought, Jeff."

"Thanks, Dick. I do appreciate it…"

———

"This is Dixie. Boys, quiet down, please. Can't you see that I'm on the phone? Thank you." Then to the phone, "Yes?"

"Oh, Dixie! Thanks for taking my call."

"Not a problem."

"Where *are* you?"

"Did you call to say something? Boys, please go into the bedroom. You can watch one of your shows. Use the DVD." Impatiently, she said into the phone, "Jeff, why did you call? After the abrupt termination of communication it was obvious that…"

"Dixieee, I didn't mean anything by not calling. It was just a busy time…"

"No. Actually it was rude and cruel and I had thought better of you."

"Dixie, you're absolutely right. I was thoughtless and if I was cruel I apologize."

"Listen, when you treated me that way it felt like you were dismissing an employee. I was *never* your employee. That wasn't *work* we were doing in your apartment for two weeks."

She sounded harder, no, stronger to him. "Dixie, of course I never thought of you as my employee. I thought of you… I think of you as… well, you know how I think… how I feel about you."

"Can't say as I do."

"Well maybe if you'd tell me where you're staying… I could show you…"

"You don't call for two weeks and you think you can just jump back into my life and upset the apple cart? Just like that?"

"Aw, Dixie. I know that I don't deserve you."

"Isn't it funny…? I used to think I was beneath you. I thought there was no chance because of our different stations in life. But you are just Jeff, inattentive Jeff, take people for granted Jeff."

"Yeah, but you're still talking to me…" his voice had dropped to a suggestive drawl.

She could hear the hope and a little of his swagger back in his voice. "Jeff, there are lots of attentive men, right here."

"Look, where are you, on this vacation of yours? Are you in the islands, like we talked about?"

"None of your business, but yes."

"You went to Grand Bahama Island? Freeport?"

"Yes."

"Dixie, I got fired."

"I know that, Jeff."

"I want to come down there and be with you and the boys."

"Jeff, I don't think so."

"Look, I have a place down there and boats, lots of stuff…"

"Well, maybe another time. I have another two weeks…"

"Two weeks, that would be perfect. Why not do it together?"

She could think of lots of reasons not to do it together. Instead she said, "Okay, we'll see you when you get down here. Bye."

CHAPTER 52
HAPPY FAMILY

"That's the third call today, Dance."

"To express interest in perhaps getting Riley Berry to come on board?"

"Yes. After appearing on the network and cable news magazines and seeing their ratings for those shows, is seems that the interest in me couldn't be higher."

"Well, except for ABS…"

"No, actually that last call was from them. I think they want me to replace Jeff Prather." She'd given out her cell phone number and it had been ringing, almost non-stop. "I'm thinking of hiring a new agent. Maybe I'll get a new start to my career."

Dance sat up, put down the newspaper he'd been reading. "That's serious stuff. Are you ready to crank up again, so soon?"

"No, I'm not ready and no, it's not so serious."

"Seems pretty serious to me…"

"I've got *lots* more serious stuff than that."

With that he turned fully toward her in his recliner. She was sitting sweetly on the couch. She gave him a direct and somewhat calculating gaze. "We need to talk?!" He said it as a question; she said it as a statement. Of course they both said it at the same time. They hardly acknowledged these simultaneous exactly alike communications anymore, they happened so often. She patted the sofa beside her; she wanted him closer, didn't want separation for this.

With a look of concern, if not outright dread, he was on the sofa now, sitting next to her. "What's so serious?" He never knew how long it was going to last. The "L" word had slipped out on a couple of passionate and emotional occasions. But he'd cautiously never assumed that she was in it for longer than it would take for her to come to her senses. Dance figured maybe she needed somebody her own age who'd be around to raise the kids, that sort of thing. The last definitive utterance on the subject had been that they were "in lust, at least." In her own womanly and intuitive way, Riley knew all of these thoughts of Dance's.

"Just come out with it?"

He set his jaw. "Just come out with it," looking deeply into those rainbow eyes, bracing himself.

He still wasn't ready for it. "I'm pregnant."

"We're pregnant?" Actually, she loved him for the restatement, almost made her cry.

"Yes, sweetie pie. We're pregnant."

He put his arms around her tenderly, carefully as though she was going to break. "How long have you known?" said into her hair as he glimpsed a changing future, right here, right now.

"'Bout a month, or so, now."

"How do you feel? We need to see a doctor? Yes, we need to see a doctor."

"A doctor would be good. I've read up and we can get a sonogram and take a peek at him."

"Him, huh?"

"Yep, he feels like a boy to me. We can find out at the doctor's office; but I'm thinking it's a boy." This was a lot to take onboard. She'd had a month or more to get used to the notion; he was dealing with information one minute old.

He liked it. Now he knew what to say. "Well, maybe we ought to give him a last name."

"He'll have a last name, not a problem." Quizzical look at Riley...

"Well, then maybe it's time we made an honest woman out of you..."

"Wrong again. We did that last month in Houston. I am an honest woman and proud of it. You were there but I pretty much did it for myself." Dance was getting uncomfortable.

"Riley, you know what I'm saying..." with a pleading sort of look.

"Dance, when are you going to get the message? It's not the baby and it's not me we're talking about. It's you!"

"Me?"

"You're always doing for others, serving others. You spent twenty years in the service. And I think you were happiest there because you took it as an opportunity to put others first, a whole country full of them."

"And?"

"And until you decide what *you* want in life for Dance, you won't reach the great achievements of which you're capable."

"But what *I* want may not be best for you!" Of course she was totally ready for this.

Tossing her head in frustration, Riley said, "And who appointed you to decide what's best for me? I'm your lover, not your child. I guess if you're going to just figure out what's best for everyone else we'll never know what you really wanted, or if you could have had it."

He stared at her and realized she was a woman on a mission. He hadn't seen her like this before.

"I *do* know this; I'm not marrying anyone who's doing it because he thinks I need respectability, or our child needs legitimacy. Dance you just need to decide what *you truly want*. That's all you need to worry about."

"I *know* what I want!" Still a little stubborn and not used to hearing any of this sort of talk.

"What do you want, Dance?" she asked, smiling teasingly and squirming on the couch.

"Well, sure. Always, you know that."

"Well, that was my last hint. In our culture, the man's gotta ask, and there's an accepted form for that."

They moved together and his mind was busy. When they'd started he'd figured it wouldn't, couldn't last. He did what any red-blooded male would do and went along for a fabulous ride, expecting it to end. It was coming to the point where he had to be serious in his thinking, he laughed to himself, like any mature, intelligent male should be. It has been more than fun. Now it was time for him to figure out what he really wanted and express himself. He had to pay his nickel and take his chances. He was amazed that it had actually come to this.

Riley, too, was thinking. *I knew I wanted him to be the one, the first. And, I didn't want a one-night stand. I didn't take precautions and as a result we're pregnant. I know that I have deep feelings for him. They started that first night. If this isn't love I don't know what is.*

"Careful! Not too rough. We've got someone in bed with us..." And they laughed and giggled. "Hey little guy... look out!"

CHAPTER 53
IT'S A...

Dance picked out some fine stones and had them made into an engagement ring. There was a perfect and large solitaire cut diamond in the middle, flanked on either side by her birthstone, smaller and equally brilliant Burmese rubies. He had picked the ring up on the way home from the site. They were headed to the doc's for a visit and a sonogram.

"Is everyone ready for some pictures, today?" He laughed.

Her smile was brilliant in return. "We're ready!" Though she wasn't really showing all that much she patted and caressed the area where she knew he was. He hugged them and looked at her as if to say, "ready to go?" She leaned up and kissed him and it wasn't perfunctory. It was wifely, but not perfunctory. He knew he'd been kissed. He hoped it would always be that way.

Another loving look exchanged and he said teasingly, "We can always reschedule the doc's for an hour or two later. . ."

"Oh, you! Can't you ever get enough?" Said with a touch of pride and a lot of joy as she reached around and squeezed his butt and pressed up against him, just to see if he was serious. He was serious. She gave him the really smoky look and played with him through his slacks a little, "Rain check?" She'd made his knees buckle that way more than once.

He laughed. "Absolutely! I also thought we might… I mean, let me start again. I want to take us to lunch at Willards after the doc's." Her look said, "You're learning, you're learning."

"Sounds good to me."

———

She didn't have to put on a smock. She just stretched out on the table and they pulled up her top and pulled down her slacks, exposing her rounded belly. The doctor was making comforting sounds and describing what they were looking for. "We're taking measurements of the head size and length of the femur." He clicked in the end points and sent the measurements to the program that stored the information. He had prepared Riley with a lotion, spread all over her abdomen, explaining that it was to get a better contact between the transmitter and her skin. They were all looking at the screen that showed the picture being formed by the sound waves as the system ranged, sonar-like, recording what it found inside Riley's womb.

He continued, "No nucal folds, no webbing, normal dimensions. Look here, see the blinking, changing of light to dark and back again? Look closely and you can see the baby's heart beating."

Riley squeezed Dance's hand, "Ohhh, look Dance. Our baby's heart. It's beating!"

"At a healthy pace, too, up around 190." He kept moving the hand-piece around her abdomen. "So, do you want to know the baby's sex?" They looked at each other.

"Yes, we want to know." Said in chorus, of course. Her laughter seemed to stimulate the tiny creature inside. It moved and turned, bringing into sight unmistakable evidence. They saw it at once. They said it at once. "It's a boy!" They laughed through tears of happiness. The doctor wiped Riley clean and printed out some copies of all of the pictures they'd recorded. Dance kissed her right on top of their little one and then she rearranged her clothes. They looked at each other and said it again, "It's a boy!"

———

The crowd at Willards was not a large one. It was a weekday and mid-afternoon, too late to be called lunch and too early for dinner. They ordered ribs and sat back to consider it all. "No champagne and no caffeine." She said.

"I'll do the same."

"You don't have to."

"I think I want to share this pregnancy with you, all of it. The hard parts as much as I can." She gave him another one of those loving looks that had been coming his way more and more often.

"Riley, you're beautiful." His mouth was dry and his voice shook a little. It wasn't what he'd started out to say, but it was true. She just sat there; she knew, at least she hoped there was more to come.

"Riley, darling. I love you and I love our little baby who we saw for the first time, today."

"Dance, I know you can tell, can't you? I love you with all my heart. I love our little one inside me." And her eyes and trembling chin spoke volumes.

"Riley, I know what I want. I want you more than anything in this world and I want our baby and to be his father. I want … I want you for my wife. Will you marry me, Riley?"

"Yes, Dance. I love you. And I will marry you." The day had slipped from one happy scene to another and so it was through tears and smiles that her ring sparkled and swam. And he slipped it on her finger and she loved it. "It's beautiful, Dance," she whispered. And she knew she deserved this much happiness and wished it for her son and her husband. For truly she already felt married to him; and she had from their first time.

And at last, at last all of those nagging fears left her.

———

The ribs came and they ate them with a special gusto. They concentrated on them and the applesauce and the fries.

"She looked up from her plate. Dance, I'm keeping my name. It's how I'm already known professionally. I'm preparing for a new career; new opportunities and I'll need to be the same person the public already knows, Riley Berry Clemens.

He took that all in, almost as a demonstration of how to say and do what you really want in life. He looked at her and her eyes were doing their multicolor dance. He didn't know if it reminded him of a moving kaleidoscope or a merry go round. All he knew was that when she did it, it was irresistible. Her smile was brilliant as she then named their Son, Huckleberry Clemens Dantes, and their happiness seemed complete."

CHAPTER 54
CLIMBING THE LADDER

"Director Peterson, it's the White House. Evelyn's holding for you to come on line."

"Hey, Ev. Pete Peterson here."

"Thank you, director; please hold for the president."

"Pete, so what's shaking? You staying out of trouble?" chuckling into the phone.

"Staying busy, trying to keep *you* out of trouble, Mr. President."

"And you're doin' a good job, too, in spite of myself. And dammit, when we both get back to Texas maybe we can knock off this Mister President stuff! Look I need a recommendation from you for an appointment. The last one you gave me was super."

"So the Secretary of State is working out pretty well?"

"You know it. Say, you got any more where that one came from? They've put together a search committee and they're getting folks all over the country heated up and excited. I just thought I'd see if you could come up with someone for UN ambassador."

"Geez, that's a thankless job. I don't know anybody I dislike bad enough for that one."

"Yeah, I totally agree. Why don't you think on it and maybe come over here around knock off and we can bat it around some."

"Will do, Mr. President."

―――

Pete Peterson and George Jameson went back a long way. Pete had been in Congress when George was still playing around with college cuties at UT. After an unsuccessful run and pretty much messing up in the oil fields, George tried again and this time made it running for Congress out of Midland, Texas. George had approached Pete and the two of them locked up and Pete showed George the ropes in the House.

Pete kept plugging away in the House, surviving Democrat redistrictings and tough campaigns while George took a shot at governor and made it. He went two terms and then ran for president. Pete was his campaign chairman. They both expected to win, which is probably why they did. The president offered him any job he wanted and Pete decided to stay where he was. That was until the intelligence dustup after 9/11. When the president asks, you go. George Jameson needed someone he could absolutely trust in that job. Other than his kid brother, that would be Pete.

He pulled up under the portico and the door popped open. He'd already been cleared in at the gate and the underside of the car checked with a mirror. They checked his ID even though he pretty much knew all of the guard detail. He was escorted to the metal detector down the hallway from the Oval Office. Through the detector he was, none-the-less frisked and given the airline treatment with a wand. The chief of staff cruised by, and then stopped when he saw it was Pete. "Director. Good to see you. The president said to clear as much time as y'all need. Would an hour do it for you?"

"Hey, I didn't want to put anybody out. He said to come by at the end of the day. You got anybody else in the hopper, run 'em in. I can wait."

"Actually, there's nobody else waiting."

"Great, then I'm good to go?"

"Yessir."

What the hell was that all about? Probably doesn't like George, oops I mean the Prez, making his own appointments. Maybe he ought to talk to his boss about that and not lean on lower level civil servants like me. If you weren't a prick when you took on a job like that you probably were if you survived long enough to finish out the term. With that thought he was ushered into the Oval Office.

———

"Pete. Good to see you. Thanks for coming. My staff pukes give you a hard time getting in?"

"Nah, they're just doing their jobs, like you'd want 'em to, Mr. President."

A look akin to actual pain flickered across the great man's face as he took the Mister almost like a blow. Pete noticed. Pete knew. He didn't particularly like his moniker that came with a "Mister" too. He'd take it easy from here on out. Probably a "Sir" every now and then would do.

He came around from behind his desk and they both took seats in comfortable chairs next to the fireplace. Pete seated himself just a second or two after the president. Neither of them would have had it any other way. It was simple respect for the office. In Pete's case it also came down to plain and simple love for the man who held that office. A Navy steward pressed with sharp creases and spit shined shoes offered them both a coffee, freshly brewed. After he left they both relaxed.

"Got any business that you want to go over that you think I need to know?"

"Before we get started? Well, Sir, we just rooted out a traitor in the Agency who had been passing information to our supposed friends the Rooskies."

"Rooted him out and then planted him again?"

"More or less. It won't be in the newspapers. All done, Sir. Is there any burr under your saddle that I need to work on?"

"Pete, it's been pretty quiet in here. I really would like to settle on someone for the job at the UN, though. It has to be someone who's tough and smart and would be willing to work himself out of a job."

"Are you saying that you don't necessarily need a diplomat?"

"Exactly. We can give him a cram course and your old buddies on the Hill can ram him through; we've got the votes. All this guy needs is a thick skin and brass balls."

"I didn't miss your comment about working himself out of a job…"

The president shrugged and tugged the corners of his mouth down with what in Texas passed for an unspoken 'fuck 'em'.

"If they can't take a joke. Right, sir?" They both laughed and took some coffee.

"Actually I do have someone in mind that just might fill the bill."

"Is this someone you could spare? I don't need to be hittin' your cupboard at a time like this."

"Doesn't work for me."

"How long you known him?"

"Long enough, Sir. Guy's name is Dance Dantes."

"Guy who runs that web site."

"Yup."

"How'd you get to know him?"

"He bailed out my best and I mean number one NOC. He directed the Operation that bagged the Russians that we're not publicizing and also handled the mole they had running against us at the Agency. Oh yeah, he finessed the TLL killer situation and got it resolved and did it anonymously."

"And he's not one of yours?"

"No sir. And he's about as smart as they come, wouldn't say shit if he had a mouthful, isn't awed by much of anything and knows how to handle himself pretty much anywhere and under any circumstances. Oh, and did I neglect to say that he's modest, loyal, is solid integrity a yard wide and six feet deep? Add to that he's…"

"Stop, already." He snickered. "Would you let your daughter go out with him?"

"Hell, I'd whistle him in and ask him to take his pick. I'd let my mother go out with him. I do think he's getting hitched, maybe soon."

Upraised eyebrows asked, anybody I know?

"It's the lucky man, not necessarily the lucky lady. The word is that it's Ms. Riley Berry."

"No kidding!"

"No, Sir."

"Lucky is the man who marries over his head and realizes it. You'd bet your life on this guy…"

"Mr. President, I think I just did."

"Anything else before I go out and hire him off the street?"

"Just one. I think it should be a package deal…" The president raised his chin and eyebrows with that way he had of inviting someone to continue. "One of the team headed by Dantes, Dick Starzinger, is a former top NOC at the Agency. I find them to be singularly suited to team together. Whereas Dantes is cerebral, deals with the big picture and delegates; Zinger is the solo operator who can execute any plan and is extremely resourceful, personally. State has its own intelligence operation, but lacks anyone remotely like Dick Starzinger. If Dantes is going to be doing what I think you want him to do over there, he's going to ruffle a lot of feathers…"

"Not to mention rice bowls…"

"Exactly."

"Thanks Pete. A package deal it is. We'll be inviting Dantes in here soon…"

"I'll give them a heads-up!"

And they would've gone on for another hour or so telling old Texas stories. But Pete knew he'd better skip out or the First Lady would get after him. Invite him to supper, maybe. Hell, George needed that time for just them. He knew how that went.

———

"Starzinger Investigations"

"Zinger, this is Pete Peterson."

"Sir. How can I help?"

"POTUS is going to hire a mutual friend of ours. On my personal recommendation.

Deferential silence…

"And Dantes doesn't know anything about it. Yet."

"Sir." And Zinger waited respectfully for the politician to get around to it.

"And I also suggested that he could use a sidekick. You. I just wanted you both to have a heads-up. You might give him the word, and if y'all have any questions, ask."

"Appreciate the director's confidence, sir." And the line went dead.

CHAPTER 55

THE ADVOCATE AND THE LIST

"Jennings, how have you been? I meant to see about us getting together for another interview and it just slipped my mind."

"Well, welcome to the *Advocate*; we're always glad to see you." Dance had looked around as he came in, noticed a couple of new employees.

"Seems like you're doing well…?"

"Dance, I think our fortunes started to change as soon as we started that first series on you. You've definitely brought us good luck. Cup of coffee?" She brought over two cups and set them on the table between them.

"I think it's more a case of your hard work and determination; anyway I'm glad to see it. Look, as I told you over the phone, I have a business proposition to offer that I hope interests you." She took a sip from her cup and set it down. Then she sat back, looking relaxed and waited.

"Jen, I'm looking for a partner, a partner in TLL." She still sat there, giving all the time he needed. He couldn't tell if she was interested, or not. "I want to take TLL public, sign up advertisers and balance the whole thing out." He took another sip and held the cup, waiting for her response.

"Dance, that's quite a mouthful and quite a change. Got a couple of questions: why the change in format and why now?"

"As to format, I think that there is still some time to run as a conservative site, but not much. I sense a change, a movement in the country. I think the American public is growing weary of extremists, extreme views, extreme entertainment, extreme politics, extreme anything. We're ready for some normalcy or whatever passes for it. You were commenting in the last piece you did that it was time for some kindness in our public discourse, remember?"

"Yes, Dance of course I remember. I'm flattered that you do. So, how would it go? What's your vision for the site?"

"I'd like to be able to leave those sorts of decisions up to you. The ideas I have go along the lines of, "If you don't have something nice to say, don't say anything at all. Instead of taking wildly inflammatory comment and putting it up there we'd search out examples of statesmanship and common heroism. We could have a section for self-identified liberals, also for conservatives, maybe one for just plain Americans…"

"I get it; by our very format we are encouraging a move away from the extreme and encouraging thoughtful examination of the other side's views."

He noted the possessive sound in the "our" word. "Yes! You've said it better than I could."

"Why now?"

"I'll tell you and I promise not to shoot you but you can't repeat this until it's wrapped up." Questioning look at Jen.

"Of course I won't divulge a confidence."

"I've been contacted by the White House. We've got to talk but I'm given to understand that they would like me to stand for UN ambassador."

"Dance! How wonderful! Will you take it?"

"If offered, yes. And if confirmed by the Senate, yes. And so you can see that I'm hoping to be too busy to take any kind of a strong hand in the running of TLL."

"Of course I'm honored by the offer. You must know that I can't come up with the cash to buy in. The bank owns most of what I've got here and we're just getting started."

"No problem. I figure that going public will generate cash in the millions, in the tens of millions. That's a task for you to learn how to do and then do it. I figure we'll go fifty-fifty on the whole deal. If you like you could throw in the *Advocate* and we'll pay off the bank loan as a first order of business. Fifty-fifty on the whole shooting match, the combined assets of TLL and the *Advocate*. Another thing, I think it would be good for you to administer the funds that are set aside for humanitarian projects. You reported on the AIDS pandemic in Africa, didn't you? Seems like you could put some of that money to very good use." He looked at her shrewdly and could see that he'd hit dead center with that one.

"Dance this is incredibly generous and the most fantastic opportunity that you are giving me. I accept!" They both stood and Dance stuck his hand out to be shaken. She shook his hand firmly and then she threw her arms around him and hugged him, for good measure.

"Jen, I'm delighted at your decision. I know this is going to work out really well. We'll get that lawyer group I use to set it all up and present the decisions to us. Here's their card, would you mind giving them a call?" She looked at him and thought, he's already set this up with them? Pretty confident and doesn't waste any time. She kinda' liked that in a man, in anybody for that matter.

"Dance, is it really 50-50? Are you saying that you don't require controlling interest?"

"Not if you don't. Do you need controlling interest?"

"Well, of course not." She laughed.

"Works for me."

"Me too."

"Plain and simple you're going to be running this and calling the shots. If I see something I don't understand or don't like I'll speak up. If you think you'd like input on anything all you need to do is call. The lawyers will write all of this down, in case either of us forgets. Welcome aboard... Partner!"

CHAPTER 56
DEFENSE WINS GAMES

"Dick! So nice of you to call! How are you doing?"

"Dixie, actually, that's what I'm calling you about. How are you and the boys doing?"

"Well, we're doing okay, I guess."

"Okay doesn't sound so good to me. What's wrong? Jeff not working out?"

"It's not that… he's okay. Well he spends a lot of time fretting over the loss of his job. I guess it was pretty embarrassing for him. He flies into some pretty impressive rages."

"I think he got what he deserved. It's like professional sports coaches. Either you deliver or you're gone. He should understand that."

"But I don't think he sees it that way. He blames others; in fact he mostly blames Dance Dantes and Riley Berry. He drinks a lot and has let himself go; he's even growing a beard. And did you know he's not actually a blonde? It's dark at the roots and he went ahead and dyed his hair brown."

"Dixie, I want you to know that any time you decide you've had enough you should use some of that thirty thousand and come on back here. I think I'm going to shut down the shop, but Dance Dantes is doing some big things with TLL. I know there is a position for you there."

"Dick, thank you so much for that. It's a comforting feeling to know you've got a big brother out there, looking after you."

"Take care, Dixie and don't wait too long to clear out of there, if it comes to that."

———

"DDO's office."

"DDO, please this is Dick Starzinger."

"Zinger, what can I do for you?"

"This has to do with the task that POTUS and DCI have asked that I take on."

"Looking out for the UN ambassador."

"Yes. One Jeff Prather is currently in the Bahamas after having been laid off by ABS News. He is highly resentful and blames Dance Dantes and his wife-to-be, Ms. Riley Berry. I believe that he has deliberately changed his appearance. I know that we don't have a large dedicated task element in a place as small as Freeport. We need to shift enough around to be able to provide surveillance on Prather. We need advance notice anytime he leaves the island, a tickler at the airport so that his name is on the watch list. I'll need to know where he's going and when. Possible destinations of extreme interest are D.C. and Houston, for now."

"We'll do it, Zinger."

"Thanks, boss. You've got my satellite phone number. I carry it all the time."

"Are you actually expecting he'll move on Dance?"

"Wouldn't surprise me."

"We have other options…"

"I understand. I would like to do some preparation of the likely attack sites. Could we send a team to the Clemens household in Houston and the Dantes home in Severna Park? It would be good to scope out the routes and potential defenses; perhaps shape the environment to our purposes."

"Zinger, we'll get right on it."

"Thanks, boss."

CHAPTER 57
THE OFFER

"Glad you could come, Dance, welcome to the Oval Office. I also asked the Secretary of State to join us," nodding in the direction of SecState. "Harlan, this is Dance Dantes."

"Mr. President, Mr. Secretary I'm very pleased at the invitation. It's an honor to meet you both." They pulled up chairs and sat easy while the staff photographers quickly got some shots of the two and then the three of them, then soundlessly let themselves out.

President Jameson faced Dance, "I understand you live over in Annapolis, and that you had a career in the Navy, Lockheed and IBM. That's quite a resume."

"Sir, you just keep bouncing around until you find something you can do. I've enjoyed the changes; don't know how often they were my idea, how often I just got run off." They all laughed.

The president took a sip from his coffee, "Speaking for myself, I know how that can be… getting run-off, that is." They all chuckled politely; he was referring to an election run-off that he had lost on his first try for Congress. "Pete Peterson, at The Agency says you're not the kind of guy that gets run off," looking directly at Dance. "In fact he had quite a story to tell me about your doings a couple of weeks ago, out in the Virginia countryside," Glancing in Sec State's direction.

"Sir, I have great respect for the Director. He probably gave me way too much credit. There were two others with me who were mainly responsible for the good things that happened."

"Not the way I heard it," Harlan Major spoke up. "Dance, I had a service career, too, Marine Corps. You get to know the ones that can be relied upon in a shooting situation. I have the greatest respect for those who are willing to bust the door down and face what's on the other side… without necessarily knowing what's on the other side."

Dance actually blushed a little and covered his embarrassment with a sip of coffee. "Thank you Sir. You're too kind. As it turns out, my best friends in the service were Marines. They all told me I'd made a mistake when I chose Navy over the Corps. I've shared many a Marine Corps birthday dining-in on 10 November, Sir." They looked at each other with that kind of military understanding, where each is totally comfortable with the other. The General had retired with three stars. No one in the Corps thought to make light of his title, Lieutenant General Major, even though to a civilian it seemed an impossible jumble of titles. Sec State's slight nod to the president said he approved of this squid.

"Dance, I'm looking to replace the ambassador to the UN; had to send him over with portfolio to Iraq. Actually, the way you've moved around makes me think this could be right up your alley. It'll be a full time job, but certainly not a career, if you get my drift. I'm looking to totally change that outfit or boot it out of the country. Actually I'm not much into trying to change bureaucracies. It's easier to just cut 'em and start over, like we do with an American Administration every four or eight years. I want you for the job. You interested?"

Here it was again, what does Dance want? He could hear Riley's question echoing in his head. He'd certainly settled that before he kept this appointment. "Mr. President, I am honored by your invitation and would welcome your nomination. I know I am just the man for the job as you've outlined it. I would willingly go through the nomination process and look forward to confirmation with the help of my new boss," and he looked in the direction of Sec State.

"Hell, that's settled, then. What say we whistle in some chow; can y'all stay for lunch?" The Secretary of State and the nominee accepted with alacrity.

CHAPTER 58
THE SLIP

"Dick, I just wanted to let you know that I am heading back home." Starzinger leaned back in his chair, still operating out of Starzinger Investigations.

"Dixie, you've got another week; take two if you need." He listened to the silence… "Hey, I'm sorry things didn't work out any better but I'll be glad to see you back here. Why don't you check in at the office until we can get you situated?"

"Dick, that sounds great. You sound great."

"So, is it going to be any problem with Jeff?"

"Jeff? No, actually he has not been around here for two days."

"You're saying he's left the island?" He hadn't heard anything about any flight and surveillance had not contacted him at all.

"All I know is that he left saying he was going on a fishing trip. He has a big boat, pretty fast one. He didn't say when he'd be back."

"Dix thanks for the call, gotta go. Looking forward to seeing you soon."

———

A quick check with the surveillance detail in Freeport and it wasn't reassuring. They'd seen him going out on his boat and hadn't informed anyone. That was almost two and a half days ago. Starzinger popped himself in the forehead, angry that he hadn't considered this possibility.

"Riley, is Dance there?" He'd called on her cell, not wanting to take the time to wade through the answering service. Dammit! Why hadn't he gotten confirmed cell phone comms with Dance?

"Hi, Zinger. No, he went off to D.C. and I don't expect him back before this afternoon."

"Does he have a cell number?"

"Sure," and she gave it to him. "You sound wound up; anything wrong?"

"Maybe not, but I need to check with Dance. Thanks for the number."

"Of course, Zinger."

————

"DDO's office."

"Dick Starzinger here. May I please speak with the Deputy Director?"

"Sorry, Mr. Starzinger, he's not in the office. May someone else help you?"

Christ, I don't know how much time I have, he thought. "Please inform the DDO that I believe Mr. Jeff Prather has left Freeport and would he please activate protection in Houston. Ask him to contact me on my satellite phone as soon as possible. Tell him that I am proceeding to the Severna Park, Maryland location. Thank you."

The phone rang three times and Dance's voicemail message came up. He must have his phone off. Zinger glanced at his watch. Probably having lunch with POTUS. "Dance, this is Zinger. We may have a problem. Give me a call ASAP. Thanks." It would take him thirty minutes to get to Dance's place in Severna Park. He spun out of the lot, going for all he was worth.

————

"Riley, I hate to do this to you."

"Zinger, what do you mean?"

"Well, I don't want to unnecessarily upset you, pregnant, and all."

"I'm sitting down," she laughed. "What's going on?"

"Well, I haven't spoken about this, but I am concerned that Mr. Jeff Prather might be moving in your direction with the intent to do very bad things."

"Oh?"

"Yes. And I need you to stay calm and follow some instructions until I can get there."

"Okay. What do I need to do?"

"Look, there's a switch that I installed next to your sliding door, the one that leads to the patio."

"Yes, I see it here."

"Please flip it to the up position."
"Done."
"Good. Lock all the doors and set the alarm system. I'll be there in maybe twenty-five minutes. I can explain it all when I get there."
"That'll be fine, Zinger. Thanks."

———

Right after she hung up the lights went out in the kitchen and the sounds of the house died down. She opened the refrigerator door and no light came on. Riley went straight to the nightstand in their bedroom on Dance's side and looked in. It was there! Dance hadn't taken his pistol with him. She picked it up and examined it. It was a Walther 9mm PPK. She pulled back on the slide and a bullet was ejected. She looked into the receiver and saw the top bullet from the magazine. Letting the slide go she stripped another round into the chamber. Then she called 911 on her cell phone. "Hello, this is…"
"I show no address, what is your location?"
"160 Round Bay Road, Severna Park."
"Yes, we have that. What is the nature of your emergency?"
"…Riley Berry. I believe that a person or persons is possibly headed here to attack me. I anticipate that they are armed."
"Ummm. I am dispatching a police unit to your location. Please remain calm." Riley locked the doors and went to their bedroom and waited.

CHAPTER 59
THE APPROACH

Jeff Prather had picked up a boat that had run in the Offshore Super Series races. It was an enclosed catamaran, 30 feet in length with twin Mercury 2.5 liter racing outboard engines. It had been fitted with extra tanks strapped to the aft deck and connected to the main fuel tank. There was also a deflated Zodiak boat with its own small motor made fast there. His boat could top out at 100 mph in calm sea conditions. With the additional tankage he could make the trip to the Chesapeake Bay in a hard day if he pushed it, easily two if he lay to for breaks along the way.

He'd told Dixie he'd be gone for a while, fishing. He'd tired of Dixie and hadn't been able to think of much other than his lost career and the two who had done it to him. He'd crossed the line from extreme resentment to willingness to take matters into his own hands. What the hell, he had a means of getting there, the gear needed once he got there and the skills, as a hunter to finish the job. How delicious the headlines would be when the sonofabitch who put that site up *also* became the target of an unknown killer! That, and the bitch he was marrying. The network had actually offered his old job to her! He smarted with the recollection…

———

Easing the throttles forward, he cleared the pier, swung into the short channel and motored quietly out to sea from the Lucayan Marina in Freeport, Grand Bahama Island. Once clear of the last buoy he'd set a course to the northwest and cranked it up to around 60. He cruised until just into the Gulf Stream. His water temperature reading shot up and he turned back to the east and ran for 20 minutes, then shut down and waited. He was ready for some sleep.

As he'd expected, he got some company. The Coast Guard hailed him and asked that he lie to. A patrol boat pulled alongside, with bullhorn, "Are you in any trouble?"

He popped the aerodynamic cockpit canopy and answered, "No, thank you. Just taking a break."

"Where from, whither bound?"

"Taking the new boat out for sea trials, heading into VaCapes."

"Mind if we come aboard and take a look?"

"No Sir, you're more than welcome." They'd put fenders alongside and lowered a Jacob's ladder as an enlisted man scampered down and hopped onto the aft deck, between the Z-Boat and the tanks. He asked permission to open the hatches forward and aft and did so, looking, no doubt for drugs and reclosing the hatches. Finding none he handed Prather a form to fill out and took it, thanked him and waved the patrol boat back alongside.

They hailed him one more time, "Mr. Prather, we strongly advise you to monitor the emergency freqs. We may need to contact you. If you rendezvous with another craft you will be stopped again." The meaning was unmistakable. Prather waved and nodded a friendly smile in their direction.

———

He'd cruised quickly north in the Gulf Stream, noting the lights at night and features along the way. It was a pleasant cruise and he was reminded of German U Boats in WWII cruising there and looking to put spies ashore or sink shipping entering or leaving the larger ports along this stretch like Savannah and Norfolk and Charleston.

Early in the morning of the second day he took Cape Henry light to starboard, heading into the Chesapeake. Making terrific speed, slowing only for small craft along the way he made the Severn River by eleven in the morning. Motoring down he picked up a mooring off of the old Severn River Naval Communications Station and shut down. Then he inflated the Z boat and started upriver until he saw the finger pier and steps up to the bluff overlooking the river. He took a careful look, and convinced that it was the place described in the report he'd gotten from Dick Starzinger he turned off his motor and glided up to the pier.

He checked his pistol, round in the chamber and safety on; then he headed up the steps. At the top he paused and seeing no one in the yard he skirted the house and found the power box. He pulled down on the lever, turning off the power and retreated back down the steps to see who might come out to turn the power back on.

CHAPTER 60
DENOUMENT

Knock, knock, knock. "Hello?" Knock, knock. "Hello!"

"Yes, who's there?" answered Riley.

"Police, ma'am. We're responding to a 911 call."

"Thank you so much, officer. I would prefer not to let you in, if you understand. I'm expecting a friend and possibly my fiancée. Either one of them will be able to explain what's going on in just a few minutes." She had the loaded pistol at her side.

"When do you expect them, Ma'am? Would it be possible for you to come to the door and show that you are not presently in any danger?" She thought about that one.

"Okay, I can see your police cars in front, I'm coming." Still standing aside she said, in a normal, conversational voice, "There's nobody in the house but me, but the power *is* off. Thank you for coming."

"Quite alright, Ma'am. Look, we'll remain in view outside until somebody you know gets here." The one who had been doing the talking sent the other one to the back to check the power and keep watch there. The power came on suddenly with a whirr of the refrigerator fan, accompanied by flashing time displays in several places throughout the house. "Ma'am, is the power on, now?"

"Yes it is! Did you just turn it on?"

"Yes ma'am," wondering what this was all about… some wacky dame turning off her own power and calling 911?

———

Prather had moved into the tall grass beside the steps and was peeking through the grass at the cop who was turning on the power.

He had a good purchase on the slope and was not visible to anyone standing at the house. The cop turned in Prather's direction and stood there, just looking, his hand resting on his holster.

Zinger pulled into the drive with the brakes on, scattering gravel and rocking to a stop right at the door. Dance came in thirty seconds behind him. They both came up to the cop and asked why he was there. "Got a 911 call from the house. Lady inside says she's okay. Either of you know what's going on, here?"

Just then Riley came out and ran up to Dance. "I'm okay, honey. After the call from Zinger I just buttoned up and got the pistol and called 911. The only thing that has happened is that the power was cut off. The policeman turned it back on."

Dantes queried the cop, "Would you say it was turned off, not a power failure?"

"Absolutely," nodded the cop. Dantes and Zinger looked toward the back of the house.

"You stay with Riley, I'll go." And Zinger pulled his piece and headed toward the back yard.

The cop out front hollered to the one in back, "Come on in front, Joe. We're finished here." Zinger did a quick survey of the back yard, checked the lock on the sliding back door as well as the switch position and came around to the front. The police had left and the three of them went inside and sat down and Dance and Riley turned to Zinger, "What's this all about?"

———

Prather, meanwhile, was having second and third thoughts. He felt lucky that Dick Starzinger hadn't flushed him and he was not eager to take him on. It took only a minute for him to work his way over to the steps and start slowly creeping backwards down toward the pier.

———

"...so when I got the word that he had adopted a disguise and was blaming you guys for his wrecked career, I got with the DDO and we put some measures in place, here and in Houston, some stuff that could be used to shift the odds in our favor if something should be attempted. I just wasn't ready for it all to go down this morning, hadn't exactly briefed you."

"What measures?" Dantes was looking at him with a small smile at the corners of his mouth.

"Well, here at the house, for instance…" CRUMP!! The sound came from down on the river. He continued, eyes wide and a furrowed brow, totally seriously, "I had them put in an explosive device under the pier," looking at Dance, "out toward the end. It had a triggering mechanism to an influence detonator that was set when you flipped that switch, Riley." They all sat there, no one acknowledging the explosion. Zinger continued, "I had Prather under surveillance and they failed to let me know he'd left the island. He came up on his own boat, not by air. His boat is one of those racers… that's why all of the last minute fuss." They kept looking at him. "We also rigged a couple of surprises at your mom's place, in Houston. Christ, I need to call some people down there and get those bombs defused!" They both laughed at him as he looked, for once, not totally in command of the situation.

"Well, you boys going down there to see what you caught, or are you going to have a late lunch, first?"

"I already ate, but I'm always ready for what you dish up, honey."

Zinger laughed and thought that they could wait until after lunch to go see what they'd "caught."

Dantes jabbed Zinger. "You know, Zinger, The Agency is going to owe me for a new pier—the end of it, at least…"

www.ingramcontent.com/pod-product-compliance
Lightning Source LLC
Chambersburg PA
CBHW070507300726
48975CB00007B/2364